Praise for the Capital Fal_ _

A Fantastic Read

"Loved the first book and could hardly wait for the next instalment, I was not disappointed. This book is fantastic, a real page-turner. I could hardly put it down. A must read for all Zombie genre fans. I can't wait for the next book."

Well, that was amazing!!

"I've never read zombie genre before but this has been absolutely brilliant! I never knew I would cry over zombie literature but I have with this, laughed, cried, every emotion possible, in me from start to finish of this trilogy. The only thing I can say I'm disappointed with is .... The End! I am now going to sit & gather myself together and just enjoy what I have read. Thank u soooooo much for the incredible journey I've been on from your wonderful work! Keep it up and if any future books come then I will be pre-ordering them irrelevant of genre, as it's become perfectly clear to me I need to open up my options now, well done, you're a star!"

Excellent again

"Another great read from this up and coming author. Superbly constructed and it had me hooked from page one. In fact, I read it over 2 nights and couldn't put it down until it was finished. Excellent stuff.... bring on the next one"

Fantastic what more can I say!

"Another fantastic book, couldn't put it down. Gripped from start to finish. Keep up the good work Lance Winkless. I look forward to a whole lot more. Please don't put the pen down for too long.."

Lance Winkless was born in Sutton Coldfield, England, brought up in Plymouth, Devon and now lives in Staffordshire with his partner and daughter.

For more information on Lance Winkless
and future writing see his website.

www.LanceWinkless.com

By Lance Winkless

CAPITAL FALLING
CAPITAL FALLING 2 – DENIAL
CAPITAL FALLING 3 – RESURGENCE

THE Z SEASON –

KILL TONE
VOODOO SUN

Visit Amazon Author Pages

Amazon US - Amazon.com/author/lancewinkless

Amazon UK - Amazon.co.uk/-/e/B07QJV2LR3

Why Not Follow

Facebook www.facebook.com/LanceWinklessAuthor

Twitter   @LanceWinkless

Instagram @LanceWinkless

Pinterest www.pinterest.com/lancewinkless

CAPITAL
FALLING 3
RESURGENCE

Lance Winkless
25/5/2022

Lance Winkless

This book is a work of fiction, any resemblance to actual persons, living or dead, organisations, places, incidents and events are coincidental.

Published by Lance Winkless

www.LanceWinkless.com

Chapter 1

Silence throbs inside Lieutenant Winters' head, like an empty cavern. A low buzz of static, the only faint noise his headset generates, starts to fry his brain.

He thought he had wanted the noise to stop. The gunfire and desperate voices from his team that radio waves had been sending from the mission and into his head had seemed endless. Now the silence is enveloping him, the cost of the mission cutting him as sharply as any knife would. Yet he barely knew Andy and Dan—so why is their loss affecting him so hard?

Fatigue is playing its part, for sure. Winters has been involved in plenty of critical missions to understand that adrenaline fades and the body relapses. But even so, he has lost team members before that he knew better than Andy and Dan, and he can't remember it immediately hitting him this full-on before.

Winters' hands rush up to either side of his head, take hold of the headset and yank it off. He throws the headset across and onto the table in front of him with force. It crashes onto the surface, sliding over the polished top and hitting the computer monitor.

The sound of the storm outside replaces the static in his exposed ears, which feel chilled in the fresh air. The wind is strong, battering the closed roller shutter door, making it rattle in its runners.

Pull yourself together, he thinks to himself, wondering where his usual deeply instilled resilience has gone. He struggles to, however, and can't seem to motivate himself to even get out of his chair; in fact, he slouches further into it.

Alone in the hangar with only the storm for company, Winters' eyes start to flicker closed, his eyelids feeling impossibly heavy. Has he underestimated his fatigue? He has been in a constant state of stress in the last two days, hardly slept and not eaten properly. Surely, resting his eyes for a few minutes is only fair and well deserved.

An image of Andy boarding the Lynx for his fateful mission flashes across Winters' waning mind. The image causes his stomach to burn and he forces his eyes open. How can he sit here feeling sorry for himself when others have made the ultimate sacrifice? Gradually, he feels his resilience start to return, together with his determination.

As he was starting to doze, the rest of the team would have been drawing closer, returning to base. Winters scolds himself for his lapse in concentration and reaches to retrieve the headset. Preparations need to be made for their return and time is short.

"Flight Lieutenant Alders, receiving, over."

"Receiving, over," Alders responds almost immediately.

"How is the team, over?"

"Quiet, over."

"What's your ETA, over?"

"Approximately nine minutes, over."

"Good, have you been given your LZ point, over?

"LZ1, over."

"Okay, follow flight instructions and I'll meet you in the landing zone."

"Received, over and out."

The dejection in Alders' voice is plain to hear, Winters thinks. He himself, embarrassingly, had nearly forgotten about the loss of Buck. How close the two pilots were, he doesn't know—but judging by Alders' voice, they were close enough.

Now he does force himself out of the chair, pushing himself up wearily on the arms of the chair, his energy not completely returned yet. Leaning over to the table and taking the computer mouse in his hand, he clicks onto the Windows icon on the screen and clicks 'shut down'. Then standing upright, he stretches out his back while he watches as the computer goes through its motions of shutting off.

After gathering his belongings from the tabletop, Winters takes one last look around the dismal hangar to check he hasn't left anything. He doesn't look back before he flicks the switch to turn off the hangar's lights and opens the door into the storm.

Outside, the wind is strong, but not as strong as Winters had assumed it would be. He had underestimated the ferocity of the rain though, which threatens to soak him to the bone, even on his short run over to the black Defender parked nearby. Jumping into the driver's seat and slamming the door behind him, Winters shakes off his soaked hair whilst attempting to dry his hands on his trousers.

The Defender's engine roars into life, but before his hand reaches the gear stick, his phone starts to vibrate in the breast pocket of his sand-coloured shirt. Pausing for a second, instinctively knowing who is causing his phone to vibrate, he debates letting the phone ring out. The

Defender's windscreen wipers swipe past his eyes three times before he gives in and reaches for his pocket.

"Report, Lieutenant," Colonel Reed's pompous voice demands.

How satisfying would it be to shove his phone down Reed's throat, Winters puzzles before answering?

"I am leaving the hangar for the landing zone now Colonel; their ETA is about five minutes, Sir."

"Good, bring the package to me directly, Lieutenant."

"Yes, Sir."

With his phone back in his pocket, Winters reverses away from the hangar, in absolutely no rush to return to it.

On the short drive towards Terminal 4 where the landing zone is situated, Winters is surprised by how much standing water there is. Large puddles dance all around as more raindrops plunge into them, adding to their size. Spray rushes up from the puddles as the wheels of the Defender cuts through the water. The sight and sound of the water cascading up and away calms him somewhat and he drifts into the bigger puddles to increase the ferocity of the spray.

His little game comes to an end too quickly as he nears the cordoned-off area of the landing zone. Strange how a little fun and games affect a person, but the self-administered therapy has helped revitalise him more, and he almost feels back to himself again.

Two soldiers are manning a row of bollards that cuts off the entry into the landing zone, their SA80 rifles held across their bodies. The airport workers in their hi-vis jackets that were manning the opposite entry earlier in the day are now nowhere to be seen. The poor chap Winters had his altercation with—and threatened to run over—probably had something to say about it and so the security was beefed up.

As he approaches the bollards, the two soldiers, who must have pissed somebody off to be given this assignment in this weather, stand their ground in front of the entry. They both look like ghouls in the dark, kitted out in their dark-green military issue ponchos, the only protection they have against the shocking weather.

Winters comes to a steady stop in front of them, not wanting to give them any cause to raise their rifles. Thankfully, once he has halted, one of the soldiers leaves his position and walks around to the driver's window. Winters really didn't fancy having to get out of his shelter to address them, and foolishly, he's left his overcoat in the command tent.

"Flight and mission personnel only beyond this point," the shivering soldier tells Winters through the half-open driver's side window.

"I am collecting a mission package that will be landing imminently, let me through, soldier."

"Flight and mission personnel only beyond this point, turn your vehicle around."

Winters doesn't come close to losing his temper this time, as the young drenched soldier is only following orders.

"How long have you been out here, soldier?"

"Nearly two hours."

"That's two hours, *Sir.*"

"Yes Sir, sorry Sir."

"I am collecting a package for Colonel Reed; move the bollards, soldier."

As always, the name drop instils the required amount of fear into the young soldier. He immediately straightens his shivering back and then waves to his partner to move the bollards.

"Thank you, soldier, how much longer are you on duty for?"

"Who knows, I think they have probably forgotten we are here, Sir."

"I'll see what I can do, terrible night for it."

"Thank you, Sir, the rain is easing off now, Sir, I think."

"Can you point me in the direction of LZ1?"

"Over to the left, toward the terminal building, Sir," the soldier says, turning and pointing in the direction.

"Thank you, soldier, carry on."

As the car window goes up, the soldier salutes the Lieutenant.

Winters, as he pulls forward towards the open entry, decides that the soldier is indeed correct, and the rain is easing off. The Defender's wipers now trigger only intermittently, to account for the sparser and smaller raindrops.

The Defender veers to the left as it enters the landing zone, taking a wide berth away from the landing points that are now on the right. Helicopters, mostly Apache Attack are constantly landing and taking off and rain or not, personnel are scattered all around. The majority are there to service the newly landed helicopters, getting them ready for take-off and onto their next mission. The rest of the personnel are either flight crew or soldiers, either disembarking from their mission or embarking ready for take-off.

The helicopter landing area has the landing point numbers painted large and bold onto the tarmac in yellow and encloses them in a large white painted circle. Each zone also has a sign next to it with its number on, making it easier for the ground staff to identify them.

Winters has entered at the end with the bigger numbers; the highest he sees is twenty-nine. Gradually, the numbers decrease as he drives. He takes it slowly, due to the number of people and equipment bustling around.

Eventually, Winters parks up a few meters away from LZ1, and he stays inside the Defender waiting for his team to land. The improving weather means that the rain is now no more than a drizzle and the wind has continued to drop, although the wind is harder to quantify with all the downdrafts taking place in the busy landing zone.

Chapter 2

A strong side-wind hits the Lynx, causing it to shudder and lose altitude before Alders reacts and compensates upfront in his pilot's seat.

Staring out of the hold window, Alice is eager to see some sign that the flight is nearly over. She knows their return to base must be close now, but it can't come soon enough for her or the rest of the team she has, no doubt, especially Josh. She is a reluctant passenger on any helicopter, not that she would outwardly show her anxieties—never mind her being squeezed into this overloaded one in a storm, having just seen one helicopter drop from the sky. This isn't nursing that anxiety at all.

Struggling to try to take her mind off it, she tries to concentrate on the view out of the window, searching for any recognisable landmarks to show they are nearly back at Heathrow. She is on the wrong side of the hold, though, and all she sees is darkness and nondescript roads. She curses her luck that she doesn't have the same view of the M4 motorway that they will have on the opposite side of the Lynx.

A wave of guilt passes over her, cursing her own luck because she isn't happy with her view out of the window when Josh is seated next to her. Her head turns in his direction, but he is still slumped in his seat with his head down; God only knows what is going on in his head. Her guilt grows.

Alice tries to think of something to say to him, to try and pick him up, if only a little. She fails though, as she can think of nothing to say that won't sound totally lame. She hopes that when this godawful flight is over and they land, he might improve.

Josh will have other things to think about, but then she remembers his sister is waiting for him and her father to return.

Feeling helpless, her gaze returns to the window, hoping to see the burning lights of Heathrow come into view.

"Heathrow is just ahead, ETA, three minutes!" Alder shouts from the cockpit.

Alice's relief on hearing those words is considerable and she isn't the only one. The low voices which are all she has heard in the noisy hold start to rise and life starts to return. Everyone starts moving to get their kit together, and it reminds her of a commercial flight after landing and the seat belt light pings off. She is relieved to see Josh's head come up as he starts to check his kit, instinctively checking his pocket to make sure the most important piece of kit is still there, and it hasn't miraculously vanished—his phone.

Sergeant Dixon seated next to Josh—and who has hardly said two words for the entire trip—reluctantly leans forward and fishes under his seat. Gradually, he drags out the cause of all this grief, the holdall containing the contents of Sir Malcolm's safe. He leaves the large black, heavily laden holdall on the floor of the Lynx and with disdain, pushes it away with his boot, towards the door and away from him.

"Downey," he says to the next man closest to him, "you're in charge of this."

Downey looks none too pleased with his new assignment of taking charge of the cursed holdall but reluctantly acknowledges his new task.

Finally, Alice briefly sees the large buildings of Heathrow Airport come into view and the bright lights of the surrounding area before her view is cut off again. Alders manoeuvres the helicopter, turning south as his flight path is directed by air traffic control.

Suddenly, the hold seems to close in on the team and everyone starts to feel slightly claustrophobic as they know their journey is coming to an end. Some of them get out of their seats with nowhere to go. They all get fidgety, eager to leave the cramped space behind.

Parked up beside LZ1, Winters is also getting fidgety as he anticipates the imminent landing of his team back at base. He can see that the landing is imminent because a squad of armed soldiers has moved into position, encircling LZ1. He was expecting a welcoming party to be in place for the landing but admits to himself, he didn't expect it to look so menacing.

Measures have to be taken to prevent the virus from spreading onto this base at all costs. A huge gamble has been taken at Heathrow. The military has invested an inordinate amount of manpower and hardware here. Should Heathrow fall, it is difficult to see how London could be saved and should London fall, surely it would take a miracle to stop the whole country from following.

Winters has played his part in formulating the plans and measures to protect Heathrow. They included these greeting parties, but times have moved on since those actions were implemented. New, nervous personnel have arrived on base. Personnel who have seen Zombies on their TVs and smartphones and have no intention of joining those ranks. The whole atmosphere on base has changed, suspicion and aggression becoming the norm and a *shoot first, ask questions later* attitude is coming to the fore.

There is one positive and hugely important development that Winters has seen in a briefing. As if by chance, a miraculous new easy method of testing people to see if they are infected has been discovered. An eye doctor from John Radcliffe University Hospital Oxford discovered he could establish if somebody was infected by scanning their eyes. The algorithm he used has now been adapted and written into an App—and now, any phone with a camera above 16 megapixels can be used to do the eye scan.

Winters is highly suspicious of how this Nobel Prize level winning discovery actually happened, but no matter; it means blood tests are no longer needed and neither is quarantine in most cases. That means that personnel returning to base can be scanned for infection immediately, and that includes his team.

Winters checks his watch. Alders will be landing anytime now. The rain has all but stopped, so he decides to get out of the Defender to watch their arrival, he opens the driver's door and starts to get out.

"Stay in your vehicle!" an overzealous Corporal shouts in Winters' direction.

"Excuse me, Soldier?" Winters replies, taken aback.

"Stay in your vehicle, Sir," the Corporal repeats angrily, not backing down. "Until the landing party is cleared," he adds, his rifle starting to turn in Winters' direction.

Winters pauses for a second, debating to pull up the Corporal for his insubordination. The second passes and Winters lets it slide, getting back into the Defender. He hasn't the time or inclination to pull him up on it now, since he has more important matters to attend to. On shutting his door, he does roll his window all the way down, however, in part as a show of defiance but mainly so he can get a better look at the Lynx now descending to land.

The Corporal and his rifle have turned back to the LZ, taking no notice of either Winters or his act of defiance.

Slowly and deliberately, Alders brings the Lynx over and down towards his allotted LZ. Noise and wind start to billow through the Defender's open window, bringing with it rain as the helicopter closes in, Winters ignores all three as he watches. The soldier's heads that surround the LZ automatically duck, their faces turning away from the barrage as the downdraft reaches its peak and the helicopter nears touchdown.

The Lynx touches down with a jolt. *Finally,* Alice thinks to herself as she is jarred by the landing, a small price to pay to be almost out of this flying cocoon.

Dixon is up and pulling at the hold's door handle almost instantly on touchdown, even before Alders has killed the helicopter's engines. Maybe Alice isn't the only one hiding their dislike of helicopters—or is it the mission that has Dixon eager to exit?

Another wave of relief passes over Alice as the Lynx's door rolls speedily back and fresh air flows into her; she fills her lungs greedily.

Dixon jumps straight down onto the wet tarmac, but he is stopped in his tracks as he is ordered to 'halt' by the agitated Corporal pointing a rifle at him.

"Fuck off, dickhead, I ain't in the mood." Dixon barks back at the Corporal.

"Stay where you are Sergeant, or I will fire!" The Corporal ducks lower behind his rifle and takes a step forward, showing he means business.

Perhaps the Corporal doesn't realise who he is dealing with or perhaps the bit of power he has been given has gone to his head. Under different circumstances, he would know not to fuck with Special Forces, or at least show them a bit of respect. On this occasion, the Corporal has decided to play with fire, risking getting burnt and burnt badly.

Dixon has played before and stays calm, even if he does have a slightly smug look on his face. He knows that his team is not going to let this pass, especially the members of his SBS patrol.

Without noticing, his concentration focused on Dixon, the Corporal is already in the line of sight of two assault rifles. Kim and Collins have their team leader covered from the shadows of the Lynx's hold.

"Lads," is all Dixon has to say.

Slowly and deliberately, Kim and Collins stalk out of the shadows, moving gradually forward showing themselves and their trained rifles to the Corporal. The Corporal suddenly wishes he had played this situation very differently. His confidence and aggression visibly wane as he involuntarily takes a step back, surrendering his pride even further.

"Tell them to lower their weapons," the Corporal shouts with little authority.

"You first, sonny," Dixon retorts, scratching his chin.

None of the Corporal's team is showing any sign of wanting any part of this standoff and look nervously on, having zero clues what to do. There will have to be a good reason for the Special Forces operatives to stand down. They can't have jumped-up regulars bandying around stories of how they faced down two Special Forces patrols, one SBS and the other SAS to boot. None of the men would let that happen and not just because they would never live it down.

"Corporal, lower your weapon; that is an order," Lieutenant Winters instructs the hapless man, who hasn't even noticed his arrival at his side.

"But Sir, they have to be screened."

"I won't tell you again Corporal, lower your weapon."

Gradually, the tension eases as the Corporal's rifle begins to lower, the man's authority in tatters as well as his pride. Once his rifle's aim is lowered away from Dixon, his team relax, and their weapons lower also.

"Sergeant," Winters says to Dixon. "Get your team formed up ready for screening."

"Screening, Sir?" Dixon asks, confused.

"Yes, Sergeant, it's the latest method to check that new arrivals haven't been infected. All it involves is a scan of your eye, nothing to worry about—and the sooner we get it done, the sooner we can let these men get on with their jobs."

"And a fine job they are doing, Sir." The unadulterated sarcasm is cutting.

"Nevertheless, let's get on with it, Sergeant."

"Yes, Sir," Dixons replies before telling his team to form up.

"Carry on, Corporal," Winters instructs the beaten man.

Josh and Alice are ushered to the front of the queue, mainly for Josh's benefit. Both teams of Special Forces have lost brothers in arms on operations and that is bad enough. To lose your father on the same operation is beyond words and the whole team want to do what little they can for their new comrade.

Josh, to his credit, is standing tall and does so as his eye is scanned by another member of the newly timid welcoming committee. Suddenly, *please* and *thank you* are the orders of the day. The overzealous Corporal stands to the side with his tail between his legs, thinking of excuses to save face with his men when his ordeal is finally over.

Dixon stands at the back of the queue, still scratching his chin and eyeing the Corporal, prolonging his suffering for as long as possible.

Josh passes the screening and walks over to Winters.

"How are you holding up?" Winters asks him.

"I'm not sure; to be honest, it's a head fuck and I'm not getting my head around it."

"It's early days, Josh, and for what it's worth, your Dad got you and your sister to safety which is what he wanted. Also, for what it's worth, he didn't have a choice but to do this mission. He did it to try and keep you safe, so don't hold it against him and don't feel guilty about it either because I didn't know him long but I do know he would do it all again.

I know it might be too soon for me to be saying that, but I don't know if I'll get another chance.

You don't have any obligations to this fight now, Josh. You've played your part and I'll make sure you are out. You've got your sister to look after now, so leave the rest to somebody else, that's what your Dad would want. Is that what you want?"

"That's my priority now, although I don't know how to keep her safe from this," Josh tells Winters.

"I'm not sure I can tell you either. If it were me, I'd get as far away from here as possible, across the sea if I could, but that will be easier said than done, I know."

"Do you know where my sister is now?"

"Yes, they are in the First-Class lounge, I'll make arrangements for you to be taken there."

"Thanks, I've got some plans and decisions to make."

"Yes, and I'm sure you'll make the right ones," Winters encourages.

"Thanks, I hope you're right."

Alice gets through screening and joins them to wait for the rest of the team. She doesn't disturb the two men talking. Hopefully, Winters has found the words she couldn't quite find. Josh looks as well as can be expected, better even, considering.

Downey, with his unwanted package—the holdall—follows Josh and Alice to screening. Winters waits patiently as Downey has his details tapped into the phone and he watches as Downey has the phone held up to his eye. The miraculous new App zooms right in on the eyeball, scanning for evidence that the owner of the eyeball is infected. The App takes its time scanning before it snaps a picture of the eye and eventually 'CLEAR' pops up in green across the screen.

"Clear," the operator of the phone announces, and Downey moves past to join Josh, Alice and Winters.

As soon as he reaches them, he lifts the holdall up, presenting it to Winters, eager to relieve himself of the burden.

Winters gives the holdall a look of disdain, as if to say, *is this what the grief's been over?* He then lifts his arm and takes the handles of the bag off Downey.

"Thanks," Winters says.

"Your welcome to it, Sir, I just hope it was worth the cost."

"You and me both Corporal, you and me both."

Winters takes the holdall over to the Discovery, opens the back door and places it onto the back seat. He closes the door and turns in the direction of the Corporal in charge of the screening team.

"What is your name, Corporal?" Winters asks the embarrassed man.

"Harris, Sir."

"You have a job to do, Harris. That doesn't mean you have to be a prick while you are doing it. Your comrades returning to base have been through enough shit without you adding to it. You can operate a tight security detail and do it civilly until it is time not to, understood?"

"Yes, Sir."

"If you don't think you can handle that, just say the word and I'll have you reassigned to another detail."

"I can handle it, Sir I don't know what came over me Sir, I apologise, Sir."

"Good, it is a very tense time, but we all have to hold it together, so carry on."

Winters salutes Corporal Harris casually as he turns away from him, and Corporal Harris returns the salute with vigour, standing to attention as he does.

Finally, Dixon receives the all-clear from the mobile phone that was stuck in his face and he joins the rest of the team, complaining and mumbling to himself.

"What are our orders now, Sir?" Dixon asks Winters.

"Mission complete, Sergeant; the cost has been great, too great and our thoughts are with the team members who haven't returned. Captain Richards, Dan and Wing Commander Buck." There is a moment of silence before Winters continues. "I have to get the holdall to Command so this is where we part ways. I have no further orders to give you, so get transport over to Terminal 5, fill your bellies and rest up, we will know where you are. Thank you, everyone."

Winters salutes the team, and they return it before Winters makes his way towards the Defender. On the way, he stops as he reaches Josh.

"Again, I'm sorry for your loss, Josh; my thoughts are with you and your sister and if there is anything I can do, get in contact with me, here, take my number."

"Thank you, Sir, I will."

The two men shake hands and then Winters makes his way over to his ride, while Josh saves his new contact into his phone.

"Right, let's get this show on the road, I need some chow. Where's my new friend?" Dixon announces as the driver's door of the Defender closes.

Corporal Harris hasn't moved from his spot, although he has been joined by the other members of his squad. He knows that he should be sorting the new arrivals out and he will, but he's just building up to it. He doesn't get the chance to stall any longer, however, because his nemesis is walking in his direction. Harris finds himself trembling a little as the tall, rugged-looking Special Forces Sergeant with the scar across his face approaches. To his credit, Harris manages to pull himself together and moves off his spot to meet him head-on.

The Sergeant doesn't slow down as they meet, and Harris thinks he is about to be in a fight.

"Ahh, there you are, Corporal," the Sergeant says as he moves around to Harris's side and throws his arm over his shoulder as if they were best of friends. Harris is both relieved and confused. "What do you say we forget about all this bad feeling, mate, and put that misunderstanding behind us. Life is too short, don't you think?"

"Absolutely, Sir," Harris stumbles.

"Good, good, so you think you can help us with a lift over to Terminal 5?"

"Absolutely," Harris again stumbles," I was just going to sort that out, Sir."

"Excellent, what's your name, Corporal?"

"Harris, Sir."

"Okay, Harris, let's get moving shall we, I'm starving?"

"Yes, Sir, we have a minibus lined up over there," Harris says, pointing.

Harris is now standing in front of all the new arrivals and he is unsure how he got there. Thankfully, the Sergeant has taken his arm from off Harris's shoulder and stands beside him, waiting for Harris to sort them out.

"Flight Lieutenant Alders?" Harris asks, already knowing who he is due to his pilot's uniform.

"Yes, Corporal?"

"I have orders for you to return to your squadron, Sir. Do you need transport, Sir?"

"Great, no rest for the wicked. No, Corporal, I can walk from here."

"Thank you, Sir. Everyone else, if you can get into that minibus, you will be driven over to Terminal 5."

Alders says his goodbyes, paying particular attention to Alice and Josh before walking off in the direction of the terminal building next to the landing zone.

The rest of the team load onto the minibus, leaving Harris behind.

Chapter 3

The drive to Terminal 5 is uneventful, although there's some banter between the Special Forces lads. Their normal post-mission buzz is heavily tempered by the losses inflicted. Voices are kept low and the jokes are small and kept to a minimum, out of respect.

"How are you holding up?" Alice asks Josh. They sit together at the front of the minibus.

"I'd be better if people stopped asking how I was holding up," Josh tries to joke.

"I'm sorry, my American insensitivity again."

"Don't worry, I was only joking. I don't think it's sunk in yet. I'm more concerned with what and how I am going to tell Emily; she is going to be devastated."

"It won't be easy, that's for sure, but have you any idea what to tell her?"

"I think I will tell her it was an accident, that he was killed in crossfire in the battle. She will ask more questions, so I will say that he was shot in the chest, died instantly and didn't suffer. What do you think?"

"That will sound believable to her and save her as much heartache as possible, I think you should go with that."

"I am not looking forward to it. And then there is Dan. I will have to tell Emily that news as well," Josh says, his head dropping slightly.

"I know," Alice says. She feels a strong urge to put her arm around Josh and to pull him into her, to comfort him. But she doesn't, as she doesn't know if she should. All she manages is to put her hand onto his back and rub it as you would a sick child. She instantly feels pathetic and pulls her hand away.

Josh looks up to her for a brief moment, their eyes meeting in the dim light. He appears young as if he were a boy and so vulnerable. Again, the urge to take him in her arms returns and again, she shies away from it and all she manages is a forced, tight-lipped smile, hopeless.

The volume of banter from the lads behind her rises for a second before they shut it down. Alice tries to convince herself that the men's presence is stopping her comforting Josh properly, but she knows she is kidding herself.

"I'll be alright," Josh mumbles and the moment passes, unlike Alice's feeling of uselessness.

A feeling of relief crosses Alice as the minibus parks up next to the huge Terminal 5 building and Josh pulls the sliding door open. Fresh air breezes into the minibus, blowing away at least some of the useless feeling she had, and she gets up from her seat.

Josh doesn't dwell on the moment he and Alice just had, and it leaves his thoughts immediately. He is too caught up in being reunited with Emily and the sense of trepidation at seeing her.

Josh and his Dad were close, very close—and when he can, he will grieve. He knows it is going to affect him terribly but right now, Josh can't allow that. He has to be strong for Emily and only hopes he has some of his Dad's strength to be able to handle it.

Josh is also concerned about Catherine hearing the news. He knows that his Dad and Catherine were close, but he isn't sure exactly how far their relationship had gone. His Dad played his cards very close to his chest on that. Josh knows he struggled with the relationship, *any relationship* because he was afraid that Emily would feel threatened by it. Emily struggled badly when her mum left, and it was made worse by the fact that her Dad wasn't as familiar to her as other fathers and daughters may be. Her father had spent so much time away from her, as that was the nature of his work.

Catherine had fallen for his Dad a long time ago. Josh was sure of that—and it was only a matter of time before it would have been reciprocated if it hadn't already. Catherine had been patient and waited. She was an amazing woman and knew the delicate situation with Emily. Josh could see Catherine thought the world of her.

Josh has his story straight in his head to tell Emily. But telling Catherine the same story is a different matter; he will play that by ear. This is going be the toughest thing Josh has ever had to do, but as his Dad would, he will meet it head-on.

After entering the terminal building, they reach the large departure lounge, where Josh and Alice had been only a few hours ago. Josh's life has been turned on its head again since they left; will it ever end?

The lounge is busy, military staff and civilians refuelling in their time window before their next task or mission. The food station is fully stocked again and has a healthy queue of eager diners waiting to be served.

Dixon and the rest of the SF team are chomping at the bit to get in on the food action but hang back with Josh and Alice—who looks lost for the moment.

"I know you've got a tough task ahead, Josh, but why don't you get some food first, it will help?" Dixon asks Josh.

"Thanks, but I can't face food right now, I need to get to my sister."

"I understand, mate; do you know where she is?"

"Winters said he would make arrangements to take me to her. Maybe he forgot?"

"Something tells me Winters doesn't forget," Dixon observes.

"Good point. Listen, you all carry on and I'll find out where she is. You too, Alice."

"No Josh, I'm staying with you," Alice insists.

"You really don't have to, Alice."

"Don't be ridiculous. I'm not leaving you to deal with it alone."

"Thanks, Alice."

"Well good luck, mate; maybe we'll catch up later but knowing our luck, we will be knee-high in shit again before our food goes down," Dixon says, then surprisingly gives Josh and Alice both a man hug.

The rest of the team say their good lucks and goodbyes before heading off to the food station where they ignore the queue, grab plates and dig straight into the food. Nobody in the line messes with them or says a word as they barge in. The military personnel know better than to get between Special Forces and their grub, and the civvies are too taken aback and frightened of the fearsome-looking men to protest.

Josh looks over to the stairwell by the escalator where officials came from earlier in the day to take everyone's details. Three military personnel are over there, two men and one woman; one of the men holds a clipboard.

"Let's try them, over there," Josh says pointing at the officials. "Are you sure you wouldn't prefer to get something to eat?" he asks.

Alice is already gone, making her way over as she tells Josh, 'no'.

Lieutenant Winters hasn't forgotten the soldier with the clipboard has instructions for an escort to take Josh to the First-Class lounge.

As he climbs the stairs and walks the corridor, Josh finds he is getting more and more nervous and that his grip on his emotions is slipping. *Stay strong,* he keeps telling himself. *You can't see Emily looking like a blubbering mess,* he steels himself again.

"Is there anywhere I can freshen up before we get there?" Josh asks their female escort.

"Are you okay?" Alice immediately asks, with a look of concern etched across her face.

"Yes, just need the loo and to wash up before I see Em."

"There is a toilet just up here," the escort tells him. "Are you American?" she then asks Alice.

"Guilty as charged, but don't hold it against me."

"I won't, where in America are you from?"

"Born in California, but we moved around a lot when I was young."

"California, very swish; wish I were there right now," their escort says, and who can blame her?

A glossy First-Class Lounge sign comes into view farther up the bland corridor. It isn't lit, however, which takes some of the shine off the desired effect. On the right of the corridor, closer to them is another sign, for the public toilets.

Josh heads into the men's without saying anything and Alice decides to take the opportunity and does the same.

Josh washes up, looking at himself in the mirror as he does. He thinks he looks okay, but he dwells for a moment, staring at himself, psyching himself up ready for his dreadful task.

The two women are waiting for him as he exits, Alice has a look of concern on her face and her attempt at a reassuring smile is not convincing. The other woman smiles a relaxed smile at Josh as he comes out, oblivious to the whole situation.

"Can you hold this for me please?" Josh asks Alice, as he holds up his rifle.

"Of course," she replies, taking it and putting it over her shoulder and behind her back with hers. "Are you ready?"

"As ready as I'll ever be."

Catherine is sitting on a tall wooden chair at one of the small square tables scattered around the lounge, facing the entry. Her phone is on the table in front of her. She is worried to death but no matter how many times she glances down at the phone, the screen stays black. She forces herself not to switch the screen on again in case she has missed a message from Andy; it's been sitting there, in front of her and she would have seen any message come through. Emily and Stacey are behind her on one of the couches, with their backs to the entry watching the TV screen mounted on the wall. Thankfully, they had managed to find something on the TV that wasn't the news. Catherine barely notices what David Attenborough is saying and what animal he is talking about, but it is keeping Emily occupied, at least for the time being.

Every time someone enters the lounge, Catherine's hopes rise only to be dashed. She was expecting Andy's mission to be finished by now and that she would have heard at least something off him, even if only a message telling her he was okay or what was happening. Asking any of the military staff on duty here is useless; they won't help at all. All they say is to wait and they will update her as soon as there is anything to report.

The compulsion to check the phone wins and she presses the screen on. All it tells her is the weather forecast and that hasn't changed either. She picks up her phone, her impatience for news now overwhelming. She is going to get some answers.

She squeezes the phone into her front pocket, leaning back in her chair to ease it in and is just about to get up when Josh comes into the lounge.

Catherine's smile at seeing Josh and then Alice enter the lounge, fades quickly when Andy doesn't join them. Her stomach tightens as she recognises the agonised look on Josh's face. She finds herself unable to get out of her chair as foreboding grips, the blood draining from her face.

Josh and Catherine's eyes meet across the room and his body stops working too as he comes to a standstill. An eruption of emotion threatens to explode from deep within him. He is teetering on the edge. He must gather his strength, and he has to do it now, but he feels it slipping away.

Emily comes into Catherine's mind and she forces herself out of her stupor; she buries her emotion, forcing herself to face the tragic news that Josh is clearly struggling to handle. Catherine falls out of the tall chair, her legs wobbly, the room spinning. She is on her feet though and some strength comes back to her. She wants to reach Josh before Emily realises he has returned, to take him back out to the corridor so that he can tell her what has happened.

Catherine must prepare herself, to be ready to be there for Emily. Her own feelings are of little consequence right now.

"Josh!" Emily shouts from behind Catherine.

Oh no, Catherine thinks and spins around to Emily, to tell her to wait there while she speaks to Josh. It is too late, however, as Emily is already springing over the back of the couch to run to her brother.

Catherine watches as Emily runs straight across the room and jumps into Josh's arms. He picks up his sister and pulls her close, her head going to the side of his as she wraps her arms around his neck. Josh looks across to Catherine, his eyes red and swelling.

Stacey comes around, standing next to Catherine, and asks, 'What has happened?'

"Where is Dad, isn't he with you?" Emily asks her brother. But he doesn't answer, can't answer. "Josh?" she questions again and pushes herself up, looking at her brother. "Josh, what's wrong, where is Dad?" Emily asks again, her voice cracking, instinctively knowing something is terribly wrong as she sees her brother's face.

Josh, struggling to talk, looks at Catherine, asking for help and she goes over to them. Emily is getting more upset by the second and desperately keeps asking where her Dad is.

"Emily, Josh is upset, let me talk to him for a minute to see what's wrong; is that okay? Catherine tries to soothe.

"I want to know where Dad is," she protests.

"I know, sweetie, but why don't you let me talk to him so that I can find out what has happened for you?"

Emily protests again, but gradually she relents and lets Catherine lift her off Josh.

"Good girl," Catherine soothes.

"Come on, Em, why don't we wait over on the couch so Catherine can see what's wrong with Josh?" Stacey says, next to them. Eventually, Emily agrees and they both return to where they sat watching TV.

Josh has already moved away, trying to hide how upset he is from his sister and has sat on another couch near the entrance. Alice follows him over.

"What has happened?" Catherine says as she sits down next to Josh, lifting his hand into hers as she does.

Gradually, Josh tells her the truth about what happened at the Orion building, from start to finish. How Dan was killed and how his Dad was infected. He tells her how he had to leave his Dad behind and the guilt he feels for doing that. It takes time to tell her as he tries to control his emotions. Catherine sits in silence as Josh tells her his awful story. She can't help but get upset as she hears it, since her heart aches for Josh, for Emily and for herself.

When Josh finishes, they sit in silence, both processing what he said.

"Thank you for telling me," Catherine says, breaking the silence, her spirit hanging by a thread—a thread that, for Emily, she won't let break.

"I'm sorry I couldn't save him," Josh says.

"Josh, you can't blame yourself, this isn't your fault; you couldn't have done anything else."

"I could have stayed with him, I left him on his own in the dark."

"You had no choice, Josh. What good would it have done if you'd stayed? That is the last thing your father would have wanted. He told you, and he wanted you here with your sister."

"Catherine is right, Josh; your dad would have failed if you had done that," Alice says.

"I know, it doesn't make it any easier though."

"What shall we tell Emily?" Catherine asks.

Josh tells Catherine what he has decided to tell Emily and she agrees that it is the best thing to tell her.

"Are you ready to talk to Emily?" Catherine asks.

"Yes, I think I am."

Colonel Reed has abandoned the command tent where Winters had left him earlier. He and his entourage have relocated to a large conference room in the Terminal 5 building. The room has been freshly kitted out with the latest tech to command and control Operation Denial. The tents acted as a temporary measure the Colonel had set up until this room was up and running.

Winters is grateful that the new command centre is operational and glad he missed the worst of the weather in that tent. He also suspects that Colonel Reed is pleased to have left the tent behind too, no matter how much bravado he would have given about being on the ground as close to the action as possible.

The new command area is bustling as Winters enters; easily fifty personnel are busily helping direct the battle to take back London. There had also been a steady stream of staff coming and going as Winters had made his way through the terminal building to get here.

A bank of fifteen large monitors has been hung onto the wall at the back of the relatively dimly lit room. Streaming onto the screens is footage from 'action areas' around London. The footage arriving from drones flying around the city, CCTV cameras and from soldiers' head cams amongst other sources. Action and fighting fill all the screens. The dark of night is masked by military-grade HD lowlight cameras, street lighting and burning fires. Only a few screens are showing darker images, but they only show the muzzle flashes and explosions in starker contrast.

In front of the bank of monitors is a cordoned-off area with a few tables and other computer monitors scattered around. Then behind that area, which Winters has just entered, is where the main bulk of the personnel are working. This area is where all the data from the operation is processed and passed up the chain of command. Some of it will reach the top brass in the cordoned-off area, including Colonel Reed.

Winters, gripping the costly holdall in one hand and his satchel-style briefcase in the other, makes his way down the centre aisle between the rows of whirring computers and busy staff, who constantly crossing over the aisle on important business that can't be delayed. Winters recognises many of the personnel working in the new command room. All are well trained and that training is constantly refreshed with exercises, drills and lessons.

Winters himself participates in many of these tasks as part of his position and rank. He makes sure he is involved with any and all new procedures and training that will keep him at the top of his game.

Winters nods at various people he sees and has had dealings with, and they all acknowledge him back. They all know he is the right-hand man of the Colonel and that affords him their respect, some envy and probably some sympathy. Winters has little time for their feelings, however, and is hardly friendly with any of the other personnel; he prefers it that way, as it doesn't confuse matters.

Sure enough, Colonel Reed is at the centre of events. He stands tall directly in front of the bank of monitors, his grey-haired head moving from side to side as he follows the action laid out before him. The Colonel is surrounded by the usual cronies and yes men, who are far enough up the Colonel, they must surely smell his crack.

Winters assumes his colleagues consider him to be one of these ass-kissing plebs and maybe they are correct to a certain extent, but they are also wrong in many ways. Winters didn't come from the same kind of privileged background as the other men surrounding the Colonel. Winters came from a family of divorced parents, went to a normal state school and worked shifts to put himself through college. After college, he had a choice, to lumber himself with debt and go to university or choose another path. Winters chose the Army and plans to get to the top of his chosen profession, even if it means kissing some ass on his way.

"Excuse me, Colonel, Sir, I have the package."

The Colonel makes a show of ignoring Winters for a moment as if something vital is happening on the screens in front of him. Winters is well used to his idiosyncrasies and waits patiently for him to respond, not letting himself get agitated or annoyed by his show.

"Put it over there," Colonel Reed says, keeping his back to Winters and indicating with his head where he wants it.

"Yes, Sir."

Winters takes the holdall over to an empty table which has been clearly set up ready to receive the contents of it. He places the bags onto the table, takes a step back and waits. The Colonel's show proceeds for another minute or two before he turns and walks across.

"A successful mission then, eh Winters?" the Colonel states as he arrives at the table, closely followed by the other officers.

Colonel Reed knows full well that completing the mission has cost three men their lives; he knows everything, or so he likes to think. The Colonel had known Andy Richards for many years, back from when Andy was in the military and more lately from his dealings with Andy through his position at Orion Securities. This is of little consequence to Reed, though, as he shows no feelings of remorse for the three men, no matter how long he had known them or what effect their loss may have on their families.

The mission is everything as far as he is concerned, and to him, the mission goal was achieved as is proved by the evidence on the table in front of him. The three men's lives are collateral damage, a means to an end that will show everyone he's indispensable and help keep him in his position of power.

The man is a power-hungry authoritarian brute and Winters debates whether to take his sidearm out of its holster and show him just how indispensable he really is.

"The mission goal was achieved, Sir," Winters says through gritted teeth.

"Very good Lieutenant, I knew I could count on you to get it done."

"Sir."

"Major Rees, let's see what Sir Malcolm was hoarding shall we?" Colonel Reed instructs.

Major Rees is the latest addition to Colonel Reed's entourage, his expert on the virus. And he is the man who oversaw the doomed facility and was at ground zero when the outbreak happened; he steps forward, extremely uncomfortable in his new position and he would be far happier back in his laboratory or behind his desk.

"Sir, the bag should be examined under controlled conditions, in a laboratory with all the necessary precautions taken," Major Rees protests.

"Poppycock, Major, the bag is here, get on with it!"

Colonel Reed has no intention of giving up his prize and Major Rees hasn't the confidence to force him to.

As if by magic, a pair of latex gloves appear in the Major's hands and he pulls them on, his fingers wriggling into them. Gently and deliberately, he places his hands on the holdall as if the contents inside are fragile and if any wrong move is made, something inside could break and cause another viral release. Slowly, he pulls the zip along the top of the bag open and pulls the two sides apart. He peers inside the bag, checking the contents for the longest time, only his head moving as he scans. If only he knew the rough handling the contents and the holdall has already received. The contents were stuffed in without ceremony and the holdall has since been thrown around, bashed and kicked.

An uneasiness has spread around the table as the men see Major Rees's caution. Nobody says a word, and even Colonel Reed's bluster is retreating. Now, he is leaning back, away from the Major's operation with a funny turned-up-nose look on his face, as if that would save him if something were suddenly released.

Major Rees's caution does not falter. He is obviously very proficient in handling delicate and possibly hazardous materials, which everyone is relieved to see. Slowly, he lifts items out and places them in order onto the table. Sir Malcolm's safe had contained a variety of different things—numerous paper files and paperwork—which the Major stacks in one pile. A passport, old photographs, an Omega watch, a box of bullets and four wads of fifty-pound notes, each wad containing at least two hundred notes.

"Bingo," the Major says quietly to himself as he lifts out a locking plastic box with a dark transparent lid. Inside the box, lined up for them all to see are floppy disks, the small hard plastic types, used before computer storage went digital.

When the Major finally finishes, the table's covered in items, and he takes a step back and clasps his hands behind him. His eyes continue to dart between the items on the table for a while until he finally looks up to Colonel Reed.

"Well Major, what is your prognosis?" the Colonel demands, leaning forward again.

"It looks promising, Colonel, but I can't say for sure any of it will be useful until we have had a chance to go through and study the paperwork and computer storage disks, if the disks are even still viable, Sir."

"And how long will that take, Major?"

"How long is a piece of string, Sir?"

"It's as long as I fucking say it is, soldier," Reed growls.

"Yes, Sir, sorry Sir; what I meant to say is, with the right equipment and the right team, two, maybe three hours until we know if there is any data related to the viral infection. We would then have to study that data if we find it, Sir.

"You have two hours to find out if there is anything useful here, Major. Lieutenant Winters will get you what you need to proceed. Understood?"

"Yes, Sir!"

Major Rees opens up the holdall again and starts replacing the items back inside, ready to take them away to wherever he will be taken by the Lieutenant. He picks up one of the bundles of fifty-pound notes, unsure what to do with all the money.

"What shall I do with this, Sir?" Rees asks, holding up the bundle just as the Colonel and his cronies turn away from the table, done with the Major for now.

"Is it relevant to your analysis, Major?"

"No, Sir."

"Then give it to Lieutenant Winters, he will take care of it," Colonel Reed says, looking at Winters for a second, before carrying on moving away.

Winters knows exactly what will happen to the money. The Colonel will leave it in his care for a suitable amount of time until it is forgotten about and then it will disappear into the Colonel's coffers. He is never one to look a gift horse in the mouth, as Winters knows well.

"What is the latest report on the progress of Operation Denial, Sir?" Winters asks Major Rees as he hands over the wads of cash for Winters to stuff into his satchel.

"Bad, Lieutenant; our forces are making little progress in clearing the city and forcing the infected people east. The area is so large there are simply too many streets and buildings to clear. Most zones are bogged down in trying to clear their areas and engaging in running battles with the infected. And of course, if our troops lose a battle or even a skirmish, they invariably turn and are added to the army of infected, so it's a double-edged sword."

"So, I take it there is a lot riding on you finding something in those files, Sir?"

"I think Command are pinning their hopes on a cure or a weapon being found in this bag. I've told the Colonel numerous times that it is a long shot, but he doesn't want to listen."

"That doesn't surprise me in the least, Sir."

"The man is an acquired taste, that is for certain," Major Rees says, nervous about deriding the Colonel in front of his assistant.

"He certainly is," Winters confirms, also keeping his opinion to himself. "Okay, let's get you set up with what you need, Sir," he adds as the Major finishes repacking the holdall.

Chapter 4

The flesh on its body burns like volcanic lava, the skin threatening to melt away and drip from its body, its organs boiling, adding to the excruciating searing pain. Encased within its melting body are its bones which feel as brittle as if they had been dipped and frozen in liquid nitrogen, and the slightest impact would risk making them splinter, crack and break.

Movement is impossible, the agony too great. The half-dead creature is motionless in the pitch black with only its nightmares for company.

The creature retches uncontrollably. Toxic, acid bile oozes out of its gaping mouth, flowing down its body and legs onto the floor to join the shit and piss already pooled there. Its retching causes its body to convulse, involuntarily sending its pain level rocketing to greater, unknown heights. Passing out from the agony, oblivion brings temporary relief from the torture.

Memories flash through the creature's unconscious mind while it is passed out, the pain blocked by its brain. Fleeting memories of its children disappear too quickly to grab and hold onto.

Images swirl around in its brain from across its life, some happy ones, ones it is unconsciously grateful to see again, but they are overpowered by images the creature would rather forget. Images from its years on the battlefield, the blood and guts of the twisted bodies of its enemies and comrades. The terrible images move out of focus, only to be replaced by other horrific images. The creature's mind had buried them years ago but now they are unlocked and gush out like blood from a slit artery, coming to torment it.

Consciousness returns, bringing the impossible agony with it. More bile bubbles from deep within the creature and starts to rise through its gut. *'No, no,'* its mind screams, it cannot go through another bout of retching, the pain is too much to bear. It can feel the noxious fluid rising though, and it cannot be stopped; the creature's dry mouth liquifies and the inevitable retching begins again. The creature tries to accept the excruciating pain the retching delivers, tries to let the fluid evacuate its guts, to get it over with. It tries to blank it all out and let it happen.

Thick fluid bile bursts from its throat in streams, following down its usual path to the floor. Revolting chunks follow the liquid and the creature has to cough them up through its throat and spit them out to stop itself choking, its pain levels soaring higher. Is the virus rejecting its body's organs? Are they being liquified and ejected through its mouth, no longer required?

The remnants of the creature's mind attempt to figure out what is happening to it, but its thoughts are a jumbled mess, incoherent, the agony overriding everything. The creature's hand twitches in the hope that the Glock is still in it so that it can raise it to its temple, squeeze the trigger and end this nightmare, but the creature's hand is empty.

A chunk is wedged in the creature's throat and it prepares for the onslaught of pain that will hit when it has to try and dislodge it. Before it can prepare, though, the creatures body spasms and the coughing starts in reflex to clear its throat. The coughing causes more retching, yet the chunk remains lodged. The creature's brain is overloaded with pain as the spasms increase and it starts to shut down.

Any semblance of balance is lost as it spasms and its body tilts and slides sideways across the cupboards behind it until its tilt goes past the point of no return. The creature's body falls slowly down onto the floor and onto its side. Thankfully the creature's brain has shut down and only its unconsciousness saves it from the agony of the fall.

This time, there are no memories or images to accompany it, only darkness and oblivion.

Chapter 5

Josh feels his sister's sobbing has calmed slightly. Emily lies against him as they sit on the couch facing the TV where Emily and Stacey were when he arrived.

Emily has taken the news of her Dad as badly as Josh had feared. She is still too young for any attempt to put a brave face on it; her emotion and feeling had flooded out immediately. She couldn't hold it back as she didn't know how to, and why should she?

Josh had cried somewhat with her, but he didn't let himself go. He did have to be brave, if that is the right word, and suppress the majority of his emotion for his loss. He had to be brave for Emily, he had to support her, since she came first now. Was he starting to unconsciously think and feel like their Dad did, thinking of his sister before all else?

If so, something tells him that that feeling is only going to get stronger as he starts to take full responsibility for Emily. Josh knows that is what his dad would have wanted, but perhaps he isn't only going to do it for that reason. Perhaps he takes after his Dad in some ways and he is doing it because he feels it, an unexplainable feeling. Is this the feeling that only a parent would know or a surrogate parent as Josh is now? Josh knows one thing for sure; he is more than just a brother to his sister. He is also her guardian.

"Emily?" Josh says reassuringly, looking down at the blonde curls below him but getting no response. "Emily, shall we go downstairs and see what there is to eat?" Still no response, but Josh persists; he wants to try and take her mind off what has happened a bit and a change of scenery will help. "Come on, Emily, I'm quite hungry, will you come with me?" He moves his body under her a little bit to help try and stir her.

"Umm," Emily growls and fidgets, and it isn't much of a response, but it is one.

Catherine, who sits with her legs curled up to the side of the couch, in an armchair, starts to stir. Her head has been down too, her hair covering her face. Gradually, her head comes up and she looks over to Josh. She wipes her nose with a tissue that has been resting in her hand for the last thirty or forty minutes. Her eyes are puffy and red, and her makeup smudged from her tears.

"Yes, Emily, let's have a look downstairs; we have been cooped up is here for a long time, so a change of scenery will be good for us all," Catherine says.

"In a minute," Emily responds, a little surprisingly, from her burrow at Josh's side.

"Good girl. I'd better fix my makeup then. I think it is going to be very smudged." Catherine tries to sound a bit upbeat.

"I'll come with you," Stacey says from beside Josh. "Do you want to come with us, Emily?"

Catherine and Stacey make a show of getting up from their seats and to Josh's surprise, Emily does start to move. Emily rises up and off Josh. Standing up, she follows the other two towards the bathroom. Her hair is a mess around her head she walks slowly, her arms by her side and her head tilted down slightly. Josh wonders how she can see where she is going.

Moving his back off the couch, Josh raises his arms and stretches before getting to his feet.

He goes around the couch and over to Alice, who sits at a table behind. Seeing Josh come over, she puts her phone on the table.

"Sorry if it's a bit morbid," he tells her.

"Don't be silly, Josh, that is completely understandable. I just sat over here because you all wouldn't want a stranger with you at a time like this."

"A stranger… Now, who's being silly? You aren't a stranger."

"Well, I'm not exactly but you know what I mean."

"Yes, I do and thanks."

"Thanks for what?"

"I dunno, you've been a good support to me, Alice."

"I'm glad I could be of service," Alice jokes, with a lovely smile.

"Are you hungry?" Josh asks, finding himself a bit flustered, not knowing what else to say.

"I could eat, for sure."

Emily's hair is back under control when they return from the bathroom and although she still looks delicate, her eyes are dry and there is even a hint of a smile when Josh holds out his hand to her.

As they all approach the exit from the lounge, the soldier who has been standing inside the door moves across it.

"I have been ordered to ask the three ladies to wait inside until further notice."

"Ordered by whom?" Josh asks.

"By my superior, Private," the Lance Corporal tells him.

Josh suddenly has visions of how his father would have brushed this soldier aside by bending him to his will or ordering him to move. Josh doesn't hold the rank to be able to give any orders, nor does Alice for that matter. After the events of the last two days, he feels totally inadequate for it. He debates how to handle the situation. One option would be to leave himself and speak to a superior, possibly Lieutenant Winters—or even better, Dixon is just downstairs. Josh is sure Dixon would jump at the chance to deal with their guard. Before he formulates any more options, Catherine deals with the situation for them.

"Move out of our way, young man," she says. "We are not prisoners; we have been in this room for hours. We are going downstairs to get something to eat and if that a problem, then I suggest you take it up with your superiors, or you can shoot us of course. Now move," Catherine instantly regrets saying shoot us, with Emily beside her.

The soldier looks like a small boy who has just been told off by his mum; he still doesn't move, though. He has his orders after all.

"Why don't we compromise?" Alice suggests. "Why don't you escort the three ladies down to the lounge area, Lance Corporal, I am sure you have had enough up here too and you're probably hungry and could eat some food?"

The mention of the word food is a masterstroke by Alice. Bribing a young squaddie with food gets a result more often than not.

After a moment's deliberation, the five of them are walking down the corridor to the stairs under the close supervision of their guard, the Lance Corporal.

Emily holds her brother's hand all the way and her grip tightens when they exit the stairs into the bustle of the departure lounge.

Although still busy, the lounge has thinned out since Josh and Alice came through it a while ago. Thankfully, however, the food is still being served and they head straight for it. There are plenty of tables to choose from after they have been served and Catherine points out a possible one.

"Josh, Alice!" a call comes from their right.

Sergeant Dixon is standing next to a table with his hand in the air.

"Who is that?" Catherine asks.

"That is Sergeant Dixon and his SBS patrol, the ones I mentioned upstairs." Josh answers.

"Okay, you go ahead and tell them to be discreet before we follow you over," Catherine tells Josh, turning her back on Emily who is beside her with her tray of food, so she doesn't hear.

"I'll go, you stay with Emily," Alice says quietly to Josh, before walking off in their direction, her tray of food out in front of her.

Josh puts his tray of food down when he reaches them, before he greets his SBS comrades.

"Good to see you all," Josh says as he shakes the four men's hands. "I thought you would be gone by now— where are the other lads?"

"They were reassigned before they had a chance to finish their nosh. Terrible luck for them," Dixon says, smiling from ear to ear about the misfortune of his SAS counterparts. "You were lucky to catch us. We are off now, just had time for dessert and after-dinner coffee though." His smile broadens.

"What's your assignment?" Alice asks.

"Can't say, my dear," Dixon answers.

"Top Secret, is it?" Josh asks.

"No, they just haven't told us yet, just been given a time and a place to report in. Anyway, forget that, who is this lovely girl?" Dixon says, bending down to Emily, who still stands with her tray, which Stacey takes off her.

"This is my sister Emily."

"Ah, I thought it must be, nice to meet you, Emily, I'm Dixon, I knew your father, he told me you were a lovely brave girl."

"Don't you have a proper name?" Emily says, recoiling slightly from the big, scared SBS operative.

"Ha-ha, straight to the point just like your father. I do but people just call me Dixon."

"Nice to meet you, Mr Dixon," Emily says shyly.

Dixon laughs again. "Nice to meet you too, Emily. Right, we better be on our way." Dixon says as he stands up straight.

The four men gather their gear together and say their goodbyes.

"Look after your brother, Emily," Dixon turns and says as they go.

"How did he know Dad?" Emily asks.

"He was on the mission when Dad died," Josh says, unsure if it was the right thing to say.

"Oh," is all Emily says before she sits down at the table with her food.

Major Rees glances at his watch with some trepidation, regretting the amount of time he had told Colonel Reed it would take to sift through all the files and information laid out in front of him. He now wishes he had added more time to his estimate.

Lieutenant Winters had instantly seconded another conference room close to the command centre to work from. He was also in the process of assigning a team to the task and arranging the requested equipment to be delivered. That didn't change the fact that now Rees had laid all the evidence out on the long black conference table, he was sure more time would be needed, time that wouldn't be forthcoming.

Sadness and regret that Molly, his brilliant and trusted Lieutenant, isn't here to assist him hits Rees and then the guilt of her death washes over him. She had warned him so many times of her misgivings with the operation to vacate the old storage facility. She had urged for the operation to be halted, revaluated and new wide-ranging precautions to be adopted. Not an hour before the disaster happened, she had burst into his office demanding that the operation be halted and saying that it wasn't being carried out safely. He had agreed with her concerns, had even protested to his superiors—but in the end what did he do? Instead of stopping the operation and refusing to carry on, he had followed orders, had ordered Molly to continue with an operation that he knew wasn't safe.

Nobody was holding him responsible for the disaster; his protests had been lodged with his superiors and were on record. The disaster, the viral outbreak and all that is now following are being blamed on a forklift driver and a young contractor fainting. Those are the CCTV images being shown by the news outlets to explain how the disaster happened.

No mention of piss-poor planning, cost-cutting or incompetent management. The cover-up is in full swing, everyone is covering their arses and that include Rees. He knows that his weakness and incompetence is to blame for the whole catastrophe. He is responsible for Molly's death and untold numbers of others. He was in charge of that facility and the guilt hangs over him like a crushing weight.

When the time is right, when he has done all he can to try and stop the outbreak, he will confess to his responsibility, confess and be damned to his fate, as he deserves.

That time is not now, though. Now, he must use all his knowledge to stop the outbreak. There are few people who have his background and understanding of the type of virus spreading in the general population. He knows how they work, and he knows the consequences if it isn't stopped. To give himself up now would be selfish. He must carry his burden and fight the virus, not for redemption. He is beyond redemption, so his only motivation now is to kill the virus.

Major Rees looks again at the files in front of him, thinks again of Molly and reaches for the first file.

"A team of six analysts will be here in less than ten minutes," Lieutenant Winters informs Rees just as he is opening the first file. "They were already on-site, on secondment from GCHQ to analyse the data from Operation Denial. Two have a medical background and the others have experience in chemical and biological weapon data. It's the best I could do within the time frame, Sir."

"Very good, Lieutenant; that is better than I was expecting. And the equipment?"

"The computers will be here momentarily, Sir, including two floppy disk readers with USB connectivity. Our best tech guys will set them up and install the software to read the floppy disks. In fact, here they are now, Sir." Winters goes over to the door and waves them in, with the hardware on two-wheeler sack trucks.

"Set the computer up there as quickly as you can," Rees says, pointing. The three men in military uniforms say, '*yes, Sir,*' and urgently get to it.

"Is there anything else you need, Sir?" Winters asks.

"Yes, an overhead projector; I have just noticed a file of films."

"We really are going '*old school,*' Sir."

"The contents of that safe were in there for many years, Lieutenant, and the only thing that could play into our hands is that they have been well protected."

"I'll get on it, Sir," Winters says, already scrolling through his phone.

Finally, Major Rees's head goes down and he starts to analyse the data in the first file he picked up. This is his forte, crunching data in his head. Biological, chemical or physical makes little difference to him; he is a genius when it comes to understanding scientific data. The text, equations and chemical compound structures are his domain and that is why he has the rank of Major. It isn't because of his people skills or fighting prowess.

Rees is virtually finished analysing the first file from page to page when the team of analysts from GCHQ arrives on the scene. The file has no data relevant to the virus and he picks up a red marker pen that arrived with the equipment to mark the front of the folder. He will have the file double and triple-checked even though he is confident it has no bearing. Each pair of eyes might see something from a different angle and come to a different conclusion. Rees does not think he is infallible, far from it, as the last few days have proven.

In rapid time, the computers are up and running, their fans working to keep them cool. And when the Tech guys, who actually consist of two women and one man, have the software installed and disk readers connected, their leader,

Lieutenant Fiona Portman, stands to attention to inform the Major.

"Thank you, Lieutenant. Let's see if these disks are still readable?" Rees says handing her the plastic box containing the old technology.

"Yes, Sir," she replies eagerly, taking the box as if it is a Christmas present.

In quick time, everyone is busy with their assigned tasks; three of the analysts sit around the table, sifting through the files, checking, double-checking before triple-checking the data. Flagging any data that could be relevant and passing it on, its final destination Major Rees.

Only one of the floppy disks is corrupted and unreadable and that disk is currently being taken apart, cleaned and reassembled to try and get at least some data off it. The data on the rest of the floppy disks is considerable and is going to take time to analyse, so there is no time to waste. Two analysts sit in front of the computers sorting the data, sending documents to the hastily set-up printer that's constantly churning out paper.

Colonel Reed suddenly strides through the door, into the conference room.

All the military personnel in the room instantly stop what they are doing and stand to attention. The analysts from GCHQ give him a cursory look to see what the fuss is about and then get back to work.

"At ease men, carry on," the Colonel orders, not wanting the work on his prize to be delayed. "Report, Major," Reed says, striding over to Rees who stands with an open file in his hand.

"We have found no data connection to the virus as of yet, Sir. There is a lot of data to analyse, however. The computer disks are providing masses of data, Sir, all of which need to be sorted and analysed. With the amount of data there is, Sir, it could take hours, if not days to get through."

"We don't have hours, and days, Major, as you well know. I don't want to hear excuses. I want to see results!"

"I understand that, Sir, we are getting through the data as quickly as possible, Sir, with the resources we have, Sir."

"If you need more resources, Lieutenant Winters will provide you with them. I expect your report within the hour, Major."

"Yes, Sir," Major Rees says as the Colonel turns and leaves.

Rees turns away from the exiting Colonel and looks at the mound of files on the conference table. New files are being added to the table constantly as the printer works overtime. New data is collated, stapled together and brought over ready for analysis. The task is daunting and as a sinking feeling starts to develop in Rees's stomach, he looks over to Lieutenant Winters, in the hope that he can offer some solutions.

Josh looks over to his little sister. Emily has hardly eaten any of her food. Her right elbow is perched on top of the table and her head is resting on its hand. Her left hand holds her fork which pushes food around her plate aimlessly. She stars down blankly at the food changing positions. She is in another world, and Josh knows what she will be thinking about; the look of sadness on her face tells him that if nothing else.

Josh had expected Emily to be much worse and more upset than she is. She was very upset when he told her, as inconsolable as Josh had expected. He hadn't anticipated how quickly she would start to recover, however. For her to be sitting down here at the table is proof of that and Josh doesn't know if he should be more worried by it. She is very quiet and who knows what is actually going on in her head?

Maybe the events of the last few days have hardened her to her loss? Perhaps it hasn't come as such a shock to her? These are not normal times and so maybe he shouldn't expect her to be affected as normal? She has seen the world in a different light now—everybody has, and that can't be undone. She has seen Stacey lose both of her parents and seen how strong she has been, so maybe some of her strength has transferred to Emily?

Whatever it is, Josh knows he has to keep a close eye on her, and that she is hurting, even if she is hiding--or worse, burying--it.

The Lance Corporal, their escort, is keeping his distance whilst keeping a close eye on them. He has finished his food and is sits at the table adjacent to them. Catherine had invited him over to join them, but he politely refused, preferring to stay where he was. That was probably a good idea for him, as Catherine had only wanted to try and get him onside.

"There is nothing keeping us here now, so we should get out of the city," Catherine suddenly says.

"I agree," Josh says after a small pause. "Have you any ideas where we could go and how to get there?"

"I have friends in Devon. They have a farm, it's beautiful down there. I have spoken to them and they have said we can go there. They have a holiday home on the farm that they rent out which we can use. What do you think?"

"It sounds too good to be true! Did you tell them there are four or five of us?" Josh asks, glancing at Alice.

"Yes, I explained the situation and they are more than happy for us to use the holiday home. I've known them for a long time, and they would say if it was a problem. They have had quite a few cancellations. Well, actually, everybody has cancelled."

"What do you think, Emily, it sounds nice don't you think, countryside and beaches?" Josh asks.

"I suppose." Emily shrugs, without looking up.

"What about you, Stacey, what do you think?" Josh asks, looking over to her.

"It sounds fine. I will have to speak to my grandparents again though. They have asked me if I want to go to theirs?" Stacey says, confused by the whole situation-- and who can blame her?

"Alice?" Josh finally asks.

"I don't know what I am going to do. I guess I will have to speak to my superiors. I am sure they will want to reassign me."

"No way," Josh says. "My Dad made a deal that if we completed the mission we would be out."

"Are you sure that included me, Josh? I'm not," Alice says, looking worried.

"I will speak to Lieutenant Winters and get him to clear it," Josh says, sounding more confident than he is.

"Well if that is the case, then yes, I'm definitely up for some sea air. Me and my parents aren't close, and they are back in the U.S. anyway."

"How are we going to get to Devon?" Stacey asks.

"I will see if Lieutenant Winters can help us, see if he can get us a car or something?" Josh says.

"I think you are putting a lot of stock in the Lieutenant," Alice says.

"When we got back, he said to contact him if I needed anything. I think he was feeling guilty, so I'll try."

"He should feel guilty, but not as much as bloody Colonel Reed, I think I'll wring his neck if I see him again," Catherine seethes and a silence falls over the table.

"Okay, we are all agreed," Josh says, breaking the silence. "I'll see if I can get hold of Lieutenant Winters."

"You tell me if you need to me talk to him, Josh. We have some history and might be able to put some pressure on him," Catherine insists.

"Okay, thanks; I will," Josh says and gets up from the table, reaching for his phone in his front pocket. He finds Lieutenant Winters' number and presses call.

Winters has been reassigned by Major Rees into helping go through the growing piles of paperwork constantly coming fresh off the printer. There seems to be no end to them. He had forgotten how much data the old 3 ½" floppy disks could actually hold. By today's standards, the memory of a floppy disk is tiny, but they can still store a mass of information, especially when it's simple forms and data.

Winters had tried to insist that he didn't know what he would be looking for. That didn't work with the Major, though. The Major used flattery to get him onboard, telling him he was an intelligent man and that all he needed to do was look for any information pertaining to viruses, chemicals or anything that sounded medical. If he found anything, he was to put it in a certain pile for further investigation. Winters' job basically was to root out the information that was definitely *not* what they were looking for.

The loudest sound in the conference room is the repetitive sound of the printer working. All of the analysts are silent, using all of their concentration to study the information in front of them. The military personnel follow suit, not wanting to break that concentration. Winters hopes that at any moment, somebody will speak up, saying they have found something he waits on.

A vibration buzzes against Winters' thigh and he pulls his phone out to see who is calling him.

"That had better be important, Lieutenant," Major Rees states.

"No Sir, it can wait," Winters replies as he presses the reject button on his phone's screen. He will call Josh Richards back as soon as he can.

Chapter 6

A faint intermittent high-frequency tone hums somewhere inside his head. Has a mosquito crawled down his ear lobe, eaten through his eardrum and burrowed into his brain to make its nest? The jungle is bursting with insects searching for a suitable dark hole to lay their larvae, to keep them safe from predators.

Andy knows the jungle well, since he has spent many nights sleeping under the stars on SAS training in Belize or Borneo. He knows that the jungle comes alive at night and is he very familiar with the sounds and noises that are frustratingly inescapable. There are no such noises tonight, only the intermittent tone that is fading as darkness returns to envelop him.

***

The tone is there again—or is it his imagination? Andy fixes on it in his dream.

Who is watching what programme on the television? Why don't they turn it down and stop disturbing my sleep? I need to sleep… my brain is too tired to wake up. My patrol will have to wait or go without me. I cannot run up that hill again… my shoulders are aching still from carrying the bergen filled with rocks. I still feel its weight dragging me down, pulling my shoulders from their sockets. Please turn that television down, let me rest.

Chatter, the blood-stained teeth chatter together, then they part, opening wide. Drool slides down over the black lips, across the grey chin and down, extending, stretching, flowing down, dribbling onto the skin of my bare exposed arm, making me shiver. The teeth move closer, opening wider for a dark rusty brown tongue to slither out, wet with drool. The dirty tongue licks across the side of my face, licking the wounds there. *Why won't my head move away? Fear paralyses me. Lick the wounds again! I want you to, the wounds you put there with your infected fingernails... clean them, you fucker.*

Its tongue slides back inside its disgusting mouth, into that dark crevice, flicking across its lips on its way in, to moisten them. Relief comes as the creature's head moves back away from me, its bloodstained teeth still on show, threatening.

The black pools of its eyes stare at me, and there is a dim reflection in them as if the moon is reflecting in the black waters of night. He looks closer, my eyes straining to see what's there, reflected in the creature's eyes. Unknowingly, I lean forward to see what is hidden. I have to see. The reflection gets bigger, gradually coming into view. Panic stuns me as realisation hits. The black eyes of another creature are hidden in the reflection, staring back at me, the reflection of me...

The repulsive creature reflected is me!

I manage to back away, not wanting to see the horrible truth. There is a wall behind me, stopping me getting away from what I have been shown. I push against it, wishing it to give way. I look around for something to grab hold of, to pull myself away. There is nothing, only blackness; it surrounds everything. The only light is in front of me, bathing the heinous creature. It sits on its haunches looking at me, studying me and waiting, waiting for what, to attack me, to devour me? I have to escape—but escape to where there is only emptiness. Something touches my wrist and I look down to see what it is, fear welling inside me again. Is this the start of the attack? The creature's hand squeezes my wrist and then slides up my arm gently, caressing. It feels good, welcoming. My fear subsides and I look up again, look into the creature's eyes. It pulls me forward, towards it, and at first, I resist, unsure. The creature's eyes blink and its head tilts slightly. It pulls again, and I give in. As I move forward into the creature's body, its other arm moves around my shoulders to pull me in closer. The creature swaddles me into its body and I welcome its embrace, its affection caring and warm. Finally safe, I can rest and as my mind relaxes, sleep comes.

***

The tone is there again, squawking quietly into my head and it wakes me from my slumber. I feel for my companion, but its embrace has disappeared; where has it gone? My eyes strain to open as my weary body and head protest. Slowly, they open, my blurred vision impaired by the darkness. Gradually my head moves, looking around the blackness for my companion. A dim light not far away shows me where my creature is.

It's crouched over with its back to me, but it knows I am awake, I can feel it. I long again for its embrace, so why doesn't it come to me? Finally, my creature starts to move around, leaving whatever it is doing. My hope rises as its heads turns towards me. It lifts its head, its face coming into view. Deep red blood is smeared across its mouth and lips and covers its chin. Its protruding teeth are coated in blood, with flesh hanging down between them as blood drips from its mouth.

My heart stops as I see below, to what it has been feeding on; the long blonde curls are unmistakable even though her face is masked. Emily!

The shock makes me jerk awake from my nightmare, adrenaline pouring through my body. Dread and fear consume me, almost shielding me from the pain that racks my body. My head spins, grasping to find reality. Am I awake or still asleep? The almighty agony tells me I'm awake. My head moves slightly, slipping my face on the slick, cold tiled floor, where I lie. Even that small movement sends bolts of excruciating pain thundering down my neck and back.

Emily; is she hurt? Is the Rabid here with me?

It was a nightmare, it must have been a nightmare, I tell myself.

Something is in my mouth, resting on my bottom cheek that is against the floor. My tongue pushes the rank chunk that was lodged in my throat out through my lips, but the foul taste remains.

My eyes stay closed, afraid of what they will see if they were to open. I must open them, however, to prove it wasn't real, it wasn't Emily, and it was all in my head. My eyes flash open quickly and widen to see what is waiting in the darkness. My eyes slowly adjust and begin to work. A flicker of light emanates from the dying torch that was left on the sink top above. The fading light is just enough for my struggling vision to see that I am alone, that there are no monsters here, tormenting me.

I am bent over on the floor, with my arm underneath me. The arm sears with pain from the weight of my body pushing it into the floor and my elbow feels like it is crushed. I have to move, but know that will only bring more excruciating agony.

A familiar high-frequency noise sounds and for a moment, I think I have fallen back into my nightmare. Dark flashbacks race through my head that I struggle to fend off. Fear of the nightmare increases my awareness and I suddenly know what the noise is. My radio headset is buzzing with interference behind me. Behind me, the torch

Josh left me lies next to the headset. Can I move, can I sit back up to reach it? I've got to do something, I can't just lie here to die—or worse, turn into the creature.

I do it, without thinking again about it. My right arm comes down and I push against the floor. Pain rips through my creaking body as my joints move, rubbing against each other. I force my back to take the strain, even though it feels like it might break in two. My right legs shifts back to help lever me upright. My burning left arm tries to help but it is dead, numb from being stuck under me, so my back has to work harder.

I scream out as my body moves up. The intense pain is overpowering, and I nearly falter and fall back down to the floor. Only the thought of how much that would hurt keeps me rising. As I reach the top, I almost blackout and nearly swing past being upright and fall down the other way to my right. I manage to catch myself though, just.

Upright again, the pain continues to wave through my body as it settles into its new position. Before I rest and let my body settle fully, my right arm flops down to the floor, and my hand touches Josh's torch and manages to take hold of it to press the switch.

Fresh bright light brings a small relief to my exhaustion and welcome confirmation that I am indeed alone in my dungeon. The pain subsides somewhat as I sit still. Only my eyes move as they look around the room. The dull ache caused by my eyeballs rolling around their sockets is insignificant in comparison to the rest of my body's torment, so I let them wander.

As I look at the kit lying around me on the floor, I decide that I am more lucid than I was previously. The agony aside, my brain is working to some extent and even without knowing if this is a temporary reprieve, I take some solace in it.

Just as my body is starting to settle and the pain with it, my eyes fall on a pack of syringes next to my helmet. At first, I wonder what they are for and why they are there? Eventually, through the haze, I remember somebody injecting me with some of them. Is it a serum to fight the virus, or something for the pain—morphine? I can't remember. Whichever it is, they have been left there for a reason. If they are for the pain, it isn't worth the renewed agony to retrieve them. I can cope now that my body is readjusting, so I might as well leave them there.

Exhaustion is getting the better of me, and the effort to drag myself up was almost impossible. Rest would be good, but the only problem is, I'm scared to close my eyes again. I'm scared to fall back to sleep and into another nightmare. What if I fall back over? I don't think I can handle either again.

Morphine would help. It would knock me out, put me too far under to remember any nightmare. It's worked in the past, in the field, when I've self-medicated to help forget the horrors of the day and when sleep had to come, to meet the horrors of the next day.

I eye the pack, which is out of arms' reach. To get it, I will have to lean over. I am confident that the risk of falling over is small, but I am sure the agony of moving will be fierce.

I calculate that the pain is worth the potential reward.

Pain rips up my back as soon as I slowly start to lean over towards the pack. I bite down hard, crushing my teeth together as my right arm rises and reaches over, increasing my agony still further. My fingertips touch the pack and I slide it closer until my hand can close around it. I flop back upright against the support behind me, my back creaking to a stop. The shooting pains up and down my spine calm gradually as sweat drips down my forehead.

Letting the pain subside before I attempt to open the pack of syringes, I don't even look at them. I sit with my head back and run through some breathing exercises to control my lung movement. Even breathing hurts, Goddamn it.

With my breathing under control, my eyes look down at the pack in my lap. Of course, it is no good! I can't read the label; my eyes are at too much of an angle to focus on it. A decision has to be made to either bring my arm up and lift the pack closer or move my head forward to look down at it. My neck is killing me as my left arm starts to lift the pack up. Shooting pain courses through my arm and up into my shoulders as it moves to bring the pack into view. The thought of the morphine flowing into my bloodstream like nectar and up to my welcoming brain excites me. It will make the pain bearable.

Favipiravir (T-705) is written across the packet in big green letters. I am confused for a moment is this a new make of morphine? My disappointment is felt deeply when I read the smaller writing which tells me the syringes are a rabies antiviral. My arms drop uncontrollably back down into my lap, taking the pack with it. There will be no imminent relief from the agony, no feeling of euphoria as my body soaks up the morphine, just more suffering in this dark hole.

The disappointment nearly brings me to tears. I had convinced myself that relief was on the way. I fight the tears away, chastising myself for letting my exhaustion let my mind run away with itself. A memory then presents itself, of somebody injecting the wounds in my face and the pain of the sharp needle puncturing the wounds returns, if only in my mind. Have the injections stopped me turning completely into a Rabid yet or have they delayed the onset? Is it still to come? Is that what I am going through now?

I should have turned by now. I have no idea how long I have been here since I was scratched and infected. But I know it is long enough that I should have turned. From the reports I remember, the turning process can vary from almost instant to a few minutes, ten or fifteen at the most. So why haven't I turned fully? Is it the injection I was given… it can't be that simple, and if it were, they would be injecting everyone at risk.

In the movies, there always seems to be somebody who is immune to a viral outbreak, and maybe that's me? I would laugh at myself if it weren't so painful. *This isn't the fucking movies, dickhead*, I tell myself.

Something is fighting the virus inside of me, I am sure of that. And if there is one thing I have learnt in my life, it's that while you're still fighting, there is a chance and that chance could be to see my children again.

My fingers fumble the packet of syringes open, there are still four inside. Fishing one out, I see that the plunger is up and ready to go. For a second, I debate reading the instructions, but I haven't the energy and decide to just go for it before I change my mind.

The stiff top pops off the syringe, exposing the long needle. I take a breath and start the painful process of raising my arm up. I'm going to inject myself in my cheek with the wounds again, that's where it was done before and must be the most effective place for the serum to go in. Am I becoming immune to the pain? I can feel it penetrating the muscles and bones of my arm and shoulders as my arm moves, but it doesn't have the same horrific effect. Or is my mind being taken away from it by the thought of the impending injection?

As the syringe appears before my eyes, level with my contaminated cheek, I turn the needle to point at the wound. My index and middle finger hold the syringe whilst my thumb moves to the top of the plunger, ready to push the antiviral serum out. I can't see the wound so I'm going to be shooting blind, I take a moment to aim as best I can. My tongue unconsciously curls out of the way as I jab the syringe into my cheek, my thumb ready to push. I barely feel anything until the needle pierces my inner cheek and sticks into my top gum above a tooth, where it is stopped by hitting something hard, either bone or the root of the tooth. Agony rushes across the gum and into my eye which immediately fills with water. I pull the syringe out as quickly as it went in.

I jab it straight back in, swearing to myself. This time, I go easier and the needle stays within the flesh of my cheek. My thumb and fingers push together, pushing the fluid out and into the wound. My thumb falters, almost coming to a stop as the fluid goes into my cheek, lighting it in burning, searing agony that spreads across the whole side of my face. The fire burns into my eye that now overflows with water, which does nothing to extinguish the flame. My thumb regroups and pushes until the syringe is spent. As my hand falls away the fire has spread to my brain, threatening to melt its soft delicate tissue to dust. The empty vicious syringe dangles down from my cheek, wobbling but refusing to let go.

Deliriously insane as my brain melts, a picture of Josh, Emily, Catherine and Stacey together, on some non-existent beach, with the sea lapping at their feet is before my eyes. I have to join them. I have to find them.

I grab the box of syringes, my whole being fixated on killing the bloody, fucking depraved virus in my body, trying to take my family from me. Syringes scatter, falling and skidding across the floor as the box rips open. One tumbles against my thigh, and it bounces but doesn't drop to the floor. It stays precariously balanced there. I grab it and in one swift motion pull the top off and plunge it into my belly. As my thumb pushes the plunger down, the fire spreads to my stomach. I don't care in my delirium though; I welcome the fire that will scorch the virus from my body and finally purge me of it.

I'm hurting and spent, with no more energy to fight. My arms flop down either side of my body, now useless limbs. My head goes back and eyes close as exhaustion takes me in. Unconsciousness comes again; nightmares or not, it doesn't matter—there is no stopping it. The vision of my family takes me into the darkness, easing my passing, overriding my agony until they too fade into black.

Chapter 7

"I have something, Major," one of the analysts across the table from Winters and Major Rees announces, lifting a file above her head as if she is at the bingo hall.

"Show me," Major Rees replies, not looking up from the file he is studying.

The female analyst, with short blonde bobbed hair and glasses, rises from her chair. Winters has found himself sneaking looks at her whenever he can, which is very unlike him. He has tried to stop himself, especially after she caught him gazing at her. She has the look of intelligence that Winters is drawn to and her pretty face only adds to the attraction, Winters has to admit to himself.

She comes around the table and stands in the gap between where he and Rees are seated, with her back to him, to show the Major the data she has discovered. Winters receives a waft of her perfume as she stands there, and he finds his eyes have left the file in front of him.

"Have you found something, Lieutenant?" Major Rees asks bluntly.

Winters finds himself staring at the analyst's bum, tightly packed into light blue jeans. Flustered for a second—which rarely happens to him—he nearly drops the file in his hand.

"No, Sir, not yet," he manages to blurt out as he regains his composure. He scolds himself for letting his concentration lapse and worse, for getting caught.

"Be sure to let me know if you do, Lieutenant, won't you?" Rees adds.

"Yes, Sir, of course." Winters feels his face flush with embarrassment as he scolds himself again.

Rees and the analyst study the file she has brought around for a good few minutes, discussing the contents, and their voices have excitement in them. Winters has his eyes under control again but still finds himself more interested in her voice than in the mundane information in front of him. He hopes that she has indeed found the data they have been searching for and that they will finally have something to take to Colonel Reed.

"Lieutenant?" Rees says.

"Yes, Sir," Winters replies, looking directly at him.

"It seems that Sam has possibly found some of the data we are looking for. That's not to say other relevant information isn't here that we haven't discovered yet, but I would say that this file is related to the type of virus we are dealing with. Wouldn't you agree, Sam?"

"Yes, from my understanding, I would agree," she says as she turns in Winters' direction.

"Excellent, Major and well done, Sam," Winters says, looking up to Sam, feeling his face redden slightly as their eyes meet.

"Thank you, Lieutenant," Sam acknowledges with a broad, enticing smile.

"I shall inform Colonel Reed immediately, Sir?"

"We still have about thirty minutes until I have to report to the Colonel, Lieutenant. I would like to double-check the data and Sam is going to go through the other files in that batch to see if there are any others that are related. Can you hold off reporting to the Colonel until then?" Rees asks but knows the answer he will get.

"I am afraid not, Sir; I am under direct orders to inform Colonel Reed the moment anything is found. Sorry, Sir."

"Well at least inform him what we plan to do now and ask him to give me until the time is up so that I can give him the most comprehensive report possible. I will need at least some time to digest what Sam has found."

"Of course, Sir. Now if you will excuse me, I will have to make the call." Winters gets up, brushing past Sam on his way out.

Winters leaves the conference room for the corridor to get some privacy for his phone call. He has a second ulterior motive for leaving.

"Yes, Winters." The Colonel answers his phone bluntly.

"Major Rees has found some information in the files that he thinks is related to the virus, Sir. He is evaluating it now, Sir and will make his report as ordered, Sir."

"Excellent, Winters; is the information going to be of help?"

"Unknown at this time, Sir. It has only just been found and there could be more information, Sir. They are checking related files now, Sir."

"Understood, make sure he is on time, Winters. I have to report to the Home Secretary." The Colonel hangs up.

The phone call went exactly as he expected. Winters is well used to short abrupt phone calls with the Colonel and gave up on expecting anything other a long time ago.

His phone stays in his hand as he moves screens to missed calls, where Josh's number sits at the top of the list.

"Thanks for calling me back, Sir," Josh answers the phone almost immediately.

"Sorry I missed your call; how is your sister?"

"She is as well as can be expected, upset but okay, I think?"

"Good, I am pleased to hear that. What can I do for you, Josh?"

"Can you arrange a car and clearance for us to leave the base, Sir We need transport out of here."

"What is your plan?"

"Catherine, my Dad's, err, girlfriend—" Josh pauses for a second, wondering if that is the right term.

"Yes, I know Catherine, please continue." Winters helps Josh out.

"Oh, okay, good, Catherine has a friend in Devon with accommodation that we can use, so we plan to go there and then see how things go."

"Sounds like a good place to start, Josh. I am sure I can help but you will have to give me some time. I am right in the middle of something."

"The contents of Sir Malcolm's safe, I take it, Sir?"

"Yes, exactly."

"Are they any use, Sir?"

"It looks like we have found something that could be useful. I don't think it was all in vain, Josh."

"That is something, I suppose, Sir?"

"Let's hope so. How many of you are travelling to Devon?"

"That's the other thing; we need your help with, Alice, Sir. We want her to travel with us, so can you arrange for her clearance too, Sir?"

"That will be trickier, Josh, but leave it with me and I'll see what I can do."

"Thank you, Sir. With Alice, there will be five of us travelling."

"Understood, Josh. I will come back to you as soon as I can so sit tight, okay?"

"Yes, Sir, I will wait for your call. Thank you, Sir."

"Thank me when it's done. I'll speak to you either way soon."

"Until then, Sir."

Winters hangs up and puts the phone back into his pocket. He is confident that arranging a car for them won't be a problem but getting clearance for Alice to go with them might be difficult. Colonel Reed made the deal with Andy for Josh to leave if he took the mission, but there was no deal made for Alice. She is still enlisted, and the Colonel will expect her back on duty, he won't lose an able-bodied fighting soldier without good reason. Winters will either have to give the Colonel a reason to give her clearance or he will have to do some creative, possibly underhanded paperwork. Winters will have to give it some thought.

"Sir, Colonel Reed has agreed to stick with the time frame for you to make your report to him," Winters tell Major Rees as he returns to the conference room.

"Well done, Lieutenant," Rees answers, back in his chair with his head buried in another file.

"That's in twenty minutes, Sir."

"Yes, I am aware of that, Lieutenant."

Sam has moved positions and is sitting in the chair Winters was occupying. She is studying files laid out on the table in front of her. It seems Winters has been demoted.

"Pull up another chair, Lieutenant, I am sure we can find something for you to make use of your time with," Rees says, pointing to a gap on the far side of him, away from the analyst, Sam.

Does he think he needs to keep us apart? Winters thinks as he moves around to retrieve a chair.

Josh turns back to the others, letting his phone drop in his hand down to his side.

He knew Alice coming with them could be a major issue and he can't help but look straight at her.

"I guess I'm not coming then, by the look on your face?" Alice presumes, looking straight back at him.

"No Josh, Alice has to come with us," Emily pipes up, the first words she has uttered in some time.

"Hold on, everybody," Josh says. "I didn't say she wasn't coming. Lieutenant Winters is going to try and get her clearance, but he isn't sure he will be able to. He is going to let us know as soon as he can. It could be a while until we know though."

"He had better say yes," Emily protests.

"We will have to wait and see, Emily, so cross your fingers," Alice says. "What else did he say?"

"He thought to go to Devon was a good idea and he is sure he will be able to get us a car; he just needs a bit of time."

"Anything else?" Alice prompts.

"He thinks they may have found some info relating to the virus, but they are still checking."

"So, it looks like we are still hanging around here for the time being?" Catherine asks.

"I'm afraid so. It looks like we either hang around here or go back up to the First-Class Lounge," Josh says.

"It's better down here than being cooped up, up there," Catherine states.

"Yes, I don't like it up there," says Emily.

"Okay, we wait for more news here then," Josh confirms as he takes a seat next to his sister, wondering how they will pass the time.

Winters glances at his watch. Five minutes until Colonel Reed is expecting the Major's report. More data and information about the virus have come to light in the fifteen minutes or so since he took his place in the naughty seat next to Major Rees, and more data is still emerging.

He has spent the last five minutes looking at some of the relevant data that have been discovered, trying to keep his mind busy and off Sam, who he can't really see from where he is anyway. Winters has to admit that he doesn't really understand what he is looking at. Science was not his strong suit at school and the complex scientific formulae and such contained in the files is like reading German. He recognises some words and phrases but piecing it together to understand the whole meaning is another matter. Winters places the file back in its place on the table.

"Are you ready, Sir? We had better go," Winters asks Major Rees.

"Yes, Lieutenant," Rees answers as he gets up. "Ready, Sam?"

"Sir," Winters says. "I am not sure the Colonel will appreciate any newcomers at this stage."

"I need Sam to handle the files and assist me. Unless you think you have a good enough understanding of the data to assist, Lieutenant?"

"I'm afraid I don't, Sir."

"Well, that settles it then. Sam?"

"I'm ready, Major," Sam says, gathering the files together.

Major Rees addresses the remaining staff before he leaves. He tells them to stick to their tasks and double-checks they know where to put new related information if it needs further investigation.

He then leads Sam out of the conference room and to his meeting with Colonel Reed in the command room only a short distance away. Lieutenant Winters follows, retrieves his satchel and brings up the rear.

Chapter 8

Corporal Harris has his hands wrapped around a nice warm mug. He lifts it to his lips now and then to slurp some of the hot instant coffee into his mouth, where he lets it sit for a moment before he swallows it to warm his belly. Harris is normally a tea man, but after the last few hours of non-stop action, he needs the extra kick the caffeine in the coffee will afford him.

Half an hour's bloody break; that is all his team has been given before they have to be back on duty. Hardly enough time to eat and get the hot drink down. It certainly isn't enough time to dry out and warm his bones, let alone have ten minutes to close his eyes. There is hardly any point in trying to dry out anyway; he will be out in the cold and wet again before he knows it.

His intellect doesn't understand that he is one of the lucky ones. He and his team have been tasked with a security detail. They secure four of the landing zones, where air transport brings back personnel who have been out on manoeuvres for Operation Denial. Once secure, they have to scan each arrival with the mobile phone scanner to check they haven't been infected. The work is constant, and they have been unlucky with the weather but the most danger they have encountered so far was when a Lynx full of Special Forces landed and didn't take kindly to being ordered around.

He doesn't consider that it could have been him in central London, out in the open, fighting Zombies. All he knows is that he is cold, wet and tired. Or perhaps he does consider it but thinks it's their tough shit for getting that assignment?

"Is it time yet?" Harris asks his team that sit around in the hangar with him, taking their break.

"Four minutes more," one of the other five members of the team replies.

Harris doesn't move to get back on duty, doesn't set any kind of example to the rest of his team. He doesn't even tell them to get ready for duty. He leans back into his seat, lifting his mug to his lips to slurp some more coffee down. He is going to make sure he takes every second of his break, and whether that means he is late for duty and holds up others from taking their break is none of his concern.

With a minute to go, two of his men get up and get their kit together, ready for duty. The other three are soon following suit, and all five privates glance at Corporal Harris. They all know they are going to be late, and that it will make them look bad and will be their Corporal's fault. What can they do? He is in charge by virtue that he has been enlisted longer.

With their allotted half an hour up, finally, Corporal Harris drags himself out of his chair and picks up his rifle.

"Come on lads, move it," Harris says as they roll their eyes.

Exiting the hangar, they go to the right, back towards the landing zones. Each of them is pleased to see that the weather has improved again whilst they were on break. The wind has died down and the rain has actually stopped completely. Standing water is still pooled all around, and they have to walk around the bigger puddles as they go. All of them know they can still expect to get wet on this duty. The helicopters will churn up the standing water, blowing it into the air in all directions as they come in to land and take off again.

"Where the hell have you been?" a pissed-off Sergeant shouts as the team reaches the landing zone area.

"On our break, Sir," Corporal Harris says in defence, standing to attention, as does the whole team upon being addressed by the Sergeant.

"Your break is thirty minutes, Corporal, not forty fucking five minutes!" the Sergeant shouts in exasperation, his face reddening.

"It has been less than forty minutes, Sir, and we have to get there and back," the cocky Corporal retorts.

"Get there and back? Are you soft in the head, Corporal? Now get back to your assigned zones and don't move until you are relieved!

"Yes, Sir," Corporal Harris replies, totally nonplussed by the whole exchange. Which leaves the Sergeant even more infuriated as he stomps off.

Harris leads his men back towards their landing zones, the men all pissed off with their Corporal, just as much as the Sergeant is. They know his attitude is going to lead to an extra-long shift for the lot of them.

They finally get back to their station next to their assigned landing zones, ready for duty. One landing zone over, the relief team who were covering for them while they were on break are in the middle of securing and scanning a new arrival. Corporal Harris and his team look on and wait while four dishevelled, weary-looking soldiers disembark an old RAF Puma support helicopter. The relief team are going through the motions of receiving the new arrivals by the book, their team leader ensuring protocol is adhered to.

With the new arrivals scanned and cleared, they are sent on their way and the relief team march over to the station to be relieved themselves.

"About time," the team leader announces as he approaches. "Where the fuck have you lot been, out for a curry?"

"Something like that," Corporal Harris says bluntly.

"Taking the piss, man," the team leader says to himself. "Here is the latest roster and the scanner," he tells Harris as he hands them over. "Next one in is a Chinook in five minutes, twelve on board."

"Are you sure you can't stay and do that one for us before you go?" Harris asks sarcastically.

The team leader looks at Harris as though he could strangle him for a second, before turning and walking away. Everybody hears him say *'wanker'*, as he leaves, without looking back. His team follow him, making their own comments and giving dirty looks.

"Okay, you heard the man; next arrival five minutes, check your weapons and get ready," Harris says, acting like a Corporal for once.

Weapons checked, Corporal Harris's team stand by for the Chinook to come in and land.

"Here it comes, Sir," one of the team announces, his head turned up to the sky.

Harris hears the distinctive sound of the big twin-rotor helicopter before he looks up in the direction of the ever-increasing din it emanates, as its rotors chop through the air. Only the raised nose and the unique rectangle underbelly of the helicopter are visible as the airport's bright ground lights start to catch it in their beam.

As the Chinook approaches, its twin engines are working hard, ready to land. Its thunderous noise starts to drown out the noise of the other, smaller helicopters on the ground that have either just landed or are waiting for clearance to take off.

Harris's team, now fully alert, spread out, ready to take up position around LZ1, the Chinook's allotted landing zone. They hang back farther than normal from the zone, however, in anticipation of the colossal downdraft the big craft will throw down.

At first, Harris thinks his eyes are playing tricks on him as the helicopter comes into sharper view on its approach. They aren't; the helicopter is wobbling strangely.

"Standby; we may have a mechanical issue," Harris states into his comms headset.

"Looks like the loading ramp is opening?" a team member on the far side of LZ1, says in confusion.

"Confirmed, loading ramp is opening," another voice sounds in Harris's headset.

"Covering positions," Harris orders as the Chinook descends, now entering the landing zone area and moving over the helicopters below.

His team is now covering the incoming helicopter, all of whom have taken a knee with their rifle pointed up and following the descent.

Still, over one hundred meters out from LZ1, the helicopter is coming down too fast, and at this rate of descent, it will fall short of its landing zone. The wobble has deteriorated, the pilot is losing control, the Chinook's nose has come down and it is swaying from side to side. A feeling of panic starts to take hold of Harris as he becomes convinced the helicopter is going to crash.

Something falls out of the back of the Chinook, out of the open landing ramp. Harris follows it down the thirty meters or so, his eyes gaping, with a look of bewilderment transfixed on his face. The flailing body drops down fast, and he sees it clearly in the bright lights and he sees where it lands.

As if in slow motion, the body drops onto the outer edge of the spinning rotors of a grounded, stationary Wildcat. The body fragments into pieces which are flung back into the air by the power of the rotors. Pieces of body shoot through the air in all directions too fast to follow, until Harris sees something travelling in their direction.

The severed arm and hand hit the ground inside LZ1. The whole team recoils as it tumbles in their direction until it comes to a stop just short of them. Harris is sure that the fingers of the hand still twitch where it lies.

There is no time to dwell on the limb, twitching or not, the Chinook is still coming in their direction and it's only a matter of time before it crashes. Did the body fall from the landing ramp or did it jump before the helicopter crashes, Harris manages to ask himself?

Now low in the air and still a distance short of its LZ, the body of the Chinook suddenly swings around at speed and out of control. A shower of bodies is thrown out of the gaping landing ramp, this time away from the helicopters below. They fall the short distance down onto the tarmac and grass areas around the left side of the landing zones.

The body of the Chinook carries on its trajectory, putting the whole helicopter into a fatal spin. Like a pirouetting dancer, it impossibly spins across the top of the helicopters below. Panicked personnel on the ground scatter in all directions, desperately trying to escape the impending crash.

After what seems like an age but is only a few seconds, the Chinooks' dance comes to a catastrophic end. The tail of the helicopter spins, sending the lowered landing ramp careering into the stationary rotors of one of the grounded helicopters below, as the Chinook loses height.

Harris sees the impact a second before the sound of the crash reaches his ears. The force of the crash sending the nose of the huge Chinook upwards and flipping it into the air, like a whale breaching out of the ocean. And like a whale crashes down into the sea on its back, so does the Chinook.

Spinning rotors first, the Chinook slams down into the hardware below. Two helicopters, both fully laden with fuel and ordinance, a fuel truck and other support vehicles are all in its path. A fierce bright white light flashes an instant before a massive explosion erupts near the centre of the landing zone area. Fuel tanks of the Chinook rupture as do the two helicopters in the crash area; the fuel truck's resistance is futile, and it explodes along with the helicopters. A fireball blasts hundreds of feet into the air at the epicentre and rushes out horizontally, sending an immense shockwave with it. Surrounding helicopters are blasted off the ground and incinerated, their ruptured fuel tanks adding to the fireball and extending it to engulf the next helicopter or fuel truck. Each new explosion has a domino effect and engulfs the next piece of equipment to it.

A chain reaction now ensues as the heat rises. Ordinance starts to explode as the heat reaches new high temperatures. Hundreds of thousands of bullets start to fire without a trigger being pulled as their cordite reaches critical mass. Bullets fly in all directions and hit the first things in their path or shoot off into the air. Bombs and rockets explode as safety mechanisms and casings are melted.

This phase makes the initial explosion resemble the ignition of a gas barbeque. Gargantuan explosions follow one after the other as the heavy ordinance goes off and spreads out from the centre, each one causing the next. Mushroom clouds rise up in every direction and melt into one big continuous one in the middle, the smoke pushed together by air rushing in to feed the flames from the outside.

Each new explosion spreads the carnage further out, to new hardware, waiting to be engulfed. The chain reaction is out of control and won't be stopped until there is nothing left to feed it.

Some helicopter pilots try to take the initiative before the destruction has spread to their craft. Those far enough away and with their engines already started hastily lift off and fly away from the danger zone, to save themselves and their helicopters. Other pilots who are either too close to the destruction or too slow to react either burn in their seats or are blown out of the sky, adding to the inferno and spreading the chaos to new areas of the landing zone.

Corporal Harris and his team were far enough away from the initial explosion to survive, and they looked on in shock and awe at the initial Chinook crash and the following fireball.

To Harris's credit, he was quick to react, seeing that the Chinook's crash would be the tip of the iceberg. He understood almost straight away what would follow that crash.

"We have got to get out of this area!" he shouts, desperately, at his men. "The whole area is going to explode."

His men don't argue; they see all the ground crews that have survived, so far running for their lives, away from the landing zone with panic across their faces. The only decision that needs to be made is which way do they go? The direction, from which they have just come back from their break, lined with more helicopters, just waiting to explode. That path only leads to the hangars laden with ordinance, which could easily go up too.

"This way!" Harris shouts as he starts to run off in the opposite direction as the bigger explosions start to ignite.

Everyone is going in the same direction, as fast as they possibly can. Harris and his men join the stream of people coming out of the landing zones, from between the masses of stationary helicopters. Caught in the expanse between the terminal buildings and the erupting landing zones, they all run straight ahead, desperately trying to get to open ground.

A shock wave travels out into the expanse, knocking two people off their feet in front of Harris. They don't stay down to lick their wounds, but scramble back to their feet straight away and are off running again, their fear driving them. The explosions are getting close to the outer edge, where lines of Apache Attack helicopters sit ominously waiting to detonate. The expanse is wide, but not wide enough; anytime now, it will be an inferno that will surely engulf the terminal building.

Harris leads his men as they try to outrun the impending disaster. The expanse narrows the farther they go, which bunches all the people up and their progress isn't helped by airport transport equipment abandoned in the middle of the tarmac.

Harris barges past some of the slower people, their panic not making their legs carry them fast enough for him. Their protests and whimpers as he pushes past are disregarded; it's not his problem they are too slow.

One panicked idiot of a man is scything his way in the opposite direction against the tide. The man's eyes are wide with terror. He won't find any escape down that way, Harris thinks to himself, bloody twat.

Progress slows as some kind of bottleneck forms up ahead. A massive explosion detonates behind, Harris doesn't turn to look. The force of the blast and the heatwave feel like they are virtually on top of him, his desperation to get clear escalating. The bottleneck is getting worse, however; what the fuck are these people doing? "Keep moving," he shouts. Suddenly, he starts seeing faces, frightened faces, coming towards him. More idiots going the wrong way; no wonder his escape is slowing down. Some people lose their minds at the slightest sign of danger, for fuck's sake.

"You're going the wrong way!" he shouts at them uselessly.

Even above the deafening sounds of the explosions behind him, Harris hears a new sound, the sound of human screams ahead. *What the hell is going on up there, the fire hasn't reached that far,* he asks himself? Whatever it is it can't be as bad as being burnt alive or blown to bits. Harris presses forward.

A small lull in the explosions allows Harris to hear a shout and the penny finally drops. The people falling out of the floundering Chinook, before it crashed, flash before his eyes. Those weren't people falling; they were infected, so that is why the Chinook went out of control. That is what Harris heard shouted; he heard someone shout 'Zombies'.

Harris comes to a standstill, panic and fear gripping him, the same as everyone else, his mind floundering. Turn back to fire and explosions or go forward to whatever awaits there? His body turns backwards, then forwards, then back again; finally, he decides and turns forwards.

People are scattering, running in every direction, some even back into the maze of exploding helicopters. One in complete panic runs into the terminal building, headfirst into the solid brick wall that runs along the bottom of the building. Her head bounces off the whitewashed wall, knocking herself out, and the only evidence left is a small red patch where her head hit.

Harris looks forward for a path through the melee. He sees one and starts his run. Only a few strides in, something flies at him from above. Harris sees the Rabid infected Zombie over the heads of the people; it is flying at him as if on wires. The Rabid's claw-like hands are outstretched ready to dig into its prey, its grey face turned to evil as its mouth opens ready to bite down. Harris tries to bring his rifle up to shoot at the vile beast, but he is too slow.

The Rabid lands on Harris, hitting him around his shoulders. Harris goes flying off his feet backwards, but the Rabid doesn't let go of its catch; its claws have dug into his prey. Harris's arms flail, trying to fight the thing off him. The Rabid is too strong and too quick and is already sinking its teeth into Harris's stomach. The beast bites out a large chunk of flesh from his belly, taking some of his innards with it.

Harris's fever-pitched screams of terror are futile but as quickly as the Rabid attacked, it is gone, jumping away, on to its next victim. Harris's screams continue only for a second, then abruptly cut off as his body starts to violently convulse, twisting and turning as the infection ravages his body. Another scream lets out from deep within his throat as his blackened eyes snap open. This time, the scream is different; it is the deathly scream of death.

The assimilation of Harris is fast and with his rebirth complete, there are only two things the creature understands; to survive, and to feed. A deep burning hunger consumes the creature completely. It jumps up onto its haunches, head darting around, looking for prey, smelling it out. The sweet smell of fresh raw flesh is all around, making the pain of its hunger heighten. The scent pulls it off its haunches, directing the creature, its legs releasing like two tightly wound springs. Flying through the air, the new inexperienced Rabid misses its target but it isn't deterred. Hunger driving it, it hits the ground, its hands and feet catching it and then it's up, its legs powering it across the tarmac, towards the closest smell of prey. Almost by accident, it slams into a victim. The woman tumbles to the ground, her pungent scent irresistible. Before the woman has a chance to scream, the Rabid bites deep into her neck, through the veins and arteries buried there. Ripping the flesh free, the Rabid gulps the sweet meat down feverishly. More, the creature needs more, before the meat turns and the virus takes hold. Its head whips down hungrily again for seconds, but before it bites, the detonation vaporises it instantly, incinerating the woman along with it.

Chapter 9

Josh leans against the handrail that runs all the way along the wide expanse of windows on the side of the Terminal 5 departure lounge that looks over the inside of Heathrow Airport. On either side of him are the north and south runways and in front of him are more terminal buildings. Away to the left are the cargo buildings and Terminal 4, the side of the airport where they were taken into quarantine and where they took off from on their fateful mission.

The airport's lights glisten in the darkness of the night and along with the landing lights from the multitude of aircraft flying in and out of the busy airport, Josh starts to get lost in them.

The departure lounge is pretty quiet, and he just had to get up for a while to stretch his legs and gather his thoughts. He strolled around for a while before he found this little oasis towards the end of the windows, where the light is dim and some of the bustle from the people that are around is cut off by surrounding plants and pillars. He has stayed in view of Emily as he said he would, and she can see him through a gap if she needs him.

Unfortunately for Josh, gathering his thoughts is not proving easy. They keep jumping from one torturous event that has happened over the last days to another, with the image of his Dad's anguished face at the forefront. In time, he may come to terms with having to leave him behind but right now, the guilt is stifling, and the image of his father will stay with him forever. Josh is trying hard to quell the new demons that have taken route inside him to haunt him, but he knows they will get a lot worse before they get better; it is going to take time.

Josh looks at his phone again, in the hope that he has missed a call from Lieutenant Winters, but he hasn't. He cannot wait to get out of this place and as far away from London as possible. This place in Devon that Catherine has arranged for them to go sounds idyllic. A good place for them all to start some healing. He has to hold it together until they get there and stay strong for Emily, but right now he feels like he is climbing a mountain with no end in sight.

"Hey Josh, are you okay?" Catherine says, coming up behind him and putting a hand of support on his shoulder.

"Honestly, I don't know."

"That's only natural, Josh; you have been through terrible trauma over the last few days. Give it some time, it's all very raw at the moment."

"I was just telling myself the same thing, but I can't help thinking about him," Josh says, his head bowing down.

"Of course, you can't, you've just lost your dad and in awful circumstances."

"Lost or left to die?"

"No Josh, lost; you know that there was no other option. It's horrible but it's the truth, there was no way he could have got on that helicopter."

"No, but there must have been another way, I could have stayed with him, but I abandoned him, I didn't even have the guts to put him out of his misery."

"From what you've said, Josh, he was still your dad when you left him, so no you couldn't do that, nobody could have. And there was no way you could have stayed with him for many reasons but two of them are we would have lost you too and Emily needed you. You did the right thing no matter which way you look at it." Catherine squeezes Josh's neck reassuringly.

"Maybe, I don't know. I know we need to get out of this bloody airport though."

"We all do, I'm sick of the sight of it. Things will look better when we've gone, I'm sure," Catherine agrees.

"Definitely, we should go as soon as we can, no waiting until morning."

"No arguments from me on that, the sooner the better. I'm sure Lieutenant Winters will sort it out as soon as he can."

"If anyone will, he will."

They both fall silent for a moment, staring out the window at the airport beyond, letting their conversation settle.

"At least it's stopped raining. Shall we go back over to the others?" Catherine asks.

"Yes, I'm ready and thanks, it's good to talk."

"I'm always here if you need to talk, Josh, it will be good for you, good for all of us to talk about what's happened."

An intensely bright light flashes into the night sky. Both Catherine and Josh's heads dart to the right, in the direction it came from. "What was," Catherine starts to say but she falls silent as in the distance, a large fireball follows the flash, rising into the sky and lighting up their faces. The light is followed by a dim booming sound an instant later, as if it's thunder following the flash of lightning.

For a moment, Josh is taken back to the roof of the Orion building and the storm that overshadowed the dire mission. His stomach drops as those feelings return with a vengeance and a horrible feeling hits him that the same nightmare has followed him here.

"My God, that was a big explosion; what was it?" Catherine asks nervously.

"I don't know, but it came from the direction of Terminal 4 where the landing zone for all those helicopters is. Maybe one's crashed. I hope that's all it is."

"What do you mean, what else could it be?" Catherine asks, worried.

"Nothing, I'm sure it is a crash or some sort of accident."

"Josh, you obviously meant something, so what was it?"

Josh looks at Catherine, who stares at him with concern written all over her face, waiting for her answer. "I just hope it isn't anything more sinister."

A look of realisation of what Josh means spreads across Catherine's face. As it sinks in for her, Josh thinks he sees a look of fear try to surface but it is only fleeting as her face turns into one of determination and resolve.

"What do you think the chances of that are? We are still a long way from the infected zone and Heathrow is supposed to be well fortified," Catherine asks.

"It is well fortified. I saw it when we flew over today. I'm probably thinking of the worst; it's probably just an accident."

"No Josh, I think you are right, we have got to think that way. Anything could be happening. It already is!"

People are gathering along the stretch of windows to see what the flash of light and noise were. Worried voices are chattering, trying to figure out what has happened. Alice, Emily and Stacey come up behind them, followed by their escort from upstairs.

"What's happening?" Alice asks as they arrive.

"Don't know," Josh says, looking down at Emily. "It looks like there has been an accident over by Terminal 4."

"What sort of accident?" Emily asks. "Are the Zombies coming, Josh?"

Josh doesn't know how to answer her because if they are, they need to be prepared. Another even brighter flash of light blazes from the same direction and an eruption of flame and sparks shoot up into the sky. This explosion looks different from the last, the fire travelling into the air faster and spreading its blast wider. The shockwave that travels across the distance from the blast hits the windows in front of them. The shockwave is much fiercer and hits with the sound of a loud crack. The windows rattle in their frames, threatening to dislodge and everybody standing at the window ducks as if they would shatter, including Josh.

"That explosion is different; that was like a bomb going off," Josh says urgently, not thinking of saving Emily's feelings.

"Josh, I'm scared," Emily cries.

The second blast is quickly followed by another and then another. The windows rattle again, visibly flexing in their mountings. Josh pulls Emily away from them, just in case they do shatter. They aren't the only ones moving back; everyone has the same fear.

Explosions keep happening, some more violent than others. The bright glow in the distance makes it obvious that whatever is going on, the carnage is spreading.

"It has to be the helicopters in the landing zone," Alice says. "One must have exploded for some reason and it is spreading to the others."

"Yes, and they were full of missiles and bombs," Josh points out.

"There had to be well over a hundred helicopters there when we landed. This isn't going to end any time soon if that's what it is? The fire teams won't be able to get near it," Alice adds.

Everyone watching through the windows goes quiet as they watch the explosions continue as if it were watching an organised fireworks display. A display that shows no sign of ending.

"What are we going to do, just stand here and watch?" Alice asks.

"I'm open to suggestions," Josh replies.

"Try to phone Lieutenant Winters, see if he knows what's happened," Catherine suggests.

"Good idea," Josh says, getting his phone out.

"What the fuck was that?" Colonel Reed demands to know from whoever is in earshot in the command room when the first explosion happens. Nobody knows; everyone looks confused and looks at each other for an answer.

Major Rees was just about to start giving his report to the Colonel but now he and everyone else is following Colonel Reed. He pushes and barges his way to the windows, shouting 'Get out of my way'. One man in his haste to get out of the Colonel's way falls over a chair that has strayed into the walkway. The man goes arse over tit and lands heavily on the floor with only the fallen chair for company. Nobody goes to see if he is okay as he struggles to get up. Everyone's attention is on the explosion that's just rocked the command room.

A new flash of light reflects in everyone's faces as they approach the windows, whilst keeping out of the Colonel's way.

Lieutenant Winters is hot on the heels of the Colonel, knowing full well that will be the easiest and quickest path to get to a viewpoint.

More explosions rock the command room as Winters and the Colonel reach the windows. No one who is already there volunteers their opinion as the Colonel finally gets to see what is happening.

The view they receive is about the same angle as Josh's and Catherine's, but the command room is one floor above the high-ceilinged departure lounge. That means they get a clearer view of where the explosions are happening.

"It is the helicopter landing zones," Winters says.

"Thank you for stating the fucking obvious, Lieutenant!" Colonel Reed barks at him.

"Sorry, Sir."

A massive blast ignites the night sky, causing everyone to duck. Everyone, that is, apart from the Colonel who doesn't flinch; he stands there staring out of the window with a fierce look fixed on his face.

"Winters!" Colonel Reed growls.

"Yes, Sir."

"Find out what the fuck is going on down there and report back to me, A-sap."

"Yes, Sir."

Colonel Reed turns away from the window, his piercing eyes moving, looking at all the personnel gathered around as they try to see what is happening.

"Get back to your stations. We have an active operation in progress. Move it!" Colonel Reed bellows.

The personnel immediately scatter, going back to work, some looking worriedly over their shoulders at the explosions as they go.

Only the Colonel's hierarchy is left standing around him, waiting with bated breath for his next move or order. He turns his back on them, as if in disgust. He stands tall, looking out of the window at the destruction taking place. His hands are clasped so tightly behind his back that his knuckles whiten.

"Major Rees, give me your report." Colonel Reed orders, not turning away from the windows.

Lieutenant Winters can guess what has happened over at the landing zones. An accident, possibly a refuelling accident or a crash has caused a catastrophic chain reaction. But as the Colonel has just torn into him, that's stating the obvious. He will want details, facts and solutions, not assumptions.

Winters rushes back to the central area of the command room, where Major Rees was about to give his report, picks up the nearest phone and dials 111.

"Central Comms," a young male voice answers. "What department do you require?"

"Flight Command, Terminal 4," Winters answers.

"Putting you through."

The line clicks and then goes silent. Winters' eyes wander around the command room as he waits to be connected. All of the personnel are back at their stations and many more are working, carrying out their tasks. As they do, Winters can see them talking amongst themselves, worried looks on their faces as they try to figure out what is going on. A few people are gathered in small groups debating and pointing here and there, mostly pointing towards the windows where flashes of light and cracking sounds are bursting through the glass. The distant battles in the centre of London that they have been watching on screens, gathering data on and reporting on, have suddenly arrived on their doorstep. Winters sympathises with their concerns, suddenly the danger is very close to home.

"Yes, who is this?" a panicked voice shouts down the phone.

"Lieutenant Winters, who am I speaking to?"

"This is Group Captain Taggart; what do you want?"

"I need a situation report, Sir."

"The situation is, we have got a breach, now I have got to go."

"A breach?" Winters says, shocked. *Is this more than just an accident?* "Explain, Sir, hello?"

The line has gone dead. *Taggart has hung up, for fuck's sake.* Winters slams the phone down and picks it straight back up, dialling 111.

"Flight Command, Terminal 4!" Winters says into the phone as soon as it is answered before the operator has a chance to say anything.

"Putting you through," Winters is told.

Winters waits again for the phone to connect. *A breach.* The words stick in Winters' mind. Taggart had to mean that the 'infected' had breached; what else could he have meant and why aren't they answering the fucking phone now? Fear and panic start to rise in Winters as he waits.

"I cannot get an answer from that connection," the voice tells Winters.

"Well try again, this is top priority!" Winters shouts down the phone.

"There is no answer to that connection."

"This is Lieutenant Winters at Command. I am ordering you to try again!"

"Yes, Sir, trying to connect."

Winters waits and waits to be connected. He looks over to Colonel Reed, who is still standing at the windows, with Major Rees talking to him. Giving his report on what he found in the files no doubt.

"I'm sorry Sir, there is no answer from that connection. Can I try another for you?"

"What other departments are over in Terminal 4?"

"Erm, there is Field Hospital 4, Sir, Air Combat Support... Engineering?"

"Try Air Combat Support."

"Yes, Sir."

Winters waits again, his impatience growing.

"I'm sorry, Sir, no answer there either, shall I try Engineering?"

Winters slams the phone down again without answering. His mobile phone starts to buzz against his thigh, he ignores it. He is too busy thinking of how to find out what is going on over at Terminal 4.

Colonel Reed sees Lieutenant Winters jogging across the command room and towards to exit. His confusion doesn't break his concentration on the report Major Rees is giving him, however.

"Lance Corporal," Winters says to the highest-ranked sentry posted at the entrance to the command room as he gets to the exit.

"Yes, Sir."

"What is your name, Lance Corporal?"

"Broad, Sir."

"Give me your phone, Broad"

"Sir?" the Lance Corporal says, confused.

"Just do it, soldier."

Lance Corporal Broad fishes his phone out of his pocket and hands it over.

"Take one of your men, find a vehicle and get as close to Terminal 4 as you can safely. I need a report of what is going on over there."

"Sir, I cannot leave my post."

"That is an order, Lance Corporal, there are enough men here to guard the door without two of you."

"Yes, Sir, where do I get a vehicle from, Sir?"

"Use your initiative, Broad. I've rung my phone from yours, so you have my number. Phone me as soon as you are in position, understood?"

"I think so, Sir."

Winters looks at Lance Corporal Broad. "Just get as close as you can; no heroics, phone me and tell me what you see. Can you do that, Lance Corporal?"

"Yes, Sir."

"Good, report back as quickly as you can. Dismissed."

Winters turns back into the command room slowly, thinking if there is another way to get information. A drone would be ideal but the place he could arrange for one of those is Air Combat Support in Terminal 4.

He wanders back into the command room, knowing Colonel Reed is eyeing him for answers. He will get his report shortly.

Winters goes over to the head of Tactical, a Captain Myers, whom Winters has dealt with on many occasions. She is a very intelligent and decisive operator who gathers all the data coming into the tactical department for an operation, in this case, Operation Denial. She then either acts on that information or if it is out of her remit, she will pass it up the chain of command and then implement any orders received.

"Have you got anything, Ma'am? I have heard that there may have been a breach?"

Captain Myers sees Winters coming and is ready for his question.

"We have nothing concrete, Lieutenant, but we think you have heard correctly."

"Please elaborate, Ma'am."

"We have a report that one of the incoming helicopters was compromised. The helicopter crashed, causing the chaos in the landing zones. The report also says that at least some of the infected people on that helicopter jumped out before it crashed. So, it looks like we have infected inside the perimeter, Lieutenant."

"Thank you, Ma'am, I will report the same to the Colonel."

Major Rees is still at it when Winters arrives to report back to the Colonel, who is walking up and down alongside the windows with his hands still clasped behind his back, listening.

"Excuse me, Sir," Winters says after waiting for a pause in Major Rees's speech.

Colonel Reed makes a show out of not acknowledging Winters immediately. He pauses his walk and turns to look out of the window as if contemplating something the Major has just reported to him. It is an act, and one Winters is well used to. So he lets him get on with his show and waits patiently until Colonel Reed has finished his act and has everyone's attention.

Major Rees' eyes give a sideways look in Winters direction. He is not so used to Colonel Reed's little games and is not sure whether he should carry on with his report or give way to Winters. The analyst Sam who is assisting Rees and standing next to him looks completely bewildered by the situation. Two of the Colonel's men are waiting to give important reports and yet he is standing gazing out of the window as if he has just arrived in his hotel on the Las Vegas strip and is taking in the view.

Finally, the Colonel turns back around but still doesn't say anything. Major Rees opens his mouth to continue but he doesn't get past the first half word out of his mouth before he is cut off by the Colonel.

"What have you got, Winters?"

"Sir, unconfirmed reports indicate that an incoming helicopter was compromised by the infected and crashed into other grounded helicopters. That caused the initial explosion which spread to other grounded helicopters and the ordinance they were loaded with, Sir."

"Is the fire contained?"

"I don't believe so, Sir. Communication with Flight Command and Air Combat Support in Terminal 4 appears cut off, Sir. Either the fire has spread to the terminal building or worse, Sir."

"Worse? What the hell is that supposed to mean? Don't speak to me in riddles, Lieutenant! Explain yourself, man."

Winters couldn't help but pay some back to the Colonel, even if it is only a small fraction and leave the best to last.

"Sorry, Sir. Again, this is unconfirmed, but we have a report that suggests at least some of the infected on the helicopter bailed out before it crashed. We could have a breach inside the perimeter, Sir."

Major Rees next to Winters isn't the only one to gasp at the news. Everyone looks shaken, and even Colonel Reed looks uncomfortable at the thought.

"We need confirmation as to whether the perimeter has been breached. An outbreak on this base will not only compromise the base, but it will also move the virus to a completely new area, way outside the current quarantine zone.

What are you doing to get confirmation, Winters?" Colonel Reed demands.

"Sir, up to now I have despatched two personnel to get as close to Terminal 4 as possible and report back what they find. I would like to get a camera drone in the air, but I can't get through to Air Combat Support to arrange it, Sir."

"Air Commodore?" Colonel Reed asks, looking at the highest-ranking RAF officer in the command room.

"I will get straight on it, Colonel." The Air Commodore leaves to make arrangements.

"Sir, we need comms to try and get in contact with anybody in Terminal 4 who can inform us of the situation there, Sir," Winters suggests.

"Yes Winters, get on it." Colonel Reed orders.

"Yes, Sir. A new perimeter needs to be installed around Terminal 4 immediately, Sir. All the troops we can muster, with heavy machine gun placements, if it's not too late already, Sir."

"Very good, Winters, I will oversee the troop movements."

"Yes, Sir."

"Anybody, anything else?" The Colonel asks, but nobody adds anything further. "Right, get to it, bring any updates to me immediately, dismissed."

"Sir?" Major Rees says.

"Yes Major, walk with me," Colonel Reed says as he moves off his perch.

"If I may, Sir, I need facilities and experts to process the data we have discovered and that cannot be done here. I need to take all the information to Porton Down, immediately, Sir."

"Indeed Major, make your own arrangements. The Air Commodore will facilitate your transport, yes?"

"Yes Sir, thank you, Sir." The relief in Major Rees's voice is plain to hear. Whether that is from a professional standpoint or because he will be leaving Heathrow that may now be compromised, is another matter.

Operation Denial has entered a new phase, one that could threaten its very existence. Winters is sure of that as he heads over to the comms stations in the command room. It was Josh who tried to phone him, his phone screen tells him as he walks. As soon as he has the task of trying to get communication with Terminal 4 active, Winters will phone him back and try to get his transport out of here arranged.

Chapter 10

Lance Corporal Broad and Private Penn descend the stairs, arriving at the ground floor of the Terminal 5 building, all too quickly for their liking. As they have come down lower, the smell of burning has increased, as has the sound of explosions. Now standing in the tight conclave at the bottom of the stairwell with only a fire exit door between them and the outside, they both look nervously at each other. Neither of them in any rush to push the steel opening mechanism that runs across the width of the door.

"I don't fancy this one bit," Private Penn says.

"Look, Colin, you heard the Lieutenant; no heroics, we just got to see what's going on."

"It sounds like a war zone out there, who knows what the fuck is going on? Lambs to the slaughter, that's what this is. And where are we supposed to get a vehicle from?"

"Calm down, Colin, let's have a lookout and see how it looks, okay?"

"Okay, let's get on with it and thanks for roping me into this, mate. My mum will kill you if anything happens to me."

"You reckon? She likes me more than you," Broad tells him, trying to smile.

"Funny fucker," Colin says. The two young mates look at each other as Broad's hand goes to push the release.

The fire exit door clicks open and the sound of chaos rushes in to fill the small area. The sounds are instantly followed by acrid smoke which fills their lungs, making them both cough.

"Bloody hell, mate, is the air any better out there?" Colin asks as Broad sticks his head around the door.

"Not really, smoke is everywhere, but the coast is clear."

"What do you mean, the coast is clear? What were you expecting to see?" Colin asks.

"I dunno; come on, let's go," Broad replies.

The two men exit underneath the departure lounge. Parked up airplanes of different sizes are parked along the front of the building a short distance in front of them with their air gates protruding out from the building above. If it weren't for the strong smell of smoke, you could be fooled into thinking none of the airplanes is moving because they are grounded due to fog. A thick haze of smoke hangs in the air and wafts around the airplanes' landing gear and the various service vehicles scattered around and parked up.

"How we going to get back in if this door closes?" Colin asks, reluctant to release the door.

"Jam something into it so it stays off the latch," Broad tells him.

"It's like a ghost town; where is everyone?" Colin asks when he finishes fiddling with the door.

"Doesn't look like any of these planes are military. They look like abandoned civilian ones," Broad points out.

"It's fuckin' creepy, like the apocalypse has happened," Colin says.

"Maybe it has happened, mate, maybe it has?" Broad answers.

"Well, there is plenty of transport here to choose from. Wonder if they need keys?"

"Let's check that baggage cart out," Broad says, pointing to a small white truck with cages attached to the back, nearby.

Broad goes over and opens the door with Colin close behind.

"We're in business; the keys are in it, get in."

"Hold on. Let me see if I can detach the cages." Colin goes to the back of the cab to have a look. "The pin is stuck."

"Stop messing around, and get in," Broad tells Colin as he turns on the cart's engine. "I always wanted a go in one of these," he tells Colin as he gets in the passenger side.

"Me too, I'll drive it on the way back, okay?"

"I'll think about it," Broad says.

"You'd better after getting me into this."

"Come on, mate, you wouldn't have missed it for the world."

The cart jerks forward as Broad puts his foot on the accelerator.

"Do you know where you're going?" Colin asks.

"No, not really. What you reckon, shall I follow the sound of the explosions or possibly the light from the fire? Knobhead," Broad laughs.

"Alright, I was only asking; you're the boss, wanker."

The cart moves steadily forward as it bounces over the lumps and bumps of the concrete taxiways in front of the Terminal 5 building. The empty cages attached to the cart behind, bang and rattle over each imperfection in the concrete. Broad resists the temptation to slam his foot to the floor to see what the cart will do, to get the mission over with and get back inside to the relative safety. The smoke haze is thick, and they could easily run into some abandoned piece of equipment—or worse, an airplane.

"Joking aside, Terminal 4 is on the other side of the runway, and I don't fancy crossing the runway. Don't want a jumbo landing on us," Colin points out.

"I seriously doubt we will need to get that close; we are going to stay at a safe distance," Broad answers.

The cart makes good progress and soon, they are nearing the end of the massive Terminal 5 building on their right. More taxiways are in front of them with the runway beyond. The Terminal 4 building and the fire are on their left, quite a long distance off, at the other end of the runway which is about two miles long. They still don't have a view of it, but it will come into view soon because the smaller terminal building on their left, which is blocking their view, is also coming to an end.

Broad turns left around the corner when he can and as he does, in the distance the bright orange glow of the fire comes into view. Broad stops the cart to get a good look. The flickering glow is still a long way off, but the fire looks massive, almost like a sunset. A bright white flash overpowers the orange momentarily as another blast goes off. Both men avert their eyes, turning their heads away slightly and they don't look back around until the shockwave stops shaking the cart's cab.

"If you ask me, this is quite close enough," Colin says seriously.

"I know what you mean, but we can't see shit from here apart from the fire," Broad replies as his foot presses the accelerator again.

"I knew you were going to say that," Colin says as they start to move again, towards the fire.

Broad drives the cart down a taxiway parallel to the runway and around one hundred meters over from it. There are no people around or any movement apart from the cart, as the taxiway is empty. Luckily for them, the majority of the smoke is being blown across the airport and away from their direction. There is still a thick haze making its way across the rest of the airport and both men have intermittent coughs. The taste of the acrid smoke sticks at the back of their throats, unmovable.

"How much closer are you going to get?" Colin asks as they near half distance.

"I don't know until we see something worth reporting, I suppose, or it gets too dangerous?"

"Something worth reporting. We could have told him what's happening from inside. There is a fucking big fire engulfing Terminal 4, simple. What else is there to report?" Colin asks.

"Let's just get a little closer, then we will phone him to report in."

"Come on, mate, this is close enough. I can feel the heat coming off the fire. It's getting bloody hot in here. What's that?"

"What's what?" Broad asks.

"There, on the runway, people are coming this way, see?"

"Oh yes; they must be survivors. I'll get the Lieutenant on the phone." Broad gets his phone out and dials.

"Lieutenant Winters." Thankfully, he answers almost straightaway.

"Sir, Lance Corporal Broad reporting in as ordered."

"Yes, what have you got to report?"

"Sir, we are still some way off the fire, probably halfway down the length of the runway. The fire is engulfing the terminal building and it looks like we've got survivors coming up the runway, Sir."

"Broad, are you sure they are people, normal people?"

"What do you mean, *normal people*? They are not that close and a bit blurry, Sir."

"What's he mean by normal people?" Colin asks from the passenger seat.

"We may have a breach, Lance Corporal. I ask again, are they normal people?"

"A breach, Sir, you mean a zombie breach, in the airport, Sir?" Panic is in Broads voice.

"Yes, Broad that is exactly what I mean; are they zombies you can see or are they normal people?"

"Hold on." The phone drops from Broad's ear and his head moves forward towards the windscreen of the cart as he tries to focus on the figures moving on the runway. The figures are blurry silhouettes against the fire raging farther back behind them and really hard to focus on.

"Is he saying there are zombies in the airport?" Colin asks Broad, desperately.

"He doesn't know; he is asking me to confirm if those survivors are people. Can you tell, do they look normal to you?"

"Fucking hell, I thought I was joking when I said we were lambs to the slaughter."

"Concentrate, Colin, do they look like normal people?" Broad scolds his mate.

Finally, Colin does start to concentrate, his head joining Broad's in a forward position as he peers out of the windscreen.

"I can hardly make them out. The fire behind is too bright, they are like shadows. I don't like the look of them, though, to be honest, mate. We've done our bit—let's go back," Colin says, his voice full of trepidation.

Broad lifts the phone back to his ear. "We can't tell, Sir. The fire is too bright behind them, but they look normal?" he says, looking at Colin and shrugging.

"We need confirmation, Lance Corporal, can you move closer?" Lieutenant Winters asks.

No not really, no, I fucking can't, Broad thinks, starting to think Colin might be right about being 'lambs to the slaughter'. "I'll try, Sir."

"Keep me on the line."

"Yes, Sir."

"You'll try what?" Colin asks.

"We need to get closer. They need confirmation."

"Oh, that's it. Let's drive towards the zombies so we can get a better look at them! You've got to be kidding; don't do it mate," Colin pleads.

"We got to, the sooner we can tell, the sooner we can get outta here. They are probably just survivors, but get your rifle ready though, just in case."

"Oh, my days. Taking the piss," Colin announces as the cart edges forward and he shifts around in his seat with his rifle.

Movement is just what the Rabids, spreading out from the burning terminal building, have been waiting for. The cart's two headlights, bouncing on the concrete—dim as they are in the haze—is all they need. The new target, potential fresh prey, re-energises the hateful creatures, springing them into action.

Broad and Colin's eyes are wide, straining as they stare out the front of the cart, trying to get a clearer look at the figures in the burning haze. The figures do get bigger in their vision and the two men soon realise the shocking truth.

"Turn around, get us out of here; those aren't people, they're coming straight for us. Turn around!" Colin shouts at Broad, his hand moving at the steering wheel to turn it for him.

Broad sees it too; the figures are running at them up the runway and across the grass verge that separates the runway from the taxiways. It doesn't matter. He still can't see them clearly and the bright orange fire behind them flashes in his eyes. The figure's silhouettes don't move normally; it is an inhuman run, intersected with leaps and bounds, like animals.

"I'm fucking going!" Broad shouts as he rakes on the steering wheel, his phone still in his hand, turning the cart around to get it pointed back to the Terminal 5 building. At the same time, his foot pushes the accelerator.

"They are getting closer. Go faster, go faster," Colin pleads to Broad.

"My foot is to the floor; this fucking thing won't go any faster!" he tells Colin as he stops turning, the cart and the empty cages behind it straightening up.

The baggage cart does pick up some speed, and it bounces violently over the imperfections in the concrete slabs below its wheels, jerking them in their seats. Behind the cart, the empty cages crash up and down, threatening to break free. Both men wish the cages would break free and stop slowing them down.

"They're gonna catch us; we're not going fast enough!" Colin declares in panic, the sanctuary of the terminal building still a long way off.

"Can you see them? How close are they?" Broad demands.

Colin doesn't want to look behind; he is too scared of what he will see. He concentrates on the distant lights of the terminal building in front of him, willing them to get bigger and closer.

"Colin! Pull yourself together man."

Colin knows he must look, but he is ashamed of the fear gripping him. He feels like a frightened small boy, he closes his eyes for a second and gathers his courage. *Fuck it*, he says to himself as he twists in his seat to look out of the back window.

"I can't see anything," Colin tells Broad with some relief that he knows is misplaced.

"What do you mean?"

"It's dark, I can't see anything."

"They are there, mate, I know it; I could run as fast as this cart. Keep looking!" Broad tells him.

Colin concentrates, his head trying to counteract the bouncing of his body as the cart jerks. Lights that point to the rear from the cab throw a dim light over the rattling cages behind, which doesn't help his view. He tries to look beyond the lit cages and thinks he sees a shadow cross the orange glow of the fire in the distance, but he isn't sure. They must be getting close to the terminal building now?

Colin thinks his eyes are deceiving him as a dark shadow crosses into the light of the cages behind. His confusion escalates as the shadow lands into the second cage at the back. The loud crash from its landing could be mistaken for a crash from a big bump in the road. The shadow disappears into the well of the cage and for a moment, Colin thinks he imagined it.

"What was that?" Broad shouts, but Colin doesn't answer. "Colin, what was that bang?"

"I think something just jumped into the back cage?" Colin answers nervously.

"What you mean, something?"

Colin doesn't answer; he is paralysed with fear as he watches the shadow rise up from the well of the bouncing cage. As it rises, it is caught in the light shining back from the cab. It faces away from Colin, and he can only see the back of its head and the green camouflage of its army uniform through the squared steel wire mesh. The thing suddenly whips around to face Colin, its hands rising to grip the mesh, its disgusting fingers poking through the mesh, pointed in Colin's direction.

The beast's evil black eyes lock Colin in its chilling gaze. Blood drains from Colin's face and drops to his boots as fear courses through him. Hideous teeth appear as the beast's mouth opens and it snarls, biting at Colin. Its right hand releases and the mesh moves up above its head, and it grabs the mesh again—and starts to pull itself up.

"What's going on, Colin?"

"One's climbing over the back cage."

"Well don't just sit there, shoot the fucking thing!"

Colin had forgotten the rifle in his hands; it had sat there like a useless toy. His hands tighten around it as if he could lose it again. All at once, he feels the security it offers and the power; it reinvigorates him. Colin bursts into action, brings the rifle up, and leans back at the same time, back towards the windscreen. The rifle nestles into his shoulder, where it has been a thousand times before. His aim comes naturally to him, and always has. It rarely lets him down. The beast is at the top of the meshed side of the cage and just disappearing out of the dim light as it comes over the top.

Colin adjusts his aim and pulls the trigger. The shot from the rifle rings out in the confined cab, making the men's ears ring. The bullet pierces through the back window, shattering it into hundreds of pieces but the pieces don't drop; they stay in position with just a small bullet hole near the top. Colin knows instinctively he hit his target, and through the shattered window, he sees something fall.

Colin can't afford to take any chances; he pokes the muzzle of the rifle forward sharply into the shattered glass. As soon as the muzzle makes contact, the glass gives way and sprinkles down, out of the frame, the pieces pinging onto the floor.

Immediately, the rifle's sight is searching for its target again. Colin moves the rifle down to where the beast has fallen. Through his sight, he sees the beast in the well of the front cage, staring at him. The creature jumps at Colin so fast he barely has time to pull the trigger again, but he does. The bullet hits the beast in the chest as it flies at the cab's small window frame, where the glass used to sit. The bullet does nothing to stop the creature and it smashes into the wire mesh of the front cage, stopping it just short of the cab's window. The creature latches onto the mesh, its crazed face level with the window; it goes so wild it tries to bite through the steel wire.

The rifle fires again, straight through the creature's forehead. The power of the bullet explodes the back of its head, sending the head shooting backwards as the beast falls down dead, back into the well of the cage. One of its front teeth hangs by a sliver of glistening flesh from the meshed wire.

"Is it dead?" Broad shouts at the top of his voice, his ears ringing.

"Yes, it's dead," Colin confirms.

"I hope you're getting all this, Lieutenant," Broad shouts into the open line of his phone, in his hand.

"He had fucking better be!" Colin exclaims. "How much farther?"

"Not far now, mate, we are just coming up to the start of the terminal buildings."

"Watch out!" Colin shouts as the eyes of a zombie shine through the driver's side door window.

The warning is too late; Colin didn't see it until the last second. Broad doesn't know what is happening as the creature hits the side of the cart, right next to him. The cart sways to the side with the force of the blow and the driver's window implodes.

"Shit!" is all Broad manages to shout as an arm and head follow the smashed glass into the cab. The creature goes to bite Broad, anywhere it can. In a pure reflex action, Broad's arm comes across his body and stops the creature sinking its teeth into his other arm. His hand pushes against the forehead of the beast, his phone still in his hand, and now squashed against the beast's head. Broad tries to push the creature back out of the window but it is too strong; it is all he can do to stop it biting him.

"Shoot it!" Broad shouts at Colin.

Colin brings his rifle around to bear, which isn't easy in the small cab. Broad's body and arms are blocking his shot to the head.

"Shoot it, fucking shoot it!" Broad shouts again in total panic.

Colin desperately tries to get a decent target. He moves further forward, squashing his back against the windscreen and taking the only shot he can find. He puts two rounds into the shoulder of the zombie which blasts it back and opens up a new target—the top of its chest. Colin fires again, hitting the zombie in the chest multiple times. Just as Colin thinks the bullets are useless, the zombie falls away, back out of the window. The back cage behind them jumps in the air on one side as its wheels hit the falling body.

"Fucking hell!" Broad shouts.

The path in front of the cart is now a little brighter as the cart moves into the lights shining from Terminal 5's buildings and they close in on the wedged open door into the building.

No solace comes with the brighter light; all it does is let them see the dire straits that they are in. The cart is being chased by creatures all around the back of them, their grotesque forms threatening to catch them at any moment.

"We're in the shit here. There are loads of them. What we gonna do?" Colin asks desperately.

"We just gotta get back to the door and get inside," Broad answers, as positively as he can, but knowing it's bullshit.

"As soon as we stop, they'll be all over us!" Colin shouts, on the edge of losing it.

Neither of them sees the creature's attack as it goes for the driver's smashed open window; it comes from nowhere. The beast bursts through, and its head, arms and body are in the cab before either of them can react. The only thing stopping it coming in further is it hitting Broad's body.

Broad screams in panic as the zombie goes to bite his arm with his hand that is on the steering wheel driving the cart. His arm shoots away from the barred teeth as they come in to bite him. The cart swerves as he releases the wheel, both of his arms flailing about trying to fight off the attack as he screams.

There is no stopping the creature; its strong arms and hands grab hold of Broad and its face buries into the side of

Broads body. The creature's powerful jaw sends its teeth clamping down, slicing through the material of his uniform and into the soft flesh of his lower body. Broad lets out a deafening, deadly scream.

As the cart swerves to the right, it hits another creature with its front quarter, the creature goes down and underneath the cart's wheels. Colin doesn't even see the second creature being hit, as his back is to it and his eyes are fixed on the zombie eating into his mate, next to him.

Colin raises his rifle again and shoots into the top of the feeding zombie's head, taking the risk of hitting Broad. The creature goes limp straight away but doesn't fall back out of the window; it stays in Broad's lap as he screams his head off. Colin, now running on instinct only, goes to grab the cart's wheel to get it back under control, but he is too late.

The cart smashes into the tyre of an airplane's wheel that is parked up next to one of the terminal buildings. The cart hits it hard and Colin is forced into the windscreen that smashes. He doesn't go through the windscreen; he is stopped by the thick black rubber of the tyre the cart has hit. The cart bounces back off the tyre, coming to a stop a couple of meters back. Colin, dazed and covered in glass, has managed to stay in the cab of the cart, just about.

Before the cart comes to a complete stop, creatures are swarming all over it, on its cages and cab. Climbing over it, fighting to get to the prize at the luggage cart's front. Within seconds, the vehicle is hardly visible underneath the plague of death.

Chapter 11

Lance Corporal Broad's phone is still active as Winters takes it slowly away from his ear. The only sounds coming from it now are those of feeding, threatening to make Winters' stomach burst through his throat. He is racked with guilt and shock by what he has just been listening to. The horrific deaths of two young men that he sent out on that mission.

Winters goes dizzy; he has to quickly sit down in the nearest chair and take hold of his head in his hands before it falls off his shoulders and onto the floor.

Winters knew what he was doing when he sent them off on the reconnaissance mission. He knew it was very high risk and still knows now that it had to be done, as there was no other way to be sure. That doesn't make him feel any better about the order he dished out to the unsuspecting men only a short time ago. Broad had looked so young, he couldn't have been more than in his mid-twenties and the private Winters saw him walk off with was even younger. His stomach somersaults again; it is going to happen, and he can't hold it back.

Winters manages to grab a bin from under the desk next to him and puts it on the floor in front of his chair. His stomach lets go and Winters urges nothing but bile into the bin. His stomach contracts violently three times before he manages to bring it under control. He spits the last dregs out and closes his eyes for a moment.

"Are you okay, Lieutenant?" a female voice asks from above him.

"Yes, sorry," Winters manages to say.

"Don't be sorry; aren't you feeling well?"

"I'll be okay in a minute, thanks, just came over all dizzy."

"Can I get you some water?"

"Yes, please," Winters replies, his head still in his hands. Slowly, the blood returns to his head, the dizziness subsides, and his wits start to return. He has to report what he has just witnessed to Colonel Reed.

"Here you go, Lieutenant," the female voice says and Winters lets go of his head, sitting up in the chair.

"Thank you," Winters replies and looks up to see Sam holding out a small plastic cup of water for him. He feels his face flush with embarrassment.

"Has it passed?" Sam asks with a look of concern etched across her face.

"Yes, thank you, Sam. It's not like me to do that," Winters tells her as his foot pushes the bin back under the desk to try and hide the evidence.

"What brought it on? Was it the phone call you were on? Have you had some bad news? Tell me if I'm being nosey, but I couldn't help but notice you on the phone and it looked serious, judging by your face."

"Yes, it was serious, I'm afraid. I have to report in with the Colonel to tell him if you want to join me?"

"Yes, okay, I'm at a bit of a loose end now that Major Rees has left. I should report back in with my superiors to be reassigned," Sam tells him.

"You will want to hear this first," Winters says as he gets up to check to see where the Colonel is.

"It sounds ominous," Sam says as she starts to follow Winters.

Colonel Reed is back at the front of the command room, standing looking at a blank screen. Winters assumes he is waiting for the drone footage of Terminal 4 to appear.

"Colonel, I have new intel, Sir," Winters announces as he walks up behind the Colonel.

"Continue," the Colonel orders without turning to look at him.

"Sir, the two men I sent on reconnaissance to Terminal 4 are dead."

Colonel Reed now does turn to look at his assistant. His arms are folded across his chest and he has a stern look fixed to his face as he says, "Continue."

"Sir, they drove a vehicle down towards the building and the fire, as I ordered. About halfway there, they were attacked by multiple hostiles. The two men retreated and managed to make it back to the Terminal 5 area, but unfortunately, they were then overpowered and killed. Sir, the hostiles were people infected with the virus."

"How did they report back to you if they were killed, Lieutenant?"

"Sir, I had an open phone line with one of the men for the whole contact. I listened to the whole thing. Sir, Terminal 4 is compromised; we now have infected directly outside this building and it is certain that more of the infected are spreading out to other parts of this base, Sir."

"Holy shit," Colonel Reed growls to himself, his eyes bulging with a look of anger on his face. "Thank you, Lieutenant dismissed."

Sam looks over at Lieutenant Winters from the periphery, now understanding what had come over him. The phone call she had seen him on was that one. He had ordered two men outside to see what was going on and they were both killed. No wonder he had been sick.

"What are they going to do now?" Sam asks as Winters comes away.

"They will activate one of the contingencies in place. I won't know until they have decided," Winters replies as he watches Colonel Reed already picking up a phone with an urgent look on his face.

"That sounds ominous," Sam says.

"It definitely won't be good news." And then Winters has a thought. "Come with me," he tells Sam.

Winters heads for the exit of the command room at a quick pace. Sam follows his exit, struggling to keep up with him, confused at what is suddenly so urgent that it involves her?

Sam follows him over to the conference room where they had come from. She assumes he is looking for Major Rees. The room is abandoned though, and all the files have gone. Only the computers and printers remain, that now sit idle.

Winters turns back towards the wide corridor. "Come on," he tells Sam. This time, he breaks into a jog as he goes down the long corridor, obviously hoping to catch the Major before he leaves. Sam finds it easier to keep up with him at jogging pace but is at a loss, as to what is going on.

They reach the end of the corridor and turn right into the lift area just in time to see Major Rees and another soldier about to go through the open lift doors.

"Major!" Winters shouts.

Major Rees, startled, turns to look at Lieutenant Winters and Sam rushing towards him. He has a sudden horrible feeling that something else has gone wrong.

"What is it now?" Rees asks quite abruptly.

"Sir," Winters starts, slightly out of breath. "I thought it would be a good idea if you took Sam with you, Sir. She is familiar with the data and would be an asset in continuing to analyse it, Sir."

Major Rees immediately suspects that Winters' reasoning for making his suggestion isn't entirely as stated. He suspects the real motive is getting her out of the danger zone more than anything. The suggestion isn't without its merits, however. Sam has proved herself to be an excellent analyst and she is indeed already familiar with the data.

Sam is taken aback by the Lieutenant's suggestion; she hadn't considered it. She had assumed she was here for the long haul, something she really doesn't fancy now things have taken a turn for the worse. It suddenly dawns on her that that is the reason Lieutenant Winters is doing this, to get her out. She has seen the way he looks at her and her feelings grow for him because of his unselfish act.

"A very good idea, Lieutenant," Major Rees agrees.

"Thank you, Sir."

"Are you in agreement, Sam?" Rees asks.

"I hadn't thought of it, Major. I am supposed to be reporting back to my superiors. I haven't been cleared to leave."

"I will sort that, Sam, but you will have to go now. Major Rees cannot be delayed," Winters tells her.

"But I haven't got my belongings?"

"Is there anything important in them?"

"Not really. My phone charger and coat. I have my wallet and ID card," Sam says, slightly embarrassed by their insignificance.

"You will have to leave them. You can get new ones," Winters tells her.

"Yes, you're right, silly of me."

"Shall we then?" Major Rees says.

"Can you give me one minute with the Lieutenant please, Major?"

Major Rees looks at the two of them before he and the other soldier go into the lift. "I will hold the door for you."

As Major Rees disappears into the lift, Sam turns to Winters. "Thank you, Lieutenant."

"There is no need to thank me, Sam. It just makes sense for you to carry on the work with the Major," Winters tells her, not wanting a fuss.

"I don't even know your name, Lieutenant?"

"It's Robert."

"Robert, I am not bragging but I am one of the top analysts at GCHQ, so I know how to read things. I know when someone is watching out for me and the reasons why. I've seen the way you have been looking at me."

Winters feels himself blush with embarrassment. He has been found out, which is not something he is used to, especially in this type of situation. To make matters worse, he tries again to hide his real motives by starting to say something too ridiculous to deflect, but Sam is having none of it.

"Robert," she says, placing her hand on his shoulder. "There is no need to be embarrassed. I've had my eye on you too and if things were different, maybe we could have explored it. It's a shame; perhaps we will see each other again, so in the meantime please accept my thanks for getting me out of here, okay?"

"Yes okay. You have caught me. I do hope we see each other again, but you had better go. The Major is waiting. Good Luck, Sam," Winters tells her.

"You too and try not to feel too bad for the orders you gave out; it had to be done." Sam leans in and kisses his cheek. "Goodbye, Robert and good luck."

"Goodbye, Sam."

Sam turns for the lift and Winters watches her all the way, her forthrightness making him even more attracted to her. She turns back to look at him as she enters the lift, smiles and is gone. Winters hears the lift doors close, but he doesn't move for a moment as he wonders if he will see her again. It's just his luck that he actually finds someone he is interested in and she is out of reach. He is sure he made the right choice to get her out while he could. However, anything could happen here now.

Winters starts to make his way back up the corridor towards the command room. As he reaches into his pocket for his phone, he decides that it is quite possible he will see Sam again. There is a chance Colonel Reed will decide to evacuate, and Porton Down is an option to relocate to. He consoles himself with that.

Josh feels his phone start to vibrate in his hand at the same time he sees the screen light up. At last, Lieutenant Winters is phoning him back.

"Hello Sir, thanks for calling me back. We have been extremely nervous here, as you can imagine," Josh says quickly into the phone, afraid that the Lieutenant will have to hang up for more important business at any time.

"Hello, Josh. I'm not surprised; things have taken a bad turn. The base has been breached and infected are outside."

"How did that happen, Sir?"

"One of the incoming helicopters was overrun. That is what caused all the explosions. We have infected outside this building as we speak," Winters informs him.

"Fucking hell, what are we going to do?"

"I don't have that information yet Josh. I will try to keep you updated if I can."

"Is there any chance of getting us some transport to get us out of here, Sir?" Josh asks, trying to hide the desperation in his voice.

"As soon as I can, I will, Josh, but it isn't going to happen just at the moment. As I said, the infected are outside the building, and we need to find out how serious it is and what decisions are made before I can let you out there. I have also still got to figure a way to get Alice clearance."

"Aren't we better off going now before it gets worse?"

"Right now, we don't know how many infected are out there, but they have just chased down and killed two men I sent out on reconnaissance. It's too risky, so give me a bit of time, Josh, to get a handle on things, okay?"

"Yes, Sir." The disappointment in Josh's voice is plain.

"Thank you. Do you still have your weapons?"

"Both Alice and I do, Sir."

"Good, see if you can find somewhere secure to wait for me to phone you again."

"How long will that be?" Josh asks.

"As soon as I know how the land lies. Believe me, I want to get you all out."

"Yes, Sir. I know that and thanks."

"Okay, Josh, be ready for my call."

"I will be, Sir."

Josh looks at his phone screen and presses *end call*. He looks around to the four ladies that are all sitting looking expectantly at him. He is going to have to dash their hopes of a quick getaway. What is he supposed to tell them—that they have all got to find somewhere to hide again? They all know how badly that seems to end up. Josh can't help but ask himself what his father would do.

Chapter 12

Another huge explosion rocks the Terminal 4 building to its core. There is no sign of the devastation ending, Dixon thinks as he looks around at the rest of his patrol, as all of their heads duck as if the roof is about to collapse in on them. All three look back at him, waiting for him to tell them what they are going to do. Dixon is at a bit of a loss, though, as the team was told to wait in the hangar for further orders that never materialised.

A strong smell of smoke has been building in the hangar since the first explosion hit and it is starting to become visible in the air. Dixon is positive that the building is on fire and spreading their way. They can just wait here like rabbits in the headlights; the orders they have been waiting for are clearly not going to arrive now.

Standing next to the table where he and his patrol had been sitting around chewing the fat, Dixon re-evaluates. Firstly, he notes that his fresh tea is fucked and full of dust, but nonetheless, he picks it up and takes a large scaling gulp from it. Nothing concentrates the mind like a fresh brew.

One thing that Dixon doesn't have to concentrate on is the fact that their position is compromised. They are in a burning building which also happens to be full of ordinance waiting to blow it to kingdom come.

The situation outside the hangar does require his brain to work as the banging on the doors and roller shutters keep reminding him. They were lucky to make it back inside and secure the doors before the Rabids got to them. That is one thing Dixon has decided, to call them Rabids. He had thought the term was apt when Andy had first said it, but since he has seen them and fought them, it is even more so. The creatures literally are Rabid people.

If it weren't so terrifying, it would be comical the way they had all run outside to look when the first explosion went off, only to hightail it back inside when the Rabids came at them. Luckily, two of the roller shutters were already down and the open one made it down just in time.

Their situation would be easier to calculate if it was just the four members of his patrol in the hangar. The patrol would gear up and get the fuck out of Dodge, but there are other people in the hangar with them. Of the seven others, some are civilians and some military, and even the military personnel are more used to loading bombs than fighting.

Dixon knows they have to evac their position, but how and to where?

"Suggestions?" Dixon asks the rest of his patrol.

"Let's get the fuck out of here!" Kim volunteers.

"Brilliant idea, Kim; any suggestions on how?" Dixon growls at him.

"We take that pick-up," Kim answers, reining himself in a bit and pointing to a dated red pick-up truck with fire written on its door.

"We aren't all going to fit in that," Dixon replies.

"Us four will. Two in the front and two in the tail; we draw the Rabids away so the rest can escape?" Downey suggests.

"Umm," Dixon sounds. *That plan isn't bad*, he thinks to himself. It could work. What other options are there anyway? He is struggling to think of another and looks around at the other people, congregated a couple of meters away from them. The military personnel have their weapons and it would give them all a fair chance of escaping if his patrol drew the Rabids away. There aren't any safe options, and the pick-up could be overrun as soon as it gets outside. If they stay inside the hangar, they are all doomed for sure; there are no other exits and Dixon has somewhere he needs to be.

"Okay, listen up," Dixon says. "We are going with Downey's plan. We take the pick-up and draw them fuckers outside away from the hangar. Downey, check that the pick-up is good to go. Kim, see if there are any other useful weapons around. Collins, get those people over here."

"Where are we going to go, boss?" Collins asks.

"I'm going back to Terminal 5. Josh, his sister Emily and Alice are there. I intend to make sure they are alright, but that's just me, if any of you need to be somewhere else then that's fine, just drop me off."

"What do you mean, desert?" Kim asks.

"I did not say that, soldier."

"What do you mean then?" Kim persists.

"I mean that I am going back to Terminal 5. This base is compromised; you might want to leave, go back to base in Poole or wherever you want."

"Well, the command room is in Terminal 5, so it sounds like as good a place as any," Collins says, and the other two nod in agreement.

"That's settled then, let's get ready," Dixon says.

The three men turn to head off to their tasks. Dixon waits, ready to speak to the rest of the people in the hangar, who Collins has started to roundup.

Dixon feels a kind of obligation to look out for Andy's two children. He may have only known him for a few hours, but Dixon liked the man and they fought together; he now considers him a brother in arms, especially as he gave his life covering their retreat. Dixon is then forced to admit to himself that he is going back for Emily, really. That's the least he can do for Andy. Josh and Alice are big enough to look out for themselves, so misplaced or not, he is going to look out for Emily.

The engine of the pick-up starts on the second attempt and Dixon hears Downey give the engine a few revs to make doubly sure it's turning over properly. The reversing lights come on as Downey starts to manoeuvre it into position. Dixon's attention is then taken over by the group of people Collins has finally managed to bring over.

"What's going on?" a middle-aged man asks. He is the highest-ranking of the military in the group and as a Staff Sergeant, he actually outranks Sergeant Dixon.

"We have got to get out of here; the building is on fire and it is only a matter of time before the fire spreads into this hangar—and I don't need to tell you what will happen then. So, we have come up with a plan," Dixon says.

"And what makes you think that is your decision, Sergeant? I am the highest-ranking person here and we were just discussing options."

"Okay, Sir, what did you come up with?" Dixon asks.

"Well, we haven't yet," the Staff Sergeant says sheepishly. "Tell me your plan and I will make the decision then."

Dixon rolls his eyes. "Sir, with no disrespect. This is the plan that we are going to carry out, and it isn't up for discussion. This is a combat situation and me and my team are best placed to deal with it. We haven't the time to fanny about, Sir."

The Staff Sergeant's eyes drop, and Dixon knows the Staff Sergeant has deferred to him, so he presses home his advantage. "My team are going to create a diversion to allow you to all escape. We are going to drive that pick-up out of the roller shutter to draw all the Rabids—sorry, infected people—to it and away from the hangar. Once the area outside is clear, you all need to get out as quickly as possible. Go left outside and get into one of the buildings farther down where hopefully you will find safety. Agreed, Sir?"

The Staff Sergeant looks unsure for a moment and looks around at the people beside him, who look even more unsure than he does.

"Sir?" Dixon asks again.

"Yes, Sergeant, that sounds acceptable," he eventually says.

"Very good, Sir. Wait until we are clear, and the infected people have taken the bait, Sir. Don't move too soon, Sir, and have your weapons ready, in case you need them."

"Okay, understood Sergeant."

"With your permission, I will get my team ready, Sir."

"Carry on, Sergeant."

Dixon leaves the group before anyone changes their minds. He heads over to the pick-up, which has been parked facing one of the roller shutter doors a few meters away, ready to go.

"Downey, you're driving. Collins, you're shotgun and Kim, you have the pleasure of keeping me company in the tail. Is everyone kitted up?"

"Yes, Boss and we have found some more ammo, so here's your kit," Downey says, passing Dixon his rifle first.

"Thank you, Downey," Dixon says as he attaches the rifle to its harness at the front of his body. "As soon as the roller shutter is open enough, Kim and I will throw a spread of grenades under it, to clear the immediate threat. Then full throttle to get us out of here, understood?"

"You got it, Boss," Downey replies with a smile on his face.

"Don't go all Mad Max on us, Downey; we want to get there in one piece! Okay, in positions. Kim, press the button on my signal."

Dixon climbs into the back tail-section of the pick-up, while Downey and Collins get into the cab. Kim takes up a position by the buttons that operate the roller shutter positioned on the wall next to it. His finger hovers over the green *up* button.

Dixon positions himself at the front of the cargo area, looking over the cab. He registers two places on the cab where he can grab hold of if needed on the ride before he bends down and retrieves three grenades from a holdall on the floor.

As Dixon comes back up, he is aware of the fear and adrenaline coursing through his body. It's like an old woollen sweater to him now; it still scratches but somehow feels comfortable.

He looks over to the rest of the personnel and gives the Staff Sergeant a nod. The man looks petrified and his rifle looks cumbersome in his grip, but to his credit, he returns the nod.

"Hit it, Kim!" Dixon shouts as he drops the pins to the first two grenades onto the floor. He doesn't hear the clatter of steel on steel as they drop, however.

Kim's finger pushes the green button and immediately, the roller shutter lurches into life, its motor straining to lift the heavy door. Kim waits next to the rising door momentarily, as he too drops the pins from the grenades in his hands. When the door reaches about six inches up from the floor, he rolls three grenades into the ever-increasing gap. As soon as the last one leaves his hand, Kim bolts for the pick-up.

Even though Dixon is well versed in the art of throwing grenades and could hit an arms dump from thirty meters out, he waits. There is no point trying to be clever; if he were to miss the gap and a grenade bounced back into the hangar, the trip could be over before it starts.

As the shutter rises on its long trip to the roof and the gap opens, Dixon throws. The first grenade is in mid-air when the grenades that Kim rolled out explode in virtual unison. Their shock wave hits the roller shutter hard and it strains and rattles against its runners, threatening to blow out of them. Thankfully, the shutter stays within its runners and keeps rising. Dixon throws his three grenades in quick succession, their strike levers springing away as they go and tumbling to the floor.

All three grenades sail through the gap and bounce out beyond the shutter which is now about a meter up from the floor. Kim has jumped into the tail of the pick-up and has taken up a position ready to cover the rear. The pick-up's engine revs. Downey isn't taking any chances that it could die while he waits for the gap to increase enough for him to plant his foot to the floor.

As the gap increases, Dixon has his rifle trained on it. He is prepared to fire in an instant if any Rabids have survived the grenade's explosions and come through. They don't, and before the gap reaches the height Dixon was anticipating, Downey floors the accelerator.

The pick-up jumps forward and Dixon has to take evasive action to duck under the shutter's bottom edge before it takes his head off. As he rises again, he slams his hand down onto the roof of the cab, partly in a rage that Downey nearly took his head off and partly to warn him to be careful.

Smoke fills the air outside and Dixon pulls up his Shemagh across the bottom of his face to breathe through, and it brings some relief. Some of the smoke is the residue of the grenades but, mostly, it is coming down from the fire and explosions that are raging away to the right at the front of the terminal building. Downey steers left out of the hangar, his way forward to the Terminal 5 building is blocked by helicopters in front of them. Dixon briefly thinks to himself that the explosions are going to travel all the way down and past the hangar as each helicopter explodes. He puts that thought out of his head; he needs to be looking out for targets, which at the moment are very sparse. That at least is good news for the personnel who remained in the hangar to make their escape.

Downey picks up some speed but doesn't go mad. Dixon is looking for a gap to get through to cut the journey time down, as well as looking for targets. He sees one coming up and bangs on the top of the cab before he shouts down the side of the cab that a gap is coming. Downey sees it and takes it, turning right and slowing as he drives through the grounded helicopters.

Thankfully, the pick-up is soon nearing the end of the helicopters. Even Dixon started to feel slightly nervous and claustrophobic driving through the dark eerie hulks of machinery where anything could be lurking in the shadows. He consoles himself with the fact that they haven't seen any hostiles yet and then curses himself for daring to think that.

As soon as Downey turns right out of the relative darkness that the helicopters cast, Dixon sees possible targets ahead, many of them. They are some way off still, up by the taxiways that lead to the long runway they need to travel up to Terminal 5. The only saving grace is that the way ahead is now wide and will keep getting wider as they go. Meaning they can stay left to avoid getting too near the inferno and explosions lighting the darkness ahead as if it were day and the sun was shining down.

"We have targets ahead," Dixon shouts to Kim behind him. There is no point in saying 'possible' targets because he knows exactly what they are; he can tell now they are only that bit closer.

Downey steers over to the left side and accelerates onto the main taxiway heading for the runway. Dixon only realises now that Downey hasn't turned on the headlights; he didn't pick it up before, even when they drove through the darkness of the helicopters. It is a good move from Downey, keeping them as stealthy as possible as they approach the figures ahead. They will see the pick-up soon enough and at any moment now.

Dixon registers the first figure change direction and starts to run at the pick-up, quite a distance away. He doesn't panic, warns Kim again and prepares himself for battle. Dixon crosses his left arm in front of himself over the cab, taking hold of an anchor point to steady himself, in case Downey takes evasive action. He then rests his rifle with his right hand across his left arm and pulls the rifle home into his shoulder. His legs move back slightly and spread to steady himself even more, pushing his weight into the cab. The pick-up bobs up and down on the road, making Dixon's aim constantly adjust to compensate.

He quickly gets into a rhythm but hitting a moving target from a moving position requires its fair share of luck as well as skill. The odds of him hitting a headshot are slim to none, so Dixon is going for the lower body and legs shot to increase the odds. He will shoot a short burst to that area to take the Rabids down. They won't be hanging around long enough to worry about kill shots.

The Rabid changes the trajectory of its run to ensure it is on a collision course with the pick-up as Downey steers.

They don't run like humans, Dixon notes as he gets a good look at the Rabid's form on the wide-open taxiway. It sways from side to side, its legs moving inconsistently, sometimes taking super-fast smaller strides which can then develop into impossibly long strides as its feet slow down and it almost glides across the ground. Occasionally, a long stride is followed by a leap and the Rabid seems to fly through the air. Dixon wonders whether it is running like that to use different muscles. Burning energy in one set of muscles until another is recovered and then switching style to use the fresher muscles? Whatever the reason, it works; the speed the Rabid reaches over a very long distance is frighteningly awesome.

The Rabid's run has attracted others to attack, as they too have now seen the pick-up driving towards them. The first Rabid closes in and is almost in Dixon's range. He knows how far these fuckers can jump and doesn't want it airborne when he takes his shots. He needs its legs in his sights. Dixon prepares to let go his first volley. He aims short of his target to account for the speed of the Rabid and the pick-up. His finger squeezes the rifle's trigger, which is switched to automatic. The five or six bullets are fired in an instant, his shoulder accommodating the rifle's juddering recoil.

The lead bullet explodes into the concrete just in front of the oncoming Rabid, missing its target and spitting up dust. Two or three of the following bullets do hit their target and as the bullets rip clean through the Rabid's legs, they are taken from beneath it. The Rabid falls forward hard, smashing into the concrete of the taxiway. Dixon sees its head bounce off the rock-hard surface as its lead arm fails to stop its fall and snaps in two.

Downey doesn't have to swerve to miss the forlorn body. He carries on straight as the body is left behind, where it fell.

Dixon doesn't have time to pat himself on the back for his shot. He is immediately adjusting his aim to the next target. That's one down but they are about to start coming thick and fast.

Targets are coming straight at the pick-up from several directions. Downey keeps the pick-up going straight on through. He doesn't try to steer to avoid them, as tempting as it may be to get out of the way of the oncoming wretches. He keeps the pick-up at a constant speed and direction to give Dixon the most stable platform possible to shoot from. He knows that swerving around will give Dixon no chance of hitting his targets, and he will only change course if absolutely necessary.

As the pick-up starts to draw level with the inferno away to its right, Dixon feels the searing heat emanating from it. They are some distance away from the burning helicopters and building but that doesn't stop the right side of his face drying out and heating up. He ignores the heat and the explosions. His focus is on the Rabids in front of him. He misses his next target and has to fire again, taking the Rabid down at the second time of asking. He readjusts and fires again, this time hitting his target first time.

Creatures are running at them from the expanse on the left. Dixon, for the most part, ignores them, however. Even at the speed they run, they aren't quick enough to catch the pick-up in time and are left behind. Kim takes pot shots at some of them who change direction and try to follow the pick-up; most give up though.

Dixon has to concentrate on dispatching the Rabids that were already within range of the pick-up and they are mostly in front and just off to the left. He tries to take them out before they get into the path Downey is taking so that he doesn't have to swerve. His rifle is firing almost constantly as he takes one out and readjusts for the next target. The pick-up does have to steer around some dropped bodies, but Dixon sees it coming and compensates.

Dixon's second magazine empties and he pulls it swiftly out of the bottom of the rifle. Another fresh mag is in his hand quickly and he clicks it into place, pulling back the action. He aims at the next target and pulls the trigger but only hears a 'dead man's click' as his rifle jams.

"Fucking piece of shit!" Dixon shouts as he releases the magazine, drops it, pulls the rifles action back to clear and obstruction and inserts another mag. By the time he aims again, his target is almost upon them. The rabid jumps at the pick-up just as Dixon pulls the trigger. This time, the rifle does burst into life and Dixon lets off a long volley at the beast.

The Rabid is hit multiple times but there is no headshot. The bullets do take some of the momentum out of the Rabid's jump and it falls short and level with the front left of the pick-up. The Rabid's head impacts with the headlight of the pick-up and it is thrown into a flat spin. The crushing blow spins the body down the side of the cab before the momentum flies it over the tail of the pick-up and over Kim's head. Hitting the ground behind the pick-up, the body slides to a stop.

"What the fuck!" Dixon hears Kim shout from behind him.

Dixon has his own problems, however. He is playing catch-up following his rifle jamming. Upping his rate of fire, he has to rely almost entirely on instinct as he guns down the Rabids that threaten them.

Passing the zenith of the heat from the inferno, Dixon barely notices his face start to cool as the pick-up battles on. His eyes start to widen as the light from the fire starts to dim as they approach the runway that will take them all the way to Terminal 5. At least the blazing light is behind them now and doesn't blind his field of vision. His eyes quickly adjust to their new surroundings and they pick out targets almost as easily. They are lit up as they run towards the pick-up, their horrific tortured features aggravated by the flickering fires' light.

Finally, the pick-up crosses the threshold and drives onto the wide runway. Downey arcs around in a large diameter as he joins the runway to place the pick-up in the middle of it. From there, he gradually picks up speed, the bumpy concrete of the taxiway having been replaced by the smooth tarmac of the runway.

"Keep your eyes peeled," Dixon shouts to Kim as they speed along the ominously quiet runway. *Maybe the Rabids haven't wandered onto the runway yet? Perhaps they are attracted by the light and noise of the fire and stayed in that vicinity?* Maybe and perhaps don't work for Dixon, though, and his eyes re-focus.

The further the pick-up travels up the runway, the dimmer the surroundings get as the fires behind have less and less effect. Downey slows down, taking more care as his view diminishes; the last thing he wants to do is turn on the pick-up's headlights.

Lights ahead start to come into sharper view from the silhouettes of the massive Terminal 5 buildings looming in the near distance. Nothing looks out of the ordinary from here, but no one is taking anything for granted and their nerves start to tingle as they get closer to the buildings.

Downey keeps on while the going is good and decides to stay on the runway for as long as possible. He ignores the exits to the taxiways that lead to the smaller building of the Terminal 5 complex. Their objective is the farthest and by far, biggest building. The main advantage with his tactics is that the darkness closes in around them, camouflaging the pick-up and keeping it out of sight.

Although Dixon understands what Downey is doing, he taps the top of the cab when he sees that it is time to turn. The pick-up veers right. There is a small bump as it leaves the runway and gets onto the taxiway leading to the main terminal building just ahead.

"I don't like it. It's too quiet," Kim says from behind Dixon.

"I know, mate, something isn't right."

Downey must be feeling it too, as he has slowed considerably and is almost coasting. Is it their new surroundings bringing on their feelings of uneasiness? They certainly aren't helping; the dimly lit airplanes that sprout up from the ground, parked adjacent to the buildings they are approaching, are creepy. The manmade light above casts shadows all around, the shadow of a wing here and a fuselage there making random patterns on the ground. The shadows occasionally weaken as a flash of light from an explosion bathes them for an instant, even from this distance. Each flash is followed by the sound of a boom or a crack that pierces the deathly silence.

Both Dixon and Kim are on tenterhooks as the pick-up moves into the Terminal 5 complex, closer to the grounded planes. Blind spots are everywhere; anything could be lurking in the shadows or behind a landing gear. Their rifle's muzzles shift continually from one blind spot to another but it's just a gesture, as there are simply too many to cover.

A loud screech sounds, sending electric chills down their spines. Their muzzles dart about quicker, looking for a target, but neither man is sure which direction the screech came from. Another spine-chilling screech lets out.

"Where is it coming from?" Kim asks desperately.

"Fuck knows," Dixon answers, unsure if the sounds even came from the same source.

"It's freaking me out," Kim says.

"Stay calm, mate, we got this," Dixon lamely tries to reassure.

The pick-up has made it to the start of the main terminal building and has slowed to almost a crawl. They need to be looking for an entry point into the building but neither Dixon nor Kim wants to give up their covering positions to look for one.

"What you reckon, Boss?" Kim asks.

"We need to get into that building A-sap."

"Have you seen a way in?"

"I haven't had a chance to look, but we are swinging in the wind out here," Dixon says from behind his rifle.

"You're not wrong there."

Dixon taps the top of the cab and leans back toward Downey's window. "Downey?"

"Yes, Boss," he replies as the pick-up comes to a stop.

"Any entry points?"

"There are doors, but they all look secured."

"Keep going and looking," Dixon orders.

Downey gently starts moving forward; he scans the building, a plane length away on their left, for any entry point.

"There," Collins says.

Downey sees it too, a single black door that looks like it has a crack of light down its length on one side.

"You're up mate, go and check it, I'll cover you," Downey orders as he stops the pick-up again and opens his door to get out and cover Collins.

Apprehension and fear course through Collins' body. He doesn't question the order though and he doesn't hesitate. As soon as the vehicle comes to a stop, he opens his door and gets out. Ducked down behind his rifle that is

136

raised and pointed forward, he moves swiftly around the front of the pick-up and on towards the door that is shadowed by the looming airplane above. He is quickly at the tail of the plane and starts to work his way down it, using it for cover while checking any blind spots.

"CONTACT RIGHT!" Kim shouts as his rifle erupts.

Adrenaline fizzes through Dixon as he swivels around from his perch on top of the cab. His rifle swings around with him to look for a target and he isn't disappointed. "Where the fuck have they all come from!" Dixon hears himself shout as his rifle opens up into the mass of Rabids that are streaming like water in and around the landing gear, in their direction, coming from an airplane on the opposite side from the main building.

They are in serious trouble—that is instantly obvious to Dixon as he fires. Their bullets are having little or no effect on the Rabid's charge and they are going to be across the expanse separating them in moments. Downey getting back into the cab and speeding off will be useless and it would leave Collins behind. Where would they speed off to? The Rabids would overwhelm them before they got very far anyway. There is only one possible salvation. To fall back to the building, hope Collins has that door open and hope they can reach it in time.

"Fall back to the building, covering grenades!" Dixon shouts to his two comrades as he pulls the pins on two grenades and throws them.

Neither Dixon nor Kim wait to see what effect the exploding grenades are going to have. They are both jumping down from the tail of the pick-up before they explode. Downey rolls two grenades under the pick-up as the two men hit the ground and then all three make a break for the building.

As soon as they are up and running, Dixon's grenades detonate and a moment later, Downey's follow. The pick-up leaps into the air from the force of the blast, its petrol tank erupting with it. All three men don't break their stride or attempt to look around when the blasts happens; they have only one objective, to get to the open door Collins is holding, down on one knee with his rifle pointed, ready to fire.

Collins sees the first two grenades explode and the blast takes out a few Rabids. More replace the fallen in their ranks, though, as they stream forward, the creatures coming at a tremendous rate. The blast from the pick-up is impressive but does nothing the hinder the onslaught. The Rabids seem to anticipate the trap and take a wide berth around the blast. Collins feels helpless as he sees the swarm of Rabids gaining on his mates. They are going to be on top of them before they make it inside.

Downey is lagging behind slightly, the screeches of the horde at his back only confirm his feeling. He knows how close the Rabids are; they are almost upon him and the door is still too far off. He rips the last two grenades from his body armour, pulls the pins and drops them down by his feet. He understands that he will probably still be in the blast radius when they go, but if he is, at least it may give the other two a better chance. The grenades away, he tries to increase his speed.

Two blasts follow one another as the two grenades explode. A searing hot piece of shrapnel hits Downey's left shoulder at the same time as the shock wave.

Downey stumbles, but ignoring the pain, he tries to gather his feet, in desperation to survive and keep going. The stumble is all the Rabid that hits his back needed. The beast's arms gather him in as Downey goes down and its teeth have bitten through the back of his neck before he hits the ground.

"Nooo," Collins shouts as Downey goes down. The horror and his sacrifice impact deep within Collins and his rage builds. Without thinking, he opens fire, his rifle spitting out bullets into the melee heading his way indiscriminately.

The only exceptions to his killing spree are Dixon and Kim, to whom Downey's sacrificial grenades may have given a chance.

Collins' rifle clicks empty just when he needs it most, when he has the best chance to cover his comrades. Cursing himself, he swaps out the magazine as quickly as he can and aims the rifle again ready to shoot. He sees Kim hit and lose his footing before he is enveloped by the oncoming Rabids, and Collins blames himself for his mistake. He doesn't dwell on it, not yet, and he fires his rifle.

Dixon is almost at the door when he registers Kim go down. He is sure he hears Kim's deathly scream or is it just more of the Rabid's sickening noise? Dixon anticipates his ghastly fate that is surely inevitable. Bullets fizz past his head, giving vital seconds and suddenly, he is amazed that he is at the door. He runs straight through it as Collins empties his magazine into the oncoming horde, giving himself critical time to pull the door closed.

Rabids smash into the closing door and actually force it shut with a bang, sealing off the entrance. Dixon has taken up a position with his rifle aimed at the door, as if he expects the Rabids to burst through. The heavy fire door holds easily and almost immediately, Dixon and Collins are surrounded by silence.

The two men look at each other in astonishment, wondering how the fuck they both survived; it's surreal. Dixon especially is finding it hard to accept that he is still alive. He thought he was as doomed as Downey and Kim. He falls to the floor of the small alcove from his firing position and sits with his back against the wall, his burning legs spread out in front of him, panting, trying to get his breath back.

"Thanks, mate, I thought I was done for. I owe you a beer," Dixon says, still panting.

"Fucking hell, Boss. I couldn't help Downey, but I should have helped Kim. I lost it and shot my mag out at the fuckin' wrong time."

"Don't blame yourself, none of us had any right to get out of that, mate. If it wasn't for your covering fire, I'd be Rabid food right now."

"I should have covered Kim, too," Collins says, his head down.

"It's a bad loss, they were two good men. If it's anybody's fault, it's mine, I led us on this wild goose chase. It's gonna take some time to get our heads around it. You did your best, that's all we can do, so head up, soldier."

Collins makes a feeble effort to raise his head, but the guilt hangs heavy.

"Come on," Dixon says as he drags himself up to his feet. "It's late and I'm knackered. Let's go and find Josh and a brew."

Chapter 13

Wherever I am, as my consciousness starts to return, I forget. I only know that I'm not surrounded by the soft sheets and forgiving comfort of my bed at home. I know it because I'm slouched with hard surfaces below and behind me. Agony aches throughout my back which feels like it would shatter if I attempted to move. My bum is dead, paralysed by my position and pins and needles shoot up and down my legs as if shards of broken glass are swirling around in my veins.

There is no sound that might help me distinguish my location—or is the throbbing pain in my head applying pressure on my brain to block it processing the sound waves as it stifles my reality?

Something tugs on the tender skin on my cheek. I manage to turn my head an inch to try and move away from whatever cruelty is pulling at it. Moving only encourages their nasty game as the tugging increases, so I keep my head still.

I am afraid to look, to see what it is that torments me. If I open my eyes and they see that I am awake, what else could they have in store for me? I have to look though; I can't avoid it forever. My eyelids twitch and try to open but they are stuck together as if they have been glued shut. I try again, the skin of my eyelids straining to pull apart, threatening to tear the delicate skin. It is impossible; they won't open—has the skin grown conjoined, to stop me from seeing? I submit and rest, conserving my energy, waiting to see what they have planned next.

My right hand has hold of something, and my fingers move discretely around it, trying to discover what it is. The object is small and round, with a raised notch, a button. I press the button and my ears hear it click, proving that I am at least not deaf. The click rouses a memory, a memory of a torch I found on the floor, where I found a box too. Slowly, my mind starts to work again. The box contained syringes, syringes that I plunged into myself, to make me well again.

The torch and box were on the floor of Sir Malcolm's bathroom. Concentrating, I slowly start to remember my circumstances. The Rabid slashing at my face and scratching my cheek; the beast infecting me. Later, waking up dazed and confused like I am now and shut in Sir Malcolm's bathroom, alone. Despite my visions and nightmares, I remember that I was alone, so what the hell is tugging at my cheek?

Reality starts to gather in my mind, slowly, as my memory returns. The thought that I have been infected is hard to fathom, so why is my brain still working? My head moves unintentionally, and again something tugs at my cheek and wobbles. It takes some courage to lift my arm. I am still afraid, but have to find out what is toying with me. My hand raises and I ignore the shooting pain it causes. The hand feels for my cheek, it moves slowly, cautiously as if something might bite it. Gently, my fingers go in to touch but come into contact with something thin and round. My fingers take hold of the dangling syringe, the needle still embedded into the skin of my cheek, dried blood sealing it in. The body of the syringe is what has been tugging as it wobbled when my head moved. I pull at the syringe and at first, it resists, but then, with a twist, the needle pops free and I drop the syringe to the floor, hearing it clatter.

My arm moves again, rising further as my hand feels for my eye nervously, to see why it won't open. Instead of feeling soft skin, my fingertips brush against something hard and crusty. The rough substance has encased the lower portion of my eye and it feels like sleep in your eye, that you can get when waking in the morning. This is on another level though, more like a hardened scab that covers an old wound.

I pick at the edge of the crust on the outside corner of my eye. My nail feels the edge of it start to slide under and lift away from the skin. It gets caught, however, my eyelashes welded into the hard substance and short of ripping my eyelashes out of the hard mucus, they're stuck.

My arms drop back down and into my lap. The agony of keeping it raised for the operation is too much. The solution to my dilemma is obvious; water, I need water to soften the hard crust and wash out my eyes.

My head flops back, resting whilst I regroup and think some more. I have no idea how much time has passed since I was infected. Hours, days? I could have been unconscious for almost any length of time; my weakness tells me that much. If I have any thought of ever leaving this place, I can't just sit here, rotting away. My eyes have already crusted over and my back feels like rigor mortis has set in. My legs and bum aren't far behind my back and I have almost become accustomed to the pungent stink of faeces from below.

Am I dead yet? I don't think so; am I dying from the fucking virus—possibly? If I remain here festering, will I die? Definitely. *Definitely, so do something, you useless piece of shit*, I tell myself.

You're blind, decrepit and covered in shit, so what are you going to do? Think, man, how are you going to move forward?

Water is the first thing I need; if I'm going to move forward, I have to be able to see. I need to clean my eyes so that I can open them. I remember, behind the box of syringes, a bottle of water stood on the floor. I concentrate my throbbing head to envisage where I saw the bottle. It was on my right, but it will be out of easy reach. The bottle was behind the box of syringes that I only just managed to stretch to retrieve. My body aches but the pain isn't as severe as it was before, I don't think. Perhaps I can stretch further this time; what choice have I got but to try?

My right arm lifts from my side and I immediately think I was wrong about my pain levels. I persist though and force my hand out searching for the bottle. All it touches is fresh air, however. I try to force a smile at the term *fresh air* when I consider the stench I'm sat in, but my bone-dry mouth protests.

Agony rips up my arm and into my back the longer my hand waves around in mid-air searching, and my arms drop as I'm forced to stop to rest for a moment. I go again, this time forcing my back to move and lean into it, using my left arm to push off from behind, to further my reach. My back cracks and creaks in agony as if it is a rusty old hinge, with every millimetre of movement. Still nothing, but I keep going forward, accepting the pain, my left arm levering me out. I brush something with my fingertips; it has to be the bottle.

My arm stops waving, now knowing where to go; I just need to lean out a bit more to grasp the bottle.

Racked in agony, I force my left arm to push me that little bit further, and it does. It pushes me too far, and my back tries to pull me back in but it spasms, unwilling to cooperate. Slowly, I tip further and further, about to fall; it is inevitable, just as the pain will be when I land. On the way down, I try to grab the bottle, not thinking about the fact that my body might shatter when it hits the hard, tiled floor. My hand doesn't close quickly enough around the bottle, it knocks it flying. I hear the bottle hit the floor just as I bang into it.

For a second, I think that the fall wasn't as bad as I thought it would be. But then cold, aching, excruciating pain waves up and down me. How many bones have I broken? My right arm tried to catch at least some of my fall; surely it must have shattered?

The right side of my face is flat against the tiles with my right arm stretched out behind my head. In my holster, the handle of my knife below me jams into my ribs. A glugging sound is also coming from behind my head as the knocked-over bottle empties its contents. The top couldn't have been on it. *Just my luck,* I think to myself as I lie contorted on the floor, wincing.

To my surprise, my pain levels drop quite quickly. Every part of my body still aches but it isn't in agony, not by the standards I have become used to. The weight has also been taken off my bum, and I feel the blood start to return to it--a small relief but I'm taking it as a win.

My hand rests on something and I feel around to find a few cellophane packets of what must be food. I reach back and forth, further around, hoping to find another bottle of water. But in amongst the other stuff, there are no more bottles, just more packets and boxes. If only I could open my bloody eyes. I try again to pull my eyelids apart and fail miserably.

Okay, next plan of action, I think to myself lying there and then the obvious answer dawns on me. Situated behind the door of Sir Malcolm's private bathroom is his shower. It's virtually next to me. Surely, I can drag myself a few feet to it, reach up and turn on the tap? The thought of a nice warm shower is bliss and nobody could argue that I don't need or deserve one.

The thought is bliss but there is no chance in hell that when I turn the tap, I am going to be greeted by welcoming torrents of warm water. If I can make it, it's going to be a cold shower for me. The building's power is out which means the boiler won't work, which means no hot water. I will take a cold shower, welcome it, anything to be able to see again and wash away the stink. It's not as if I haven't had plenty in the past while on duty, sometimes under the stars. Once you get over the initial shock, they are very refreshing and invigorating, I kid myself.

I get my body into position to slowly start the pain-stricken, arduous task of pulling myself across the floor, in what I am sure is the direction of the shower. My muscles burn and protest fiercely and my joints creak, rubbing together like sandpaper as I go. The grimace on my face is fixed as is the determination. My legs are still dead, useless, and follow my body on a free ride as my hands and arms manage to do the work. Eventually, the shower door rattles in its runner to itself as I touch it. My sense of direction hasn't failed me, and I pull at the bottom of the door to roll it back. The small ledge up into the shower is tricky but soon mounted and I turn over and grab whatever I can to help me sit up so that I can pull my legs in.

Sitting with my back against the back wall, I rest. Could it be that using my body has loosened it up a bit? The trip hurt, that's for sure, but it could have been worse.

I try to remember where the tap to the shower is. I haven't been in this bathroom many times and barely took any notice of the shower cubicle. With a creaking back, I reach above my head, to find the tap.

Before I turn the tap, I prepare myself for the onslaught of cold water, ensuring my body knows to expect the assault. Nevertheless, my body goes rigid with shock as the water starts to rain down. My clothes give me some protection at first, but they soon soak through as the water penetrates through to my skin.

Almost immediately, I put my head back and rest it onto the wall behind me, allowing the water to splash directly onto my face and crusty eyes.

A loud crash reverberates into the bathroom, from one of its outside walls. The shock makes me jump, my head springing upright as if to look what is going on. All I see is darkness and panic grips me. The noise from the shower has alerted the Rabids to my presence. Visions of them bursting through the bathroom door play across my closed black eyelids and my panic grows.

My hands come up to my eyes as fear flows through me. I put my head back again and my knuckles rub the water into my eyes, desperately trying to wash away the globules of sleep. Another crash is followed by muffled screeches and then another crash. Are they coming through the wall? I keep rubbing, massaging the water into my eyes. Taking my hands away. I urgently try to open my eyes and feel the corner of my left eye pop apart slightly. I rub again, encouraged that it is working. I can feel the hardness of the crust start to soften. I go to open them once more and both eyelids do prize apart. My eyelashes linger, stuck in the goo but I persist, straining to get my eyes open. Gradually, the eyelashes slide free and at last, my eyes are open.

Darkness still fills my vision though, and for a moment I think that I have lost my sight. My hands wash the last of the residue away in the hope that will bring my sight back, but it doesn't. More crashes and screeches sound out and in a futile act, I slide my Sig out of its soaking wet holster, ready to defend myself. I don't even know if it is loaded, I can't remember—and I don't fancy my chances of hitting a headshot when I'm blind.

The feel of my trusted weapon in my hand brings with it reassurance and my panic subsides a bit. Enough to let my brain work at least and realise that I haven't lost my sight. The room is in pitch darkness, I think?

At least my sudden panic has taken my mind off the shower's cold water, which actually isn't that cold. The commotion outside the bathroom continues but I just sit there waiting for something to happen and letting the water wash over me.

The Rabids don't burst in and eventually they settle down, obviously having gotten used to the new noise of running water.

After a time, I realise that they aren't breaking in and my guard starts to drop. I put the Sig down and start to undress. The process is a struggle and painful. My muscles have relaxed more as my skin has soaked up the water, but my joints haven't; they are still in turmoil with every movement. I place the important pieces of kit close by, just outside the cubicle, like the Sig's holster and my body armour. All the clothes I am wearing, however, I throw as far as I can out of the shower. Especially my soiled trousers and underwear, which were a nightmare to get off, as were my boots.

Finally undressed, I have one more thing to try before I can fully relax for a while. I have been afraid to try it in case my body rejects it but I can't put it off any longer if I mean to carry on. My head leans back, and I open my parched mouth to allow water into it. My dried-out tongue tells me immediately that the water is welcome as it soaks it up like a new sponge. The water slides down my throat and into my stomach like nectar, and it feels amazing. I drink in the most refreshing water I have ever had, even though it is travelling through pipes that are not meant to carry drinking water. I have to stop myself from gorging myself, a few gulps are all I allow myself. I have to take it easy and see if the water will settle into my infected body.

That done, I lower onto the floor of the shower, again taking the pressure off my bum. I curl up on my side and let the shower do its job, thinking how pleased I am that the water is staying put in my stomach.

Dozing on the floor of the shower, but not sleeping, I am still aware of the water washing over me and the sound of the shower. I think about the horrors of the last few days.

The carnage is brutal and horrible to remember, and I can't help playing it back in my mind. The blood and guts stain my thoughts and are hard to escape. Friends and colleagues butchered, many in front of my eyes, fill me with sadness and guilt. Especially Dan, my best friend, he could have made his excuses and got the hell out of Dodge. Instead, he was by my side until the end, fighting my fight and always with a smile on his face. I don't feel the tears I shed for him; they simply join the water raining down on me to be washed down the plughole as if they were never there.

Minutes pass and my thoughts threaten to overcome me. I have to suppress them and change my train of thought. Rolling onto my back, under protest from my body, I open my mouth again to let some water in. After a few gulps, I roll onto my other side, determined to think ahead and not back. Getting comfortable, I control my thoughts, making myself concentrate on what I am going to do next despite my tired head.

A chill shudders through me, waking me. I must have drifted off to sleep. Thankfully, almost immediately, I remember where I am for a change. I shiver again, the water is pulling my body temperature down. I have no idea how long I have been here, but it's time to get out.

I manoeuvre myself and sit back up. My body is still hurting all over, but I think—hope--it is improving. I look at my wrist in a hopeless attempt to see what the time is. My military-grade watch's hands have lost all of their luminosity, useless. If I couldn't feel the watch around my wrist, I wouldn't know it was there. How long have I been in this room, I wonder to myself?

My shivering is increasing. I need to finish up. My hands search around the outskirts of the shower cubicle and soon find a bottle of shampoo or shower gel, I have no idea which. I squirt a large dollop into my hair and start to give myself a thorough washdown.

With some relief, I finally turn the shower off; if only it had been hot. Now I just need to get to one of the towels that I know hang on the right, on a rail, on the wall.

I am forced to rest yet again when I finish drying myself, sitting on top of the damp towel, just outside the cubicle. My body aches and my energy levels are low, I feel so weak, but at least the shivering has stopped.

The Rabids are quiet; there was a bit of commotion when the shower went off, it didn't last, however. My legs are better and have feeling in them. I move them around on the floor to try and get them working better. Any minute now I am going to have to try and stand on them; I can't keep crawling, although my confidence isn't high.

Through the glass-walled cubicle, a glimmer of light shines through the water droplets that cling onto the glass. It has to be coming from under the door. Is the sun coming up? Have I been here that long? It wouldn't surprise me. I have been in a terrible state. If days had passed, I would have no trouble believing it.

The prospect of light spurs me on. The time has come to see if I can stand and use my legs, no matter how much it is going to hurt. I use the wall and the glass door frame of the cubicle to steady myself and for leverage. My arms scream as I pull up on the door frame, trying to get onto my knees. My legs are not playing along, and the assistance they give is feeble. What hope is there that they won't buckle under me when I go to stand? With my head against the glass for balance, my right arm pulls under my right knee to move that leg into position, onto its foot to stand me up. The effort is nearly overwhelming. I am panting, out of breath like I've just run the hundred meters. Controlling my breathing, I take a deep couple of breaths and go for the big push up.

A funny wailing noise escapes my throat as the muscles in my leg contract. The strain is enormous as my right leg pushes and my arms pull against the door frame. Pain shoots to my brain from every part of my body as I slowly rise. As I go, I try to get my left leg involved to help but it won't cooperate, I can't bring it into position so that the foot is flat on the floor. My arms pull harder to compensate and my right leg keeps pushing. Determined not to give up and fall back down, gradually my leg straightens until finally the knee goes back and it locks into position with one last agonising jolt.

Fuck me, how the mighty have fallen, I think to myself. I powered across the roof above me not so long ago, running from a horde of Zombies. Now it takes every ounce of energy I have to just about stand up.

At last, my left foot decides to get involved and I manage to get it grounded. Now, my breathing takes on the sound of someone who has just run a marathon, rapid and harsh. I daren't move until it calms down. My head is dizzy, and I cling onto the door frame for dear life. I doubt I'd have it in me to do that again if I fall or collapse back down.

After an age, my head clears and my breathing recovers. With my hands still gripping the door frame, I try bending my knees, one at a time at first. The right one performs pretty well, but the first time I try the left, it trembles and almost gives way before it does lock back into position. I try it again and again before the bloody thing remembers what it is doing, and it stops trying to collapse. Finally gripping tightly with my hands, I bend both legs at the same time and then straighten them. They complete their task; I won't be taking part in any races right now, but my legs are working.

I'm eager to get to the door, to get to the light, but I need something before I dare to crack the door open. My Sig, which is still inside the cubicle, on top of the well, just inside the door. I thought about bringing it up with me but decided against it. I needed both hands free to get me upright and as I'm stark bollock naked, there was nowhere else to put it. I don't delay this latest challenge and with a few dramas along the way, the Sig is soon in my grip.

With no more excuses, I start shuffling over toward the door, using the cubicle to steady myself. I am full of trepidation about opening the door even though I am all but sure there are no Rabids behind it, in the office. If there were, they would have made themselves known by now. I don't take it for granted though; my guard is up, not that I'm in any state for a fight, not by a long chalk.

The bones in my feet feel so fragile, giving the impression they could crumble and snap with each shuffled step. In my hand, the Sig knocks against the glass as my hands support me on my slow journey. I keep averting my eyes to look at the light at the bottom of the door, like an addiction, afraid it could disappear. I can't wait to get out of this tomb, and I hope I never have to return to this godforsaken place. I will have to come back inside though; when I'm ready, I will need to get my belongings and equipment.

Coming to the end of the cubicle, I turn the corner and my hands move onto the wall that the door is built into. I am now very close to the door which I feel in just a few steps and my anxiety rises. My last few shuffles bring me to the other side of the door and to the door handle, and my left-hand curls around it, ready to open the mechanism. Before I turn the handle, I take a moment to prepare myself as best I can. I look down at the dull light that comes under the door to try and get my eyes adjusted to light as much as possible. I don't want to be squinting as the door opens because my eyes haven't seen light in so long.

Naked in the dark, I am totally underprepared if anything unexpected does happen when the door opens. I gather my courage and tighten my grip on the Sig. It's now or never. Slowly, the handle turns in my left hand until the mechanism frees from the door frame and the door is poised to swing in. Moving further to the right, so that my eyes are in line with the edge of the door, I crack it open.

Light streams into my eyes and for a moment, I can't see anything as they squint and rush to adjust to the blinding light. My exercise to get them adjusted prior to opening the door proves to be an almost total failure.

Fresh air chases in the light and while my eyes may complain, my open mouth and nostrils certainly don't. They breathe in the new source of air greedily, filling my welcoming lungs to capacity.

Quickly, my blinking eyes recover and start to focus as the fresh air gives my brain a new lease of life. The first thing I register is that the light in the room beyond the door isn't as bright as I first thought and is actually quite dull. The initial assault of light had played tricks on my eyes. Now that they are adjusted, I see that the sun coming through the windows is weak. Whether that is because the sun is on its way up or down, or because it is still blocked by cloud and smoke, I don't yet know.

The Sig is raised next to my head ready to defend myself. My trusted pistol isn't needed, however, not yet. I scan the office, taking in the horror laid out before me. Two contorted bodies in the centre of the floor make up the centrepiece of the carnage. One is face down in virtually the middle of the floor, the first Rabid I shot as it followed me down from the roof. The second body is face-up with its shoulders and head propped up on the legs of the first body, and its legs are bent and twisted to one side. It is the first time I get a proper look at the Rabid that sliced my cheek with its nails and infected me. I look at the dead face with dread and its dead eyes stare back at me, its mouth gaping. Chills run down my spine as I look at the bald middle-aged bearded man who put me where I am now. He scared the shit out of me when he attacked, but now he looks like an averagely built dead corpse. Hard to believe the terror and power he once possessed.

The rest of the office is as I expected, a mess. The equipment we brought down to get into the safe is strewn across the floor where it was left, along with the rubble from the roof. Wires still run up to the safe door which is wide open, and ropes hang down the singed black wall from the hole above. The cleaners are going to have one hell of a time sorting it out, I joke to myself.

At the far side of the office, the door is still blocked by the desk, giving me the confidence to open the bathroom door and move out into the office. I shuffle around the opening door, being careful on my aching feet. My eyes are fixed on the hole in the roof. I don't know what happened up there in the end and what the current situation is. For all, I know Rabids are still alive up there and could attack through the hole at any moment.

Moving out into the office, steadying myself on the door frame, I feel my head go light and my legs go weak from the exertion and need to rest for a moment.

I nearly jump out of my skin as I go to sit on the arm of the couch next to me. Sir Malcolm's body is lying across the couch as if he is taking a nap. I wasn't expecting it and didn't see the body until I went to sit. Dried blood stains his cheeks either side of his yawning mouth, the remnants of shooting himself through the roof of his mouth. I am sure if I looked, I would find the back of his head blown away. I don't touch the old fella though. I just take a perch next to him on the arm of the couch, rest for a moment and wonder how it came to this.

Sitting there, I look over my battered body. My skin is absolutely covered in injuries. Scrapes and cuts on my skin are overwhelmed by the bruises. My arms and body have multiple bruises over them. From small light-coloured shallow ones to big deep ones that range from dark grey to almost black in colour at the centre of them. One on the right side of my belly is particularly black and red raw around the edges, with a small scab in the centre of it. That is where I stabbed myself with the syringe, in my frenzy I vaguely remember, flinch from the memory of the agony it brought.

Either side of the couch arm, my legs protrude down to the floor and it is they that have by far the biggest bruises. One virtually covers the whole side of my left thigh in a rainbow of colours, but bruises flow across both legs melding together, especially down the sides. My skin is almost as camouflaged as if I still had my combat uniform on.

Trying to look on the positive side, I take solace in the fact that my meat and two veg are still intact, resting between my legs on the arm of the couch.

Chapter 14

I've made it out of the darkness and look at the only other piece of equipment I have on me, apart from the Sig. I am pleased to see the second hand on my watch is still moving, so I assume that the time the watch shows me is accurate. The time is coming up to ten past five, but is that in the morning or afternoon? I have no idea—and what day? I look again and the date on the watch tells me it is only the day after the mission, which is some relief. I have been out of it for hours, not days, but that could be about fourteen hours or twenty-six hours? The dull light coming into the room doesn't tell me what part of the day it is. The sun could be coming up or going down and I can see out the window that smoke still hangs in the air, only adding to the mystery.

I look at the time again and log it. Then I fumble to pull out the winder on the side of the watch. I wind the time forward until it passes twelve, but as it does the date doesn't click to the next day. It is ten past five in the morning, meaning about fourteen hours have elapsed since I was infected and since I last saw Josh. I wind the time back to ten past five and press the winder back in.

Josh must have gone back to Heathrow, back to Emily. Are they still there, and how can I contact them or get to them? I've got to work that out, but in the meantime, I've got to get myself together. I'm going to have to move the desk away from the door and leave the office. I'm weak and naked, and if I'm going to find my children, I need to get my shit sorted.

An audible rumble emanates from my stomach which takes me by surprise. I don't feel hungry—in fact, I feel queasy and sick. Is my body calling for food, can it handle it? Is the sick feeling caused by hunger? I hadn't considered that; I had just assumed I was nauseous because of the infection.

Pushing myself up from the arm of the couch and back onto my delicate feet, I am still extremely weary. I have never been so drained. Nothing comes close, not even the culmination of SAS selection. I shuffle steadily over to the wall of the office on my left and then with one hand steadying me on the wall, I make my way along the office until I reach the blocked door that leads out into the lounge of this floor. I make my way around the desk to get to the side of the door that opens. My feet feel the debris and dust that covers the floor. I'm careful not to tread on any lumps, the thought of the pain they would cause my feet sending a shiver down my spine. The carpet and rug are rough and crusty in places with dried black blood, which is impossible to avoid stepping on.

Sir Malcolm's desk is heavy and in my weakened state, it takes considerable effort and pain to shunt it off the door. With the desk away from the door, enough to allow it to open slightly, I carefully open it a small amount so that I can see out into the lounge beyond. I daren't move the desk any more until I am sure the coast is clear.

Through the open gap, I see in the dim light that the lounge is in the same condition as it was left in. No Rabids have broken into the area. Satisfied, I heave at the desk a couple more times until the door opens enough for me to get through.

As I leave the office into the larger area, I am suddenly self-conscious of my nakedness. I am used to it being a busy bustling workplace and here I am with my tackle out, about to streak across the lounge. At least the CCTV isn't working, I hope!

My plan was to go straight to my office and make use of the change of clothes I keep in there. My stomach wants to direct me to the kitchen, though, which I suppose is a good sign. I am split between covering my modesty or going straight to the kitchen to try and eat something. In the end, I decide on the kitchen. I need energy, so I will attempt a small snack and then go to my office. If the snack goes down okay and settles while I'm getting dressed, I will return to the kitchen.

Crossing the lounge is a struggle and I have to pause at different islands of chairs and couches to lean on and rest. Finally, I make it to the kitchen and as tempting as it is to sit in one of the chairs as soon as I arrive and get my breath back, the first thing I do is go to put the kettle on. Stupidly, it isn't until I have lifted the kettle to fill it with water, that I remember there is no power. *Bloody idiot*, I think as I drop the kettle back down, my craving for a coffee making me want to scream.

The kitchen table still has the remains of the food on it that Catherine arranged for our arrival. None of it looks very appetising now after having been there for a couple of days. I've eaten worse but decide to check the fridge. Excellent; there is a plate of cellophaned sandwiches on the middle shelf. My left hand manages to pick it up and I turn and place it onto the table, the Sig isn't about to leave my right hand.

Every tooth in my head hurts as I chew the two sandwiches that I allow myself and my throat protests as it swallows them down. The food does go down though, despite a couple of urges and I have to make do with a can of coke I discovered in the fridge. Whether it settles or not, time will tell.

I could quite easily take a nap when I finish eating, and my eyelids weigh heavily. The caffeine in the coke is no substitute for a coffee and does nothing to combat my tiredness. I force myself out of the chair, however, ready for the long trek to my office.

At a slower pace than a decrepit old man, I eventually open the door to my office. On the right, next to the small two-seater couch is a tall cupboard. I open the door to the cupboard and retrieve the sports bag that is sitting at the bottom and take it over to the couch where I sit down.

The formidable struggle to get dressed takes time but is worth every strain of my body. I almost feel human again dressed in the black jeans and dark grey sweater. Pulling on my socks and tying the laces on my boots takes the most effort; my feet feel nice and snug in them once they are on, however. Maybe I am still human after all. The food has stayed in my belly and I believe it has given me some of my energy back. The clothes have warmed me and helped return some confidence.

I still feel like shit, just not as shit as I felt before.

Getting up from the couch, I go over to the mirror that hangs on the back wall. I look like death warmed up and I wonder if I actually am? The scratches down my cheek feel worse than I had feared they'd look. The three scratches are about an inch long and are quite thin, and the red swelling around the dark red centres makes them look wider. I touch one with my finger; the scab is dry and rough. If there are scabs, that must mean my body is healing them, mustn't it? Perhaps they will heal up nicely over time, or perhaps I'm kidding myself?

My shuffle has developed into a slow, short-stepped walk as I go over to the windows that look over the city behind my desk. The morning is very dull outside, and the visibility is poor. Smoke is rising from buildings in the Paddington area and from buildings beyond in the city. It doesn't look like the new dawn has brought any relief to London.

How on earth am I going to reach Heathrow through the chaos or at least try and contact Josh or Catherine? Turning away from the windows, I think that there may be a slim chance to contact them. I leave the office and instead of going back over to the kitchen, I make my way back towards Sir Malcolm's office and his bathroom. I pause on the way, both to take a breather and to listen at the barricaded door to the stairwell. The door is still ajar a little bit, the barricade still doing its job though and it has stopped the gap increasing. Controlling my breathing so that I can hear beyond the door, I listen carefully. I think I can hear faint noises or is it just the sound of the stairwell—I'm not sure? There is a strange smell in the air that I can't quite place. Lifting the Sig up, I tap one of the filing cabinets with the barrel of the gun lightly. The metallic ping immediately raises groans from the other side of the door, from the creatures hidden there. The groans don't last, they die down quickly and have stopped before I move off again.

Standing at the half-open door to the bathroom, I am not keen to re-enter. Memories of my torturous night in there return and are heightened by the foul smell that drifts out to me from within the hell hole. I try to laugh it off and tell myself it's just a bathroom, but the memories are still raw. I have never known such pain and suffering as I experienced in there. It was a nightmare of epic proportions and one I am sure I will relive on dark nights to come if I survive.

My hand pushes the door wide open slowly. I half expect something to jump out at me from the darkness as the foul smell grows stronger. Nothing jumps out, only more stinking air as light brightens up the bathroom.

Moving to the left of the door, I get my body out of the way to let in more light so that I can see inside better before I enter. As my eyes adjust to the darkness, I see what a revolting mess I made of Sir Malcolm's bathroom. There are pools of liquid excrement on the tiled floor below the sink where I had been sitting and it is smeared across the floor around that area. The pool has a wide trail leaving it, going over to the shower where I had dragged myself across the floor. My old contaminated clothes sit in wet lumps near the back by the toilet where they landed. Thankfully, most of my equipment seems to have escaped the filth, but my phone, however, is swimming in the main pool and will have to be fished out.

I enter the cesspit and carefully retrieve the equipment I need, trying to avoid the filth. I throw or kick most of it out into the office, where I will sort it out. It is hard going, especially the bending down, when I have to brace myself against something to get back up. The final thing is my phone and I debate whether to just leave it? It has been sitting in that foul liquid for hours and probably won't work. The battery will be dead for sure and I have no way to charge it anyway.

In the end, I get it, I use my rifle to drag it out of the liquid and then pick it up with a towel from beside the sink for inspection later.

With everything out that I want, I'm grateful to leave the bathroom behind and close the door. I wipe my boots off, on the carpet outside the door and then go to sit on the office floor, using the couch to help me down and rest my back on.

After taking a short rest, the first thing I retrieve from in front of me is my helmet, my best hope of communication. A quick test tells me the fucking battery pack is spent and the radio is dead, for God's sake. That's both my phone and radio out of action, so what now? Sir Malcolm's phone will be dead, but at least it may not be damaged, and I remember it was in his pocket when I searched him for the files. I'll get it when I get up.

I gather up the rest of the equipment; my holster is still damp, but I put it on nevertheless because it will free up my hand from continually holding the Sig. Some of the equipment goes in my pockets, but most of it I put away in the wet body armour, which I don't put on. With everything stored away, I put the helmet up onto Sir Malcolm's legs so that I don't have to bend down again and then lever myself up using the couch. I find Sir Malcolm's phone easily, which does prove to be dead. I pick up the helmet and my rifle and go to leave the office, retrieving Sir Malcolm's phone charger from a socket on the way.

Getting to the kitchen, I empty some of the equipment from the body armour, that I need to check, onto the table. I use the kitchen roll to dry off the body armour as best I can before hanging it over the back of the chair to dry some more. That done, I wash my hands off with soap and cold water in the sink before salvaging whatever food is left in the fridge, and a drink, and finally plonk down on a chair exhausted, to eat and consider my options.

The task ahead of me is considerable and seems almost impossible. The more I think about it, the more daunting the whole scenario becomes. I will be lucky if I make it out of the building alive, never mind reaching Heathrow. I have to break it down into segments to try and make it manageable in my head.

How can I exit the building? I stumble at the first hurdle. The lifts are out, and the stairwells are overrun with Rabids. Even if I had the equipment, I wouldn't have the strength to abseil down the outside of the building from the roof. My mind works, but I can't see a way out.

Then I have a thought. I know for sure that the stairwell off the lounge has Rabids blocking it, but I can't say that about the back stairwell. We just assumed they were coming up both stairs when the power failed and the shit hit the fan, so we blocked it and left it, without checking it, though. Since then, the battle on the roof happened and so if they were in the back, the noise of the battle may have caused them to move? A glimmer of hope rises in me as well as impatience to get out of here. I finish eating and go about checking my gear on the table.

Opening the towel containing my soiled phone, I don't hold out much hope that it will work again. I clean it off with some kitchen wipes from under the sink as best I can and push it into my pocket, next to Sir Malcolm's. My main task, however, is emptying the magazines for the M4, drying them out, checking the spring mechanism and reloading them. I do the same with the Sig and the Glock ammo, as well as checking over all three weapons. I can't afford any misfires.

A new lease of life seems to be gradually growing inside me. Whether it is the energy from the food, the thought of getting out of this building or my body rejecting the virus, I don't know. I don't ask too many questions, but I just go with it and keep my fingers crossed that I don't relapse.

The gear checked, I am eager to move. I load everything into where it should be and stand up. Firstly, the holster for the Glock goes around my waist, then taking off my shoulder holster, I pick up the body armour. The quick-drying material is still a little damp but it will do, and my arms go through it and I pull it on, adjusting the fastenings so that it fits tightly, but not too tight. I adjust the shoulder holster to allow for the body armour and that goes on. Finally, I pick up the M4, slip its silencer from my body armour and screw it to the M4's muzzle before attaching the rifle to my front. All three weapons are exactly where they need to be, with my knife to hand completing the set. My confidence grows again when I'm fully kitted out and my determination is undiminished.

I decide to leave the helmet behind. The radio is dead in it and I am going to need every sense unobstructed; it's a risk but one that is worth taking.

Ready to move out, I take a second to think if there is anything I've missed. There isn't anything I can think of, so I exit the kitchen and head for the back stairwell, and don't look back.

Furniture is still piled up between the door and the wall opposite. The door is still closed, and it doesn't look like anything has tried to get through it, which is a good sign. Before I touch anything, I put my ear as close to the door as I can to listen for any tell-tale signs of Rabid activity. I don't hear anything, so very carefully and quietly, I start to deconstruct the barrier. The process takes time, not only because I don't want to make any noise. My strength may be returning but I am by no means back to full strength yet. I keep having to stop to get my breath back and rest my arms. I also take the opportunities to listen again for activity, I hear nothing new.

I keep the door blocked with the last couple of chairs while I take a seat and wait to recover from the excursion. As keen as I am to get on, there is no overextending myself and finding I have no energy when I need it most.

Recovered, I get up and dig out the torch from my pocket, turning it on. The new batteries make the torch shine bright, too bright. My first look through the glass panel on the door is without the aid of the torch, and I see only darkness. I bring the torch up and shine only the edge of the beam through the glass. It brightens the top of the stairwell up nicely and the area is clear. I could be in business.

After I move the last couple of chairs away from the door, I attach the torch to the right underside of my M4. Slowly and gently, the door handle turns down until it comes to a stop and I go to pull the door.

The bloody door is locked. I'd completely forgotten, Stan has locked it; shit, where are my keys? I can't remember. They must be either in the kitchen, in my office or Sir Malcolm's office, but I didn't have them when I got to Heathrow. They could be in the lounge area somewhere—I just can't remember.

I haven't got the time or the inclination to go and hunt for them, so I decide to take a gamble. I replace the two chairs to block the door, move back and aim the M4 at the door frame where the lock will be embedded. The silencer does its job as the M4 spits a bullet out. The wooden frame disintegrates where it hits. Chippings and splinters fly into the air like confetti, the cracking sound short-lived. I check the damage without moving, waiting to see if there is a reaction from beyond the door. There is no reaction and metal glints at me from within the door frame. Lowering the M4, I move forward and try the door again. It moves slightly but gets caught in more splintered wood. I give it a quick fast tug, and the wood gives way and the door comes free.

Millimetres at a time, I ease the door open, constantly listening at the widening gap for any noise, but there isn't any. The gap widens until it is big enough for me to slip through. I listen one last time before my body goes through the gap. Behind me, my left hand eases the door closed, without a sound.

Darkness closes in around me as quickly as my fear rises. The feeble light coming through the glass panel in the door behind me does nothing to illuminate the area directly in front of me, never mind the stairs that fall away on my left. Silence seems to echo in my ears, and it is the only thing stopping me from panicking. No noise equals no movement, so nothing is coming to attack me, I assure myself.

Satisfied no Rabids are about to attack, I take another necessary risk and turn on the torch attached to my M4. As I stand in the corner, my rifle raised, I'm ready to push the door back open and retreat as the torch illuminates the top of the stairs. Again, nothing happens, no new noises rise up from below and I wonder if the Rabids were ever in this stairwell.

I take a step forward to the stairs proper, the light from the torch following my aim, which turns down to the first flight of steps. My finger hovers over the trigger ready to fire but the steps are clear. I move my aim over the top of the handrail on the left, shining the light down firstly to the next flight of steps, which are also clear. I move the beam of light around, looking down the whole stairwell. My view is restricted as the flights cover each other but no new noises sound and no Rabids jump out. I'm not sure how these creatures react to light so I'm not going to get complacent. I will descend methodically, pausing at each level's door to revaluate and using the door if a quick exit is needed.

My aim comes back down and reverts to the steps in front of me. The light shines off the steps and I notice debris on them. Dirt and dust litter the stairs here and there, and it can mean only one thing. Every inch of the Orion building is kept spotless, including the stairwells. Rabids have been on these stairs, I am sure of it. I climb down slowly but surely, even more warily now, the M4 showing me the way. I arrive at the bottom of the first flight of steps and into no-man's-land; there is no door here for a quick exit if I need it. I don't rush, but I don't delay leaving this area either. I scan the area below and start to descend to the next level which has the door to floor six.

Not wanting to see beyond the door to floor six in case any of the horrors that happened down here are visible, I have to force myself. It is too big of a risk to just ignore it and not to check for threats. Firstly, I make sure the area of stairs around the door is clear and then I slowly peer through the panel of glass in the door. My view is very restricted through the narrow panel but unfortunately, it is enough to give me an idea of the terror. Debris litters the area of the floor I can see and in amongst the debris are mangled unrecognisable human body parts. Sadness and nausea rise in me as I look. The far wall is singed from searing heat and peppered with shrapnel from one of the grenade explosions we heard go off while we stood above, listening helplessly as the carnage was unfolding. At the very edge of the visible area, is what looks like a ball and I have to strain to see properly what it is. I am nearly sick when my brain works out and registers what I am looking at.

Jill's severed head is lying on its side in amongst the debris, looking in this direction. Her eyes stare wide into oblivion, the skin of her face next to the floor burnt black. I have to quickly look away before I am physically sick, panting uncontrollably as if I'm having a panic attack. I'm at risk of losing it completely, my body trembles and I start to see stars in the darkness. Control your breathing, I tell myself, but it is easier said than done. I've seen it so many times in my past, in and around the battlefield, soldiers losing the plot. Good, solid, reliable soldiers who were joking around only the day before. Ones that you couldn't imagine breaking are suddenly overwhelmed by the exhaustion and horrors of it all and instantly snap. I was never immune to it, but I always managed to square it away in my head; maybe that's why it haunts my dreams so badly of late? I have never been this close to snapping in the field before, but I'm not the same man I used to be.

Using the techniques I've learnt over the years, gradually my breathing slows and my heart rate comes under control. Both my body and mind are fragile, that much is plain. I have to accept it and deal with it; I've no choice, as there is nowhere to hide and recover properly right now.

To push forward, one foot at a time, is my only option. Floor six is clear of targets, my rifle comes up and I recheck my path down before continuing.

The rest of the floors look as if I've come into work in a deserted building on a Sunday. If Rabids are on those floors, I didn't see them through the narrow glass panels in the doors. That doesn't mean they aren't there, and I focus my concentration up as well as down as I descend.

Only two more floors to go, I think as I leave the door to floor two behind. Halfway down the next flight of steps, shock and terror grip me. I go to retreat and nearly fall backwards, up the stairs. I catch myself and manage to refocus the aim of my wayward M4 ready to pull the trigger. Caught in the beam of the M4's light, a female Rabid stands in the corner of the no-man's-land, its black eyes staring at me. My peripheral vision looks for others, I don't see any. The trembling of my body races in time with my heart rate. I manage to keep it together though, just. Its mouth opens slightly to make a chilling low groan in my direction, the heinous sound rising from beneath its long straight hair that hangs around its grey face. I aim, ready for its attack. No attack comes though, it just stands there staring straight at me, groaning. The wretched creature stinks to high heaven, and I can smell it, even from where I am. Why doesn't it attack? Is it injured? Not that I can see. I almost feel sorry for it as my finger squeezes the trigger on the M4 and I shoot it, straight through its forehead. The Rabid drops like a sack of spuds into a pile on the floor, its groaning noise instantly cut off.

My confusion over the Rabid's behaviour is overridden by my reaffirmed concentration of looking for other Rabids that may be lurking in the shadows, ready to attack. Holding my breath as I step around the corpse to save me from the stench, the light from my M4 searches every corner as I proceed, eager to leave the dark stairwell behind.

I can see nothing of use through the panel in the door of floor one, it only shows me a blind corner of the corridor. Rabids are certain to be somewhere on that floor; it is the floor they broke in through the windows when the building was compromised. Grief for lost friends wells up, as does relief. I was so close to not making it off that floor when they broke through. It was Dan who arrived just in time to save me, a debt I will never have the chance to repay.

I take the last two flights down extra carefully, feeling sure that Rabids will be waiting down at the bottom. To my surprise, it is clear and the exit to the ground floor awaits. That is the easy part done, I remind myself as I go to see what I can through the glass panel. As soon as I exit, I am going to be out in the open spaces of the building proper, without anyone to cover my back.

Somehow, I've got to exit the stairwell, move down the corridor and get through the door into the storeroom. The door will be open because its electronic lock will have failed, along with the building's power. There is another problem however, in our wisdom, Dan and I parked one of the trollies, loaded with arms in front of the doors of the storeroom when we brought it up from the armoury. I'm going to have to move it before I can get through the doors. Under normal circumstances it wouldn't be a problem, I could just take off the brakes and wheel it out of the way. That type of problem is the last thing I need right now. It could start drawing unwanted attention and the delay could prove fatal. Even so, only if there is a minimal risk I will wheel the trolley into the storeroom with me. I need to restock with ammo for one, and a few grenades wouldn't go amiss either.

Again, the view out of the panel is very limited and doesn't show me much. I've no choice but to push the door open and hope Rabids aren't lurking nearby. Gently, I start to ease the door open with my foot, my hands poised, gripping the M4. The door's well-oiled hinges are silent but the air piston in the door's closing mechanism above the outside of the door makes a low hiss as it extends.

With the gap almost big enough for me to get through, I stop and listen for any sign of movement in the corridor. No noise comes so I peer out of the gap and down the corridor, which is the direction I need to go. The corridor is clear, and I can see the edge of the trolley protruding out, where it is parked in the alcove of the entrance to the storeroom. Swivelling my foot whilst keeping it against the door, I turn to look through the panel in the door to get a view of the other end of the corridor. The short run behind which goes nowhere and is a dead-end is clear also. Carefully, I open the gap slightly more and slip out into the corridor, my left hand stopping the door closing too quickly behind me.

Out, I double-check my rear and then hugging the left side wall, I stalk down the few meters to the end of the corridor behind my rifle. Just to my right now is the entrance to the storeroom with the trolley blocking the doors. Around the corner on my left is the longer corridor that leads up to the main entrance to the building and the reception area. I get my breathing under control before I attempt to look around that corner. Hopefully, when I get into the storeroom,

I will be able to rest-up. My legs are waning, and my arms are struggling to cope with the weight of the M4.

Cursing myself for thinking too far ahead, I get my head back to the present and the immediate challenge ahead. Pulling the M4 up and in, parallel with my body, my head eases over so that I can get a look around the corner. The enclosed corridor starts to come into view, the bright white walls and ceiling reflecting the little light there is. As my view increases, I start to see debris sprinkled across the floor. Most of the debris is shattered glass and rubble and as my sight focuses farther along, up to the reception area, the clutter on the floor worsens. My heart jumps as two Rabids come into view.

The two creatures appear as dark shadows, the dim light coming from above and behind them from the tall walls of windows in the open area of the first floor. Both of the creatures are in a state of stasis. They barely move, standing still as they wait for new prey to awaken them. I don't plan to be on their breakfast menu and reposition myself to bring the M4 to bear, pointing the rifle down the corridor at them.

Before I take a shot, I use the sight of the rifle to scan the reception area closer, checking for other Rabids that could be hidden in the dark patches where the light fails to penetrate. I can see only the initial two targets and focus the sight on the Rabid that is slightly further away. This Rabid is considerably bigger than the second nearer one. This Rabid is not facing this way; it is turned facing the stairs leading up to the first floor, that is out of my field of vision. My rifle travels to the right to get the other Rabid in its sights.

My heart stops in sheer panic and fear when the rifle's sight fixes on the target. The Rabid is awake and staring directly down the M4, its head tilted menacingly forward as its mouth begins to open. I can't afford for it to make any sound, not even a groan. If it alerts the other Rabids that are sure to be covering the first floor, they will be swarming down this corridor in no time.

The M4's trigger depresses, and a bullet spits out. The shot muffled by the silencer screwed to the muzzle of the rifle. The Rabid's head bursts open like a soggy old fruit, splattering brain and bone everywhere before it drops to the floor. I am taken aback by the eruption and struggle to understand why the head exploded. I can't afford to dwell on it now, and my aim moves to the other Rabid but my second of delay is too long. The Rabid screeches a bone-chilling noise as it turns in my direction. It is moving already, so I flick the M4 to auto and fire, filling the Rabid's neck and head with bullets; it drops. Sound enters the reception and travels down the corridor to me, the sound of Rabids on the move. Dropping the M4 to my chest, I push off from the wall. Moving across to the trolley as quickly as I can, my foot kicks off its brakes and I push. Straining against the heavy trolley and the doors behind, the trolley starts to move, pushing the doors open with it. A stampede has started, coming for me. The rumble of feet hitting the floor and screeches reverberate down the corridor, getting louder with each passing second. Adrenaline gives me strength that was lost to me moments before and fear drives me to push harder. The trolley picks up some more forward momentum, the doors hissing as they swing in, widening out. Rabids are into the reception; I hear them and feel them down there, racing forward behind me.

"Move, you fucking bastard!" I shout at the trolley, desperate for it to listen. Amazingly it does, the doors straighten out, fully open and the trolley glides into the storeroom.

Rabid noise is close, virtually on top of me. The trolley inside, the doors are free and start to swing back closed. I slip through between the trolley and the closing door, which isn't hard as the doors are moving at a snail's pace. Looking up, I see the swarm of beasts halfway down the corridor, their twisted faces riddled with ferocious hatred. They will burst the doors back open and tear me to pieces before the doors have even closed. I ram forward into the trolley, and it judders from the blow and jerks forward, hitting the closing doors. The pistons above hiss louder and the doors swing in quickly. I keep pushing, my eyes fixed on the lead Rabid at the threshold to the storeroom.

The Rabid crashes into the doors, stopping their inward momentum instantly, its snarling head jutting through and jamming in the gap. The black mouth of the creature snaps its long teeth at me, rage burning in its evil eyes. My right hand closes around the Glock at my side and pulls the weapon up and over the top of the trolley. I fill the beast's face with bullets, and it drops limp in the gap.

I keep the pressure on the trolley with my shoulder and jam each foot down onto the trolley's brakes. They help but they won't stop the building pressure from the desperate Rabids pushing to get inside.

My minds works like a well-oiled machine and I turn my back on the trolley, pushing against it for all I'm worth. I bend my knees so that I can reach one of the trolley's lower drawers and I pull it open. Jackpot, a bevy of grenades show themselves in the drawer, alongside numerous ammo mags.

I grab magazines and shove them into any available pouch in my body armour, two going into my back jeans pockets. Two grenades are shoved into my front jean pockets too; it is tight, but in they go. All the while I'm pushing back, but my knees are bending as the trolley gradually slides back from the Rabid's force, even with the brakes on.

With three more grenades in my hands, I check my exit route and then pull the pins. I slide back up and place two of the grenades on top of the trolley. The scene I see through the gap beyond the door is terrifying. Countless Rabids fill the corridor, baying for blood, ravenous to burst through. Releasing the grenades, the levers spring out. I have seconds to evacuate before they detonate.

I'm running before the ejected grenade levers have settled, dropping the last grenade where I stood. I can't feel the pain that must be charging through my legs as I sprint for the fire exit on the other side of the storeroom. Adrenaline courses through me, carrying me and I welcome it as sure as a junkie welcomes the needle. The trolley's wheels squeal against the floor as it is pushed inwards.

I reach the fire exit as the two grenades explode. The shockwave from the explosion hits me and forces me forward. I hit the fire exit door, smashing into the door's emergency release mechanism. The door flies out, taking me with it and suddenly I'm outside. Hot gas follows me out of the door from the explosion and manages to singe my hair. I whip around and slam the door closed, anticipating the secondary explosion of the grenade I dropped to the floor. I'm just in time, as the door slams shut, the second blast hits and is massive. I can tell, even from outside. The grenade I dropped to the floor takes the whole trolley with it, including all of the other grenades it was carrying. The fire exit door visibly bulges in its frame from the force of the blast. For a moment, I think it is going to shear free and explode out. It doesn't, it holds in place to my relief, just. I'm not under any illusion that the two blasts will have killed all of the Rabids; they don't die that easily and I don't want them to see where I went. If they did and they come through the fire exit after me, that would be the end, I'm sure of it.

I have to keep moving before the adrenaline wears off and my body starts to shut down. I'm on a path at the back of the Orion building. In front is the water of one of the Paddington Basins canals. Bodies still float in the water and some of those bodies still move. My only option is to go left, away from the building. Right is a dead end, with only more water.

The small bridge crosses the canal at the end of the path on my left, and that's where I go. A familiar ache starts to form in my legs, and walking is going to be very hard any time now. I've got to rest. Approaching the bridge, the span of which is across from me, I see a possible place to hold up for a while. There is a gap under the bridge, between it and the concrete bank of the canal. It'll be tight but I'll fit.

Chapter 15

Somehow, it is comforting to be enclosed under the span of the bridge, lying on my back and chilling. I felt exposed and vulnerable in the open space of the outside when I exited the Orion building. I couldn't wait to get out of that building when I was in it, and I can't work it out. Maybe it's because I was entombed in the dark for so long? I had better get used to it and quickly if I'm going to make it to Heathrow. I can't hide under here for long.

The rush of adrenaline has subsided from my body and my body aches at its passing. My limbs have tightened up, especially my legs. They had no right to get me out of that crisis, but they did. I was sure they would be in far worse shape than they are now after their desperate excursion. They ache and hurt but to my surprise, it is manageable, I think?

I pull out the two grenades I salvaged from my front jeans' pockets, which makes me even more comfortable. Putting them on the ground next to the two magazines I have already extracted from my back pockets, I roll onto my side, looking over at the canal.

Ripples hit the concrete bank below me. The water would be still if it weren't for the Rabid bodies churning it. None of them are close and I try to ignore their movement, looking over them to the buildings and sky beyond. The sky is a reddish-orange colour in the areas that aren't filled with black smoke. If it weren't for the smoke haze, it could actually be a nice September morning. The British weather never fails to surprise; it was wind, rain, thunder and lightning yesterday evening. That strong wind has done nothing to clear the air of the smoke this morning, though. It hangs all around, staining everything, including my lungs.

I retrieve an energy bar from a pocket in my body armour and it is only when I take my first bite that I realise I haven't got any water. How the fuck can I forget water? I'm not too hard on myself, though. I have been through the shit and if that's all I've forgotten, then I've done well. I will have to locate some, sooner rather than later, however.

The other thing I've come away from the building without is a radio, but that couldn't be avoided. My plan to pick one up from the storeroom didn't quite work out.

A fast jet streaks across the sky above the buildings I'm looking over and it pulls me out of my daydream. A loud Rabid screech echoes out as the whining noise of its engine fades, bringing me right back to reality. Operations in the city are obviously still ongoing and I wonder if Operation Denial is proceeding as Colonel Reed planned. I hope so, as I am relying on running into one of his units and arranging transport back to Heathrow. My hope doesn't belay my doubts, however. I've seen no evidence of troop activity in this area. When I looked out of my office windows there was nothing, and I didn't even see a helicopter.

Rolling back onto my back, I sit up, in a fashion. My back is bent forward, my head is ducked down beneath the low bridge above. Taking the last mouthful of the energy bar, which is going down like sawdust, I start to check my gear. How could I forget water, I ask myself again? It would ease this dry concoction in my mouth down. There are plenty of ammo magazines loaded into my body armour, seven and with the two on the floor next to me, that gives me nine. I look for a space to get the two mags on the floor into, and one squeezes in but the other will have to go back into my jeans pocket when I get up. I attach the measly two grenades onto my body armour and I'm ready to go. I'm still taken aback by how fit I'm feeling but I don't question it, I just go with it. Grabbing the last mag off the floor, I shuffle on my bum over the edge of the bridge where I climbed under. Checking the surrounding area, my right-hand grips the M4 in case it is needed. The coast is clear, and I ease myself from under the bridge, backing against it while I slip the spare mag into my back pocket and scan again.

Smoke is seeping out from the edges of the fire door I exited, back down the path from me. It rises up and away from the building. I wonder if there is a fire in the storeroom, and that will prove to be the end of the Orion headquarters?

I turn my back on it, my concentration moving to work out the best direction to go. Heathrow is south-west from my position, and I want to get onto a main road. The last thing I want is to get caught on a narrow street with limited exits. A main road will also give me the best chance of coming across a military unit. With any luck, they will arrange transport, and if not, they will have comms—or at the very least, I can get some intel off them.

My brain calculates, running through a myriad of different directions I could take. I decide Bayswater Road is where I need to get to, that runs along the top of Hyde Park. Surely, Operation Denial has progressed as far as that by now, so I'm bound to find a military presence in that area? So, if I cross the bridge, I only need to move down one side street before I get onto Sussex Gardens, a main road that runs straight down to my objective, Bayswater Road.

My route decided, I prepare to move. Normally, it would be slow and low as I move; my back and legs won't take that posture for the distance I'll be going, though. So, it'll be slow and upright and with no one covering my six it could be very slow. The M4 rises as I set off.

Moving from down the side of the small walking bridge, my head is soon level with the bridge's walkway. I scan the approach to the bridge, which is clear, as is the bridge itself. My aim turns to the exit of the bridge, on the other side of the canal. There is a small courtyard with shops encircling it, positioned slightly back from the embankment. One of them is a convenience store and my dry mouth reminds me I need water. I don't like the look of it, however, so my mouth will have to wait. Left will be my route off the bridge and then down to the small road which leads out of the basin and into the streets beyond. I scan the area on the other side of the bridge and immediately see one Rabid on the left side of the embankment opposite, directly on my route. It is standing in a state of stasis as they seem to do when there is nothing for them to attack. The rest of the route is clear, so I take aim, for a shot that is just inside the distance I am confident with. The silenced M4 hits its target, a direct headshot and the Rabid drops. There is no reaction to the kill shot and so I quickly move, lowering the rifle and mounting the bridge. Crossing the bridge in double time, constantly looking for new threats, feeling exposed and out in the open as I travel over the water. No new threats present themselves and I drop to take cover behind the end of the bridge as soon as I'm over, to rescan, the M4 raised in front of me.

Satisfied, I move again, across the embankment and past the dead Rabid, to the sidewall of one of the shops. Then I move left down the side, to the back corner of the building, where it joins the road.

My movements are once more second nature to me. After years of neglect, the last few days have re-sharpened my technique, my body moving in reflex. No targets are present along the path that carries on along the canal in front of me. I quickly re-check my six before concentrating on scanning around the corner of the building and the road that leads out of the Paddington Basin. The M4 leads my view as I slowly turn it around the corner of the building and onto the short road. My immediate impression is that the road is deserted. The dark, smoky overcast morning is deceptive though, and I take my time checking every dark corner possible, logging blind spots that could have anything lurking behind them. I pick my next hold point, which is behind a green broadband junction box and move, leaving the Basin behind.

So far, I have been lucky, deserted streets and one Rabid. Have the Rabids gone from this area having overhunted to find better feeding grounds, leaving a few stragglers behind, who couldn't keep up or who got separated from the main pack? The state of the road tells me that chaos has ensued here. Rubbish is strewn all over the road, blowing around in the breeze from the numerous upturned rubbish bins. Windows in the houses and shops on both sides of the street are smashed and crashed, abandoned cars block the road. Time will tell, but I am certain my easy ride won't last. Drama is near, and I can feel it.

Reaching the broadband box quickly, I scan again from the new angle, pick the next hold point, check my six and move. My next hold point, about a third of the way down the road, is behind a parked car. On the other side of the road, a house smoulders, smoke rising from a hole in its tiled roof. The fire must have been extinguished by the heavy rain last night. A body is face down in the road at the front of the smouldering house, half of its clothes burnt away, exposing charred blistered skin. My eye, through the rifle's sights, linger on the morbid scene for a moment. Not to take any sick form of fascination from the burnt body, but to make sure the body isn't moving. The body doesn't even twitch and I decide it doesn't pose a threat. It is properly dead.

At my next stop, halfway down the road, a small convenience shop is nestled in between two houses on my side of the road. The door to the shop is wide open, inviting me in. I've got to get a drink from somewhere; is it worth the risk? The door is open but inside looks dark and dingy—it does look empty, though. The road is deserted so I gamble that the shop is too.

Outside, the shop is littered with packets of food trodden into the pavement as if the shop has been hastily ransacked by a mob, which it probably was. What are the odds of me finding anything to drink in there? Surely, it has all been looted long ago? This time, my dried-out mouth wins out, and I really do have to find some sustenance.

I move both slow and low towards the entrance. The windows on each side of the door have advertisements for beer at bargain prices, to tempt customers inside. It may be early in the morning, but an ice-cold beer would go down a treat right now. My parched mouth dries out further, to remind me of its urgency. I ignore it, taking my time.

From the right side of the open door, the opposite side to where the door hangs, I get the best view inside. The place has been stripped bare by the looks of things. A small counter is just inside the door with a till sitting on top of it. Next to the till is an angled display rack which was once full of chocolate bars and other treats, designed to elicit impulse buys off unsuspecting customers. The plastic rack looks forlorn and stands empty with every single bar of sugar stripped from it. Behind the counter, the tobacco display cabinet and next to it the shelves that would have held bottles of spirits stand just as empty. Perhaps someone decided to have a massive party to welcome the apocalypse, I joke to myself.

Crossing over to the other side of the open doorway to get a view of the other side of the small interior, my hopes of finding a bottle of anything liquid diminish. Aside from damaged packets of food discarded on the floor, everything edible looks like it has been seized by the desperate residents of this road.

The shop looks clear, but before I enter, I pick up a squashed loaf of bread in a plastic wrapper off the pavement and throw it inside. The loaf slaps onto the floor halfway down the centre aisle. This is a tactic I believe I've seen on a Zombie film or TV show, designed to see if any Zombies jump out when they hear the new noise. Nothing moves inside and suddenly I feel slightly ridiculous for trying it. Dan would be pissing himself laughing at my display and I would just have to cower in embarrassment. I do miss the banter and his sense of humour.

I cross the threshold into the shop in hope, more than an expectation, of finding a missed bottle or can. The M4 moves around in front of me, checking corners and blind spots. Before I look for anything to quench my thirst, I make sure I'm alone inside the gloomy shop.

The shop is clear as are the two tall Coca-Cola-branded fridges. I don't have to open their doors; I can see that I'm too late, looking through their glass fronts. In fact, it is just as I thought from outside, that the place is empty of anything edible and there are definitely no beers. I'm wasting my time here, so I go to leave. On my way out, already glancing out of the door, I notice a bottle of shampoo on the floor, half-hidden by the shelves. If a bottle of shampoo can fit underneath the shelves, maybe a bottle of drink could have rolled under them. In the scramble, one could have easily been dropped and inadvertently kicked under.

Stopping, whilst still watching the door, I lower onto one knee and then put my left hand down onto the floor. Quickly, my head goes down to look underneath the steel shelves. I feel totally exposed as my eyes go down to look, but it's worth it. When I get back up, I have two bottles in my hand, one plain old water and the other fruit infused water.

Saving the trendy fruit-flavoured water, which goes into the only free pocket I have in the front of my jeans, I twist the top off the plain bottle and gulp half the bottle down. My dried-out mouth swills the last mouthful, letting it soak in before swallowing. After a second's consideration, my arm comes up again and I finish off the bottle. There was nowhere to store it anyway, what with all the ammo I'm carrying.

Exiting the shop, I carry on down to the bottom of the road, going through my manoeuvres without incident.

Stopping just shy of the end of the road, before it joins Praed Street, I take cover behind a telephone box that is standing on the corner of the junction, next to a wall.

Praed Street looks like a war zone, compared to the side street behind me. The commercialised main road, with its shops, restaurants and more than its fair share of hotels, due to its proximity to Paddington Station, line both sides of the street and has been a battlefield. Burnt-out buildings and cars are everywhere I look. Smoke clogs the street and my view. Dead bodies are dotted around in countless contorted positions and mutilated states. Women and children were not spared the nightmare, harrowing images entering my brain from every direction. Across the street, the body of a woman mounts the tall spiked railings of an iron fence. Three spikes protrude out of her back. Her doubled-up body must have hit the spikes with tremendous force. The hotel above her has an open window, from which she must have taken her desperate jump to escape. Blood has stained the grey railing red bellow her body. The trail continues down to the wall the fence is mounted on and further down, to the pavement.

I wish I couldn't comprehend the horror that had unfolded here, but unfortunately, I can, I know it well and it fills me with dread. I have to put all of my dismay to one side though, gather my resolve and concentrate on my objective.

I've got to head right and follow this long street all the way down to Bayswater Road. I do my work, scan the path of the next part of my journey, pick a hold point, check my six and move, rinse and repeat.

Steering clear of the buildings, especially the ones with open doors or broken windows, I flag them as high risk of hiding Rabids ready to attack. Progress is slow, but as my mother used to say to me when I got my driving licence, better late in this life than early to the next. A motto I never heeded back then or for most of my life.

At the second hold point, a Rabid presents itself. The creature is stumbling around aimlessly in the middle of the road. The young teenage girl, in light blue jeans and trainers, has long blonde hair that reminds me of Emily. She swerves around until she bangs into something, causing her to change direction until she hits another immovable object and changes her direction again.

I bring the M4 to bear, aiming at the back of her head. My sights are filled with her blonde curls as my finger hovers over the rifle's trigger. *Shoot, for God's sake, put her out of her misery*, I tell myself. I can't though, as much as I try, I can't shoot her. "Fuckin hell," I whisper under my breath and look for a way past the young girl.

Drawing the rifle in, I drop down, out of sight behind the rear of the car I am using for cover. Staying down low, I edge to the side of the car and peer around its corner on the opposite side to the floundering young Rabid. The pavement is passable if I work around the dead body that spans the width of it. If I time passing the gaps right, the cars lining the side of the road will give me cover. The young Rabid doesn't look like she is taking much notice of her surroundings, anyway, judging by how many times I've just watched her bump into things.

Staying low, I go around to the side of the car and move down its side. Without pausing, I carry onto the next car, but the gap is too small to worry about. The next three cars are also behind me before I reach a piece of road with no cars parked on this side. It is about two car lengths' gap with no cover to the next parked car. Looking at the road from behind my cover, I cannot see the Rabid, so quickly move to traverse the empty space. Back behind cover, I keep working my way down until I am nearing the Rabid's position in the road. I know I'm near without having to look. I can hear her feet dragging on the road and an immature growling sound. Typical of any teenager some might say.

A smell is in the air also, one I am becoming over-familiar with. The distinctive stink of Rabids. I can't remember my nose being so sensitive to the smell before today. Apart from when that one retched virtually in my face as Alice and I entered the Tower of London. I can even smell it over the aroma of rotting bodies that are also in the air. Is it caused by the infection; is it one of the side effects that you can smell these fuckers from a distance? If it is, as much as the smell churns my stomach, I can see how it could be useful.

Another empty space at the side of the road appears, just at the wrong time. I am virtually level with the young Rabid and there is no cover to move forward behind. I have two options, to either do what I couldn't do before and shoot her or wait until her back is turned and go for it.

She has gone quiet, stopped moving. Peering carefully over the bonnet of the car to see her exact position, it takes me a moment to find her. My nerves suddenly fizz in fright as my eyes meet hers over the top of the bonnet to my left. My head stays perfectly still, hoping I'm mistaken, and she hasn't actually seen me. My hands tighten their grip of the M4, ready to bring it up as my finger curls around the trigger. A second or two passes and the girl turns away from me to carry on her sad dance in the middle of the road.

Ever ready, I move quietly and quickly down the pavement to the next parked car and away from her. As soon as I reach the body of the car, I stop and drop to my haunches, pressing my back against the car's doors, the M4 across my body. I take a breather and try to work out what just happened. I was sure the young Rabid was looking straight at me, but then why didn't she attack? The only explanation I can come up with is because she can't see. That must be why she is stumbling around aimlessly in the middle of the road? Our eyes meeting must have been a coincidence.

Putting the confusion to bed, I move to continue working my way down Praed Street. My passage is going as well as can be expected. Occasionally, I rest up for a minute behind one object or another. The rest is more to allow my concentration to recover than my body. I am flabbergasted at how quickly my energy and strength have returned. There is no substitute for getting your muscles moving to get them back to normal; the body is a wonderful thing.

Of course, just as my confidence rises, I begin to see a problem coming up, one I should have expected as I know the area well enough. The problem is the reason that there are so many hotels on this street: Paddington Station. The station backs onto Praed Street, ahead on my right and is the location of one of its main entrances. The same location is also where the biggest hotel on the street is, the Hilton Hotel.

I hold up well short of the area outside the station and hotel to take in the carnage. The wide façade of the hotel was once beautiful. The building always reminded me of a French chateau, with its two tall protruding towers at each end, topped with intricate grey slated, arched rooves and spires. The gorgeous building is now a shell of its former self. The limestone body is blackened from fire and peppered with bullet holes. Curtains blow out of the building through the smashed windows and there is a hole in the side of one of the towers, probably caused by an RPG.

Bodies fan out from the building, littering the road and pavement outside the hotel, too many to count. In amongst the bodies, I can see camouflaged uniforms. The scene is unreal, heart-rending, and that isn't even the main reason I've stopped.

Rabids are mingled in with the dead, at least six or seven of them. Only two are on their feet, the others are down on their knees, hunched over bodies, gnawing at the meat and bones of the dead.

Trying to contain my feelings, I search for a way through the disgusting butchery as my anger grows. There isn't a way through that won't get me seen. I'm either going to have to go back to the nearest side street and go around or make a stand.

Anger and disgust override my reason and I shift to a better firing position. my rifle rested nicely as I look through its sights. Taking aim at the first standing Rabid, I fire, and the beast drops, lost in the other bodies below. The second standing Rabid hasn't noticed anything as I fire again, killing it. Even more oblivious are the hunched-over gnawing Rabids, and I take another seven shots to kill the five of them.

There is no reaction from anywhere else to my cull and as far as I can tell, there aren't any more Rabids to add to my tally. I've been lucky, as my action could have resulted in giving away my position if there had been any more around. It was stupid. I should have circled back and taken a back road, but then there would have been the guilt for letting that feast continue.

After double-checking for any sign of new movement, I leave my covering position. First off, I cross the wide road to the opposite side of the street to the hotel and station. It's marginal but there are fewer bodies to step over there. The road crossed, I take cover and scan the area in front of me once more from the new angle before I attempt to carry on. Dead bodies are still plentiful on this side of the road; the harrowing scene doesn't end just because I've crossed one road. Shops line the pavement, their customers now slaughtered in the street. At the entrance to the underground station, there is a concentration of the dead piled up, some caught in the crossfire of the fight, but many are mutilated.

In the near distance, a screech pierces the relative silence. A gunshot rings out after the Rabid sound and I look past the harrowing scene in front of me to see if I can spot where it came from. The low light and smoke haze spoil my view of seeing anything in the distance, however, and my eyes return to the carnage in front of me. The gunshot reinvigorates me somewhat though. There is at least somebody else out there fighting, so could I be nearing the troops?

Moving forward, I enter the bloodshed. Taking it slow and steady, there is no chance of averting my eyes from the disfigured bodies I have to traverse. They may look dead but that doesn't necessarily mean they are. Each one within striking distance has to be looked at to see if it's a threat; the gore is endless. The muzzle of the M4 cuts through the hanging smoke, crisscrossing from target to blind spot and back to check my six, as I go forward one step at a time.

Another screech, closer, stops me dead in my tracks, I crouch down, reducing my presence. I'm caught in the open and the nearest cover, a bus shelter, is still meters away past the entrance to the tube station. Only my head moves as I search for the source and the chilling noise. Time passes with no repeat of the noise or sign of movement. My legs straighten and I take another step, desperate to get out of this abhorrent area. Out of the corner of my eye, I see movement near the tube station entrance. An arm reaches into the air from low down on the ground, a head coming up to join it in slow motion. I actually feel sorry for the mangled Rabid whose body is almost obliterated. The young man's eyes look like they are caught between fierce evil and agonising pain.

A shot to its head ends its torment.

Carefully, I pick my way through the grim path, between the bodies, eager for it to finish. I stay well clear of the tube station entrance where the lights have failed. The darkness inside offers nothing but terror. I'm almost too scared to look into the shadows out of fear of what I might see lurking there, I must, though.

My relief is palpable as I cross the intersection with Spring Street, leaving the mass of bodies behind and finally reaching the cover of the bus shelter. My breathing is heavy when I lean my back against the shelter, my guard still up. I don't know how much more of this tension I can take; my nerves are nearly shot.

Taking a minute to get my breath back, I reach behind and pull out the fruit water from my pocket. The bottle is damp with the sweat that has soaked through my jeans and the liquid is warm, but gratefully received.

I look at the terrain ahead, and the carnage doesn't end but it isn't as bad as the hell I've just come through. Praed Street has ended, I notice from the street signs, I'm now on Craven Road. *Let's see how I get on, on this road*, I think as I push my back off the bus shelter.

Hold point follows hold point on my never-ending journey. My technique makes it slow going but it's working well. I scan each area until I'm satisfied it's clear, then I make the short hop to the next hold point. Eventually, I see the end of Craven Road approaching. The morning hasn't got any brighter thanks to the smoke and the sound of Rabids has been intermittent. I've had to shoot my rifle four times since leaving Paddington Station behind. Each shot was a kill shot, all of the Rabids half asleep. I'm sure I am closing in on the troops because I can hear the fighting, and the sound of gunshots is drawing nearer.

Bayswater Road is close now, as I reach the end of Craven Road. There is a short side street off to the left that joins onto it. Dark green treetops are visible at the end, as I turn the corner, even through the smoke. The trees are on the outer edge of Hyde Park, one of London's many green open spaces. I will come out near the opposite end to where I watched the chaos start to unfold on the corner of Hyde Park and Oxford Street. Back when I was happily oblivious, sitting in my towel on my bed, fresh out of the shower, watching the news on television. That seems like a previous life now, but so much has happened since that morning.

Emily was next door getting ready for school; now where is she, at Heathrow? I hope so, or somewhere safe at least.

Chapter 16

"We are evacuating." Colonel Reed announces to his inner circle of cronies. "RAF Heathrow has been compromised and we cannot afford to let the command structure be compromised, especially with Operation Denial continuing and making progress."

Lieutenant Winters had been expecting the announcement all night. He is not surprised that Colonel Reed has delayed his decision; he doesn't like to admit defeat. Not that he has now; he will consider this a tactical retreat. Winters did think that the announcement would have been made before now. It was obvious it had been coming all night, despite Colonel Reed's efforts to retrieve the situation. Perhaps the cold light of morning has cleared the Colonel's mind.

Winters must be hearing different reports and seeing different data to the Colonel. Operation Denial is certainly continuing but—in his opinion—far from making progress, it's bogged down and stalled badly. Nonetheless, Winters stands at ease at the back of the forward command area, letting the Colonel and his top brass carry on their delusion, waiting for his next orders.

Josh and his sister Emily are on his mind. He has let them down. He had told Josh he would arrange transport out of here, but he has failed. They are all still holed up in the

Terminal 5 building. Transport would have been easy enough to arrange but getting them outside and to it safely had proved beyond him. Twice, Winters had tried to divert the new troops in the building to escort them to the transport, but each time Colonel Reed had demanded more troops for one task or another, and Winters' troops had been re-tasked.

Now that Colonel Reed has announced the evacuation of the command structure, Winters is struggling to see how he is going to get them to safety at all. Colonel Reed won't be bothered who is left behind, as long as his chosen few are evacuated safely. Captain Richard's children certainly won't be near the top of any priority list for evacuation.

Winters has completely tuned out of Colonel Reed's blabbering; he's had enough of the fucking idiot. Winters has seen it happening gradually over time, Colonel Reed losing his edge. Ever since this crisis started, he's been all bluster and bravado, with little or no substance. Reed's perceived status overrides every decision he makes, and those decisions are becoming more and more atrocious.

"Winters," Colonel Reed says, but Winters doesn't respond. "Lieutenant Winters!" Colonel Reed shouts.

"Sorry Sir, yes Sir?"

"Wake up man! Is the transport in position?" Anger flares from Colonel Reed.

"Yes, Sir, two cars and the Defender are in the loading bay ready to go, I have the keys."

"Let's move then, Lieutenant." Colonel Reed demands. Far from remaining to oversee the evacuation of everybody, he is leaving one of his cronies behind to deal with it.

"Yes, Sir." Winters turns about-face, ready to lead the chosen few down to the loading bay on the ground floor.

Lieutenant Winters picks up his satchel and makes his way through the command room and towards the exit. An idea to get Josh and Emily out is forming in his mind. He feels sick as the thought develops, and he feels the blood rush from his head. There is a possibility, but it is going to be high risk. If it goes wrong, he will pay dearly and if he goes through with it and it works, he will pay too. He has to act now if he is going to go ahead.

"Private Moody, receiving over," Winter says into his radio as he leads them out of the command room.

"Receiving, over," Private Moody answers.

"Private, the top brass are on their way down, vacate the loading bay."

"Sir, are you sure?"

"Yes, that is an order, thank you Private."

"Yes, Sir."

A short burst of gunfire sounds out from inside the building somewhere, as they all march down the corridor after Lieutenant Winters. Concerned, pompous voices are raised behind Winters. There is no concern for the safety of the thousands of personnel in the Terminal 5 building, not to mention the untold numbers outside the building and beyond. These cretinous men are only concerned for themselves. This is the moment that Winters decides that he is going to go through with his risky plan to get Josh, Emily and the others out, come what may.

"Move it, Winters!" Colonel Reed presses, on his shoulder. A tone of fear is in Colonel Reed's voice and Winters wonders whether the Colonel realises it.

The men stomp down the corridor, bunching up behind Winters in their eagerness to vacate the building. Winters does increase the speed of his walk as more gunfire vibrates through the walls of the building; he doesn't want to run out of time. He turns the corner, closing in on the lifts where Sam left him to go with Major Rees.

Winters looks at the faces of the ten high-ranking officers, including Colonel Reed, as they gather around waiting for the lifts to arrive. All of them have a look of concern on their faces, concern for their own wellbeing. Winters has a feeling of disdain for each and every one of the officers; he knows them all very well; after all, they were all hand-picked by Colonel Reed. 'Yes Men', only here to solidify Reed's position not because they are the right men for the job. Some of the officers are looking quite frightened, giving away their soft underbellies at the first sign of danger.

The first lift 'pings' its arrival, its door sliding open. Winters checks the digital panel above the second lift and sees that it is close, only two floors away.

"Stop dawdling, man," Colonel Reed scolds Winters as he barges him into the first lift.

Winters bites his lip and he is pushed to the back of the stainless-steel lift's interior. He is jammed between the back of the lift and Colonel Reed's shoulders.

"That's enough, the rest of you, get the next one!" Colonel Reed barks.

Winters takes the chance to run through his plan as the lift descends. Butterflies circle his stomach and his palms sweat as he finalises it in his head. He doesn't rush to get out of the lift as it reaches ground level and the doors slide open. He ignores Reed's rantings as he slowly and deliberately bends down to pick up his satchel, that he had intentionally dropped to the floor.

Exiting the lift, he glances at the digital panel above and sees that the second lift is about to arrive.

"Get a move on, Winters, what is wrong with you?" Colonel Reed asks.

"Sorry, Sir, this way," Winters replies as the lift doors to the second lift open to reveal the rest of the officers.

Taking the lead again, Winters shows the officers the way to the loading bay that is positioned on the side south wall of the Terminal 5 building. The loading bay, that is used by suppliers to bring goods into the building, is a long walk from their current position, down wide corridors.

Winters doesn't delay now; his stride is long and quick, out in front. Gunfire and the sound of fighting echoes into the corridor, the noise is much louder now that they are on ground level. Various doors and adjoining corridors sweep past as Winters goes. The doors all have signs mounted on them with a number and the name of the shop or restaurant that the doors access. They are the back doors to the retail outlets of Terminal 5, where the goods arriving at the loading bay are brought to resupply the outlets.

The five-to-ten-minute walk is nearing its completion. Winters can see the end of the corridor and the loading bay is just next to it. His nerves heighten at the prospect of reaching it.

"Are we nearly there, Winters?" Colonel Reed asks breathlessly from behind.

"Yes Sir, just down the end here."

Winters turns the corner and sees the side access door to the loading bay. He slows his pace down slightly to prepare himself.

"Here we are, Sir," Winter informs the Colonel as he reaches the door.

"Good, get the door open, Winters."

The officers bunch up again, waiting for the door to open. Winters keys in the access code for the door and pulls it open. He blocks the door with his body for a second and then moves inside. He is checking to ensure everything is as it should be, and it is. The two cars and the Defender stand waiting to carry the officers away and to safety. The journey away from the building when they drive outside will be risky. The infected are all around the building, including the long roller shutter at the front of the loading bay that Winters is standing next to. The cars are on the other side of the loading bay, a short walk away. Apart from the cars, the loading bay is empty; there are no personnel and Private Moody has left as ordered.

Colonel Reed and the other officers push past Winters. Desperate to get to their transport, they head straight for the cars. Colonel Reed making a beeline for his beloved Land Rover Defender.

Winters watches them reach the cars and start to pull on the door handles. None of the doors open however, all the cars are locked. The officers protest at the delay and look around in confusion.

"Winters!" Colonel Reed shouts, looking back at him. "Open the bloody doors; where are the keys, WINTERS!"

It is now that Winters executes his plan. His fear and anticipation peak as his head turns from the gaggle of protesting officers to the wall on the left. His hand comes up and he presses the bright green button next to the roller shutter. The roller shutter jumps into life immediately. This is not an old juddering shutter, but a nice smooth quick one. Fresh air blows under the shutter as it rises nice and quickly. The air is carrying the loud screeches of the infected as they go into a frenzy, excited by the new movement and the light streaming out of the loading bay.

Adrenaline pumps through Winters. His head turns back to the officers as they realise what is happening and go into a panic. Some bolt back towards him and the safety of the door, terror etched across their faces. Others draw their sidearms to defend themselves, whilst others freeze in sheer panic and fear.

The first beast is through the gap before the roller shutter has risen even a meter, the creature throwing itself under the edge of the shutter before it springs to its feet to attack the nearest piece of new meat. Shots ring out around the loading bay from the officers who have pistols in their hands as they try to kill the intruder. They miss and the creature lands on its prey, biting down into it. More beasts quickly follow the first one under and the feeding frenzy goes to a new level. The officers running at Winters are taken down as they are hit sideways off their feet screaming at the top of their lungs. And teeth sink into them, their eyes pleading at Winters to help them.

Winters is unrelenting, however. His hand drops from the green button to press the button below it. The roller shutter goes into reverse and the door starts to close, just before it has reached two meters up. There are more than enough creatures inside to deal with Reed and his cronies.

Across the bay, Winters looks for Colonel Reed. He is backed up against the side of his black Defender with his arms outstretched. A creature has him pinned back as he tries to stop the creature's teeth from biting into his neck or face. For a moment, Winters thinks the once-mighty Colonel might succeed in stopping the creature from feeding on him.

The beast changes its tactics though, turns its head and sinks its teeth into Reed's arm. Colonel Reeds face instantly changes from fighting determination, to shock and to fear as he realises he has finally lost.

Winters has seen enough and not a moment too soon. Down on the floor, a creature's eyes meet his as it looks up from the red-stained bleeding body below it. Winters doesn't hesitate, and quickly backs out through the side door, pulling its handle as he goes. The door swings shut just in time for the beast to slam into the closed door.

Head spinning and body trembling, Winters has to drop to his knees before he passes out, the second time he has had to take action recently to stop himself fainting. He drops further down, forward, onto his forearms bringing his head down to get blood into it.

His curled-up position works, and he feels the arteries in his neck pump fresh blood to his brain, taking oxygen with it and the spinning slows. Feeling better, he rises back up to his knees and stays there, contemplating what he has done.

He has just slaughtered a big proportion of the military's highest officers and the command structure of Operation Denial. Does he feel guilty? Yes, but for the loss of life, not because they were officers. The military will be better off and more effective without those men; he has no doubt about that. Many in the higher ranks of the military would thank him for taking Colonel Reed and his web of lies, deceit and bribery out of the game.

As for Operation Denial? Winters will communicate the unfortunate turn of events up the chain. Nobody is irreplaceable and a new command structure will soon be in place to take control of the operation. A structure that perhaps will actually improve results; they can't get much worse.

As his wits return, Winters hears the screaming coming from beyond the door behind him as the slaughter continues. He may be mistaken, but he thinks he hears the rasping voice of Colonel Reed shouting, "WINTERS!"

Winter has no remorse for Colonel Reed. Some of the other officers that Reed had suckered into playing his game, maybe, but the Colonel, no. Reed has sacrificed countless troops today, desperately trying to cling on to his power and would have continued to do so, without a second thought—and that is just today. When he thinks back to all the operations in places like Afghanistan and Iraq in which Reed has tried to play God, Winters shivers. Some—no, most—of the operations were ill-thought-out and planned by Reed and his go-to tactic to rescue the situation and try to save face was more often than not to throw more troops into the lost cause. Reed had gallons of blood on his hands, was well past his sell-by date and today got his comeuppance.

As he gets to his feet, Winters contains no sorrow in him for the slaughter of Reed. If anything, he feels sorry for the infected beasts who are going to have him to contend with now.

Recovered, Winters starts the long walk back to the lift area to get back up to the command room and get on the phone to military command. He needs to make sure they know that the temporary command structure in place for Operation Denial, while Colonel Reed is relocating, will have to cope until they find a new commander to take charge of the operation—because Colonel Reed will not be doing it.

Once he has made that call, Winters can put into operation phase two of his plans to get Josh, Emily and the others out of harm's way. Phase two is just as fraught with danger as the start was, if not more so.

An explosion rocks the wall of the corridor on Winters' right, the doors to the outlets rattle in their frames. Urgency grips Winters and he picks up his pace, starts to jog and then to run up the long passageway. Nobody will be going anywhere if the infected get inside the building.

The two lifts are in Winters' sights as the gunfire continues. As he gets to them, he slaps his finger on the call button and gets his phone out.

Chapter 17

Josh feels his phone vibrating in his pocket. A ray of hope flashes through him as he goes to get it out. *Please let it be Lieutenant Winters with some good news*, he thinks to himself. Josh's hope grows when he sees that it is him calling.

"Hello, Sir," Josh answers, bringing his head up with his phone to his ear. Josh feels the weight of expectation as Emily, Catherine and Stacey look at him from their seats with hope and desperation on their faces.

"Listen up, Josh; I'm about to get in a lift so I'll have to be quick in case I lose signal," Lieutenant Winters says.

"Sir."

"Are you still in the First-Class lounge?"

"Yes Sir, but we were just about to evacuate to a higher floor," Josh answers.

"I've sorted out transport, but it won't be straightforward. I need you all to meet me outside the command room, one floor up from you. Leave there and go right, up the corridor to the lifts. Take the lift up to floor five, then, out of the lift, go right then first left. The command room is at the end of that corridor. Understood?"

"Yes, Sir, we will leave immediately."

"Is Dixon still with you?" Winters asks.

"Yes Sir, and Collins."

"Good, make sure they come and bring all the firepower you can, okay?"

"Yes Sir, I would have a job to stop Dixon coming."

"Good, wait for me outside the command room. I'll meet you there, don't try and come in. I've got to go." Josh's phone clicks and Winters is gone.

"What's happening?" Catherine asks as soon as Josh's phone leaves his ear.

"Lieutenant Winters has got transport, so we have to meet him on the floor above us. Get ready to go, we have to leave now," Josh says and then turns to speak to the others.

Dixon, Collins and Alice are at the barricaded door to the lounge. No one else is in the lounge now. Dixon managed to get rid of their guard, with a few choice words. They have already started to disassemble the barricade and are in the process of lifting furniture away as Josh reaches them.

"What you saying?" Dixons asks Josh.

"Lieutenant Winters has arranged transport; we need to meet him on floor five."

"That's what I like to hear. I knew he would come through in the end. Let's get moving," Dixon Replies as he shoves some furniture out of the way of the door.

"What kinda transport?" Alice, asks.

"He didn't say. He did say it would not be straightforward, though."

"Sounds like more fun and games," Dixon says ominously.

"Yes, yes it does," Josh replies. "I'll make sure the others are ready," Josh says as he leaves them to finish off clearing the door.

Catherine, Emily and Stacey are up, have gathered their few belongings together and are ready to leave.

"Josh, are the Rabids outside the door?" Emily asks, taking Josh by surprise at her use of the word Rabid.

"No, Emily, but we are going to take it very carefully, okay?" Josh answers as best he can.

"Why is there so much shooting then?" Emily asks.

"That's downstairs and we are going up, so we will be moving away from the shooting, okay?"

"Okay, will you stay by me?" Emily asks worriedly.

"Yes, of course, little sister, I'm not going to let you out of my sight," Josh tells her, picking up his rifle and checking it.

"Okay, let's go then," Emily announces.

The three move over to the still-closed door out of the lounge.

"Right, listen up," Dixon says. "We haven't got far to go, but eyes open, everybody. Collins will take point with Alice. I will take the rear with Josh and you ladies will be in between us. If we run into trouble, stay together and listen to what I tell you, okay?"

"Okay, Mr Dixon," Emily says.

"Good girl," he replies with a smile on his face.

"Has anybody got a spare sidearm I can use?" Catherine asks.

"I'm not sure that is a good idea," Dixon informs her.

"I didn't ask if it was a good idea, Mr Dixon. I asked if you had a spare sidearm? I am well trained if that's what you're worried about." Catherine retorts.

"Are you sure?" Dixon asks.

"Yes, my father used to take me shooting in South Africa and I shoot regularly when I go back."

"Fair enough," Dixon says as he reaches for a holster in his body armour, on the left side of his chest. He pulls out a Glock and hands it to Catherine.

Everybody watches surprised as Catherine checks the safety, releases the magazine to inspect, reinserts it and pulls back the action.

"What, have you never seen a glamorous PA with a gun before?" Catherine jokes as she finishes checking her weapon and sees everyone looking at her.

"No, not since Miss Moneypenny, but I like it," Dixon jokes.

"Steady on, cowboy," Catherine fires back. "Let's get going, shall we?"

Dixon nods once at Catherine and then at Collins, giving him the go-ahead to open the door.

"Wow, that was brilliant," Emily says to Catherine as Collins slowly opens the door.

As soon as the door opens, the volume of the constant shooting increases considerably. The gunshots echo around the cavernous departure lounge before they travel the relatively short distance up the corridor to them. Emily moves close to Josh and tries to take his hand in hers.

"I need both hands, Emily, stay in front of me but hold Stacey's okay?" Josh tells her, and Emily complies.

Collins's head goes out of the gap of the open door to check the area is clear before he opens the door fully and moves out into the corridor, his rifle up and his knees bent. Alice mirrors his stance and follows Collins out, her rifle swinging one way and then the other. Satisfied the corridor is clear, she signals for the rest to follow.

Catherine is the next one out, her head looking one way, then the other, Dixon's Glock held in both hands. Her arms are straight, pointing the gun at the floor in front of her, ready to bring it up at a moment's notice.

Emily and Stacey are up next but just as they are about to cross the threshold, an impossibly loud Rabid screech pierces the air above the noise of gunfire. Emily immediately takes a step back away from the door, moving back into safety.

"Emily, we have to go now; come on, we can do I," Stacey says, looking at her and pulling her hand gently.

"I'm right here, Em," Josh reassures.

Emily takes a step forward again and this time, she keeps going. Stacey guides her out and takes her to the right, so that Josh, followed by Dixon, can start to move.

Alice has waited, covering the corridor on the left, her rifle aimed directly down it. As soon as Josh emerges, he replaces her, and she quickly moves up to the front with Collins. Josh then rolls away to follow Emily, allowing Dixon to cover the rear.

The group moves quickly up the corridor with Collins showing the way on point and Josh and Dixon working in tandem to cover the rear. Sounds of gunfire and Rabids are constant and only quieten marginally as they move away up the corridor.

Collins presses the button for the lift as soon as he reaches them, before taking a covering position just past the lifts. Dixon has taken a knee and is covering the rear as they wait for the lift to arrive.

"Pack into the lift tightly. We don't want to split up," Dixon instructs from over his shoulder as the doors ping open.

Collins and Dixon load onto the lift last. It is tight but not too tight, even with their weapons. The lift whisks them up to the next floor quickly.

In sync with the door sliding open, Collins's rifle sweeps down, the butt rising to meet his shoulder and his head moves to its sight. He steps out of the door before it is fully open, and he covers Dixon's exit which is just as well choreographed. The two men ensure the area is clear and cover all angles before signalling to Alice to lead the others out. She comes out rifle raised, joining Collins and taps him on the shoulder without dropping her aim to tell him to proceed. Collins moves forward immediately, back towards the sound of fighting, before he hangs left onto the adjacent corridor that leads up to the command room. Alice stops at the intersection, covering until the three women are past and Josh reaches her when she breaks to join Collins again.

They move quickly along the corridor until it opens out into a foyer with a room at the end. Outside the room, hanging on the wall by the side of the entrance is a sign that reads *command room.*

Two soldiers are stationed at the entrance and they both look confused by the arrival of this odd group.

"This'll do," Dixon orders as they reach the end of the corridor and get just inside the foyer, well short of the command room.

Collins has already stopped and taken a covering position at the corner of the corridor and the foyer. His rifle is already aimed back down the relatively narrow corridor. He knows as Dixon does, it is the best defensive position if anything decides to attack up the corridor.

"Why don't you take a seat ladies, while we wait for Lieutenant Winters?" Dixon says, motioning with his head to a row of nearby seats from his covering position. "Josh, see if the Lieutenant is in there; we can't hang around here in the open."

Josh doesn't need asking twice. Gunshots are constantly ringing out, but their noise is gradually being overtaken by the unmistakable sound of Rabids.

Josh rises from his knee, leaving Alice to cover the middle of the corridor. She moves to lie down on her front, her elbows resting on the floor holding her rifle up, her legs splayed out behind her.

Josh approaches the entrance to the command room, the two guards outside looking wary.

"Can we help you, Private?" one asks, a Lance Corporal.

"Sir, Lieutenant Winters ordered us to meet him here, I just wanted to check he is in there?" Josh replies, his neck stretching to try and get a good look inside to see if he can see him.

"We cannot confirm that, Private."

"Sir, this place is going to be overrun soon, I just need to know if he is in there? We have women and children with us, Sir," Josh says, trying to pull on his heartstrings.

Josh can see inside the command room; there are only a few people in there by the looks of it. He can't see if Lieutenant Winters is one of them, however.

The two guards look at each other for a moment and then Josh's ploy works.

"He is in there, Private, but we can't let you in."

"No Sir, thank you, Sir. I'll wait with the others, Sir." Josh salutes and turns back.

"CONTACT!" Alice shouts, and at the same time she opens fire, letting off two rounds.

Emily's scream is masked by the noise of Alice's rifle, but Josh hears it. Panicked, he sprints across the foyer to where she is sitting gripping onto Stacey. He stands next to Catherine who is already up and guarding his sister, Dixon's Glock pointing at the enemy. Josh puts his body between Emily and the corridor, his rifle aimed ready to fire.

Chapter 18

With extreme care, I edge nearer the junction that leads onto Bayswater Road. The normally busy thoroughfare that carries traffic into the shopping mecca of Oxford Street and the West End only carries the mangled shells of burnt-out cars. Battle noise travels up to me, making me more cautious. As I reach the junction, it is obvious in which direction the action is taking place—on my right, west, further along Bayswater Road or just past it in Notting Hill Gate.

I have a decision to make, either stay on the built-up side of the road with its hotels and embassies or cross the road, to the Hyde Park side. The Hyde Park side looks more inviting with the trees and greenery behind the border fence, but it could easily hide Rabids in its leaves.

There is no contest as I peer down Bayswater Road. The built-up side has bodies and other obstacles filling the pavement and gutter. The buildings that line the street are scorched by fire, with window broken and doors gaping open. *No thank you, I'll take the other side of the road*.

Rising from my covering position at the junction, I go to move and cross the road. I glimpse it out of the corner of my eye, on my left like a shadow. At first, my brain processes the image as a tall man running across the junction—and for a split second, I delay, but it is not a man. A giant Rabid, by far the biggest I've seen, flashes towards me at tremendous speed. Fear and reflex take over and I whip around, my M4 turning quickly with me as I bring the rifle to bear on the target. My split-second delay has cost me dearly, however, the rifle turning too slowly to get a shot away. The Rabid slams me back off my feet and we both hit the ground, the M4 pointing at nothing but air. I scramble to recover myself as gravity directs the Rabid to the side of my body. I am nowhere near quick enough; the Rabid's scramble is quicker and it springs onto me, its powerful arms pushing down onto my arms' biceps. The massive beast pins me down, its ugly head floating above mine. I struggle uselessly to free myself, hardly noticing its depraved stink, but I can't break the Rabids' unrelenting grip. Petrified and unable to move, all I can do is look with fear into the terrifying eyes of my assailant and wait for its teeth to strike.

The Rabids' mouth starts to open, its infested yellow teeth getting ready to slice into me. My eyes locked with the creature, it stares at me, studying its prey. The beast's head tilts back, its mouth opening further and then the head comes swiftly down into my face and it screams an ear-piercing high-pitched screech an inch away from me. Its hot breath and spittle shower my screwed-up face as my eardrums threaten to burst. I wait for the inevitable pain of its teeth ripping into me, my fear rising, but it doesn't come.

My arms feel the giant Rabids' claw-like grip loosen around my arms, and it then pushes against them. The Rabids' weight almost crushes my arms as it hurls itself up and off me, jumping to its feet. Before I can react, it runs off, careering down the road in the direction of the sound of fighting.

The beast has deadened my arms, they feel weak and floppy; without looking, I know my biceps have already started to bruise. What just happened, and why didn't it bite? It had me powerless in its grip. The temptation to lie on my back to rest and recover, to think more about the reason, is strong. I can't though, I'm too exposed, my stomach muscles manage to pull me up into a sitting position. With some feeling returning to my arms, my left hand moves to my face, to wipe off the remnants of the Rabids' spittle from it as best it can, in the hope the vile smell will go with it too.

An idea starts to form in my head as my arms feebly help me to my feet again. An explanation as to why the Rabid didn't bite. I churn it over in my brain as I bring the M4 up so that I, at least, have a chance of defending myself if I'm attacked again. Out in the open, I find a hold point and move to it, finally making it across the road. An Apache Attack helicopter powers over my head from behind, heading straight down the road. I barely hear it as my ears recover from the Rabid's assault, but I welcome the sight of it.

Do the Rabids think I am one of them? Do they take me for a Zombie? I had assumed the female Rabid in the stairwell at Orion hadn't attacked me because it was alone in the dark or because there was something wrong with it. It was the same with the young infected girl in the street earlier. She didn't attack me because she didn't see me; she looked straight at me for fuck's sake. Can they smell me as I smell them now? I couldn't smell them so easily before I was scratched, I am sure of that.

I was attacked by the hoard in Orion, yes, but I started that episode. The building was nice and quiet, until I started shooting; that caused the commotion and they reacted to it. There was no other reason for the giant Rabid not to bite, to take its pound of flesh. Was his display a display of power to show me he is the alpha, the king of the jungle?

My mind reels as I try to work out what I am now. Am I a Rabid or do I just stink like one? I have my faculties and my one driving force isn't to eat people. So, at least for now, I must just smell like one. Is that the only similarity I have to them, I wonder? My body has recovered extremely quickly from the virus. I have had colds that have lasted longer. I feel myself recovering, my body growing stronger as each hour passes. Perhaps I will get some of their inhuman strength; now, that would be handy!

I force myself to put the ifs and buts about my condition to one side, at least for the time being. It will have to be investigated further; I don't want to be a risk to anyone but now is not the time. My concentration has to be focused; I won't change my tactics based on the possibility my smell may mask me from them. That sounds a sure way for my journey to come to a fatally quick end.

The path ahead is clear, and the hold point picked so I move, staying low, behind the sights of my rifle. Leaving a wide berth from the perimeter fence of Hyde Park, I follow its path along to the next cover behind a parked-up Audi. The car, hastily parked, skew-whiff to the curb on double yellow lines, is near one of the entrances to the park. Unbelievably, the car is sporting a parking ticket stuck to its windscreen. Obviously, the Zombie Apocalypse has not deterred the diligent parking attendants of London.

Moving down the side of the black car, on the park side, I reach the bonnet. Resting the M4 on top of the bonnet, I scan the area ahead. The battle in the distance is loud, unrelenting and drawing closer. In the distance, I spot a drone in the air. The unmanned aerial vehicle is much lower than it would normally fly, the pilot not having to worry about an attack from the ground.

The vehicle looks like it is circling, I assume, over the battle taking place ahead. Judging by the vehicle's position, it looks like the fighting is taking place in Notting Hill Gate area, still a fair distance away. A streak of faint smoke emanates from the drone as it fires a missile down at the ground. I don't see a flash or any evidence of the explosion from the missile, but a few seconds later a muffled boom travels through the air to me. I'm going to have to be careful as I approach that area, as the fighting is fierce; however, it is my best chance of joining up with the troops and I haven't seen evidence of others.

Just as I go to move, I see something out of the corner of my eye again. This time, my brain isn't fooled, and I react immediately. I drop down low, turning my back to the Audi, bringing the M4 down swiftly. Wandering out of the gate of the park, a Rabid emerges, as if it has just finished its morning walk. I quickly have it in my rifle's sights, ready to shoot. The creature strolls onto the pavement and looks at me without stopping. A much smaller Rabid than my last encounter, the dishevelled creature carries on looking in my direction, not pausing its stroll. Amazingly, it takes little or no notice of me, no show of strength or aggression. In fact, it turns its head away. Totally nonplussed by my presence, it turns left and carries on its walk along the pavement, in the direction of the sound of fighting.

On the spur of the moment, I decide to try something and get to my feet. Keeping the back of the Rabids head in the M4's sights. I let out a short sharp wolf whistle. The Rabid now does come to a stop and turns sideways to look at where the noise came from. Looking straight at me, the creature still shows no aggression, quickly loses interest and turns back to continue on its way.

Dipping the M4 to move the sights from my view, I study the creature for a moment. Can it really be true that they think I'm a Rabid? Whether it's true or not, I can't let this one carry on its journey. The beast is heading for the battle in the hopes of finding one thing, prey. I pull the rifle back up and shoot the Rabid in the back of its head in quick succession, before lowering it again as the Rabid falls into the gutter.

I go back down to take cover behind the Audi, the thought playing havoc with my mind. I'm overthinking it; my concentration's been distracted from the task in hand. My head goes back and I take a breath, enjoying the slightly fresher air coming out of the park across from me. I look through the entrance into the park, attempting to remember one of the numerous times I've taken Emily in there on a weekend after I've had to 'pop' into work. I'm hoping the memory will focus my mind on what I need to do and where I'm going.

Another dark figure walking along the grass, some distance away and past the entrance, ruins any nostalgic memories my mind tries to conjure up, however.

Get moving for Christ's sake, I tell myself, *there isn't time for these delays*. I force myself up, rescan the area and head to the next hold point, ignoring the dead Rabid I have to step around.

Events out of my control happen around me, as I cautiously continue along Bayswater Road. Rabids appear from every nook and cranny of the road, drawn out by the sound of fighting. They stumble out of the buildings that line the right side, many in a state of semi-coma and tripping over themselves if anything gets in their way, especially flights of stairs. I witness one emerge from a dark doorway at the top of a stone staircase. The creature, half asleep, doesn't seem to register the stairs at all and walks out on to them as if they aren't there. The scene is almost comical as its foot meets fresh air, it falls forward and tumbles down the flight. The sound of cracking bones as the Rabid hits the stone stairs hard quickly quenches any of the humour I'm feeling. For a moment, I think the creature is incapacitated, but it starts to move and tries to get up. One of its arms is horribly broken though, its forearm snapped in two at a disgusting angle with bone sticking through the skin. I put it out of its misery.

The sounds of explosions and gunshots are like the music from the magic pipe of the Pied Piper calling the rats out. Rabids emerge from the buildings and the park in increasing numbers and they all move in one direction, the direction of the battle. I have no choice but to go with the flow. It's too late to turn back; they are behind me. I keep my distance as far away from them as possible. As unnerving as it is, one thing is for sure; my question has been answered, and it is as if I am invisible to them. I wouldn't stand a chance if that weren't the case.

The roar of a helicopter engine bursts into the road, as it swoops out over the buildings in front of me, without warning. Both of the Wildcat's hold doors are wide open and I can clearly see the face of the door gunner as the helicopter hovers just above the height of the buildings and across the road.

I come to a stop as my hand goes up above my head and I wave at the gunner, letting him know I'm in the area. A look of determination is etched across the man's face as I wave at him frantically. A Rabid runs past my right shoulder from behind, careering down the road as if it knows what it about to happen. The gunner has to have seen me, but it makes no difference; the door gun erupts, sending a hail of bullets down. Just in time, I jump to my left and roll away from the barrage. The road is ripped to shreds where I had stood from the ferocious onslaught, as the gun cuts down anything in its path. *Fucking wanker,* I think to myself as I roll to my feet and run to take cover behind a stone wall at an entrance to the park. *He saw me and fired anyway.*

The gunner sprays the area with high-calibre bullets, indiscriminately. Rabids are torn to pieces where they stand and the same is happening on the other side of the Wildcat as the second door gunner sprays the opposite side of the road.

Bullets smash into the stone wall behind me, cracking it, raining chippings onto me. Around my feet, the slabbed pavement disintegrates, blown apart and I fear getting hit by a ricochet. The gunner is targeting me deliberately; does he think I am a Rabid too, is he stupid? Rabids don't stand and wave, they bite. Let's see if this idiot prefers Rabids that shoot back, that'll really freak him out. I edge right away from the road and the hail of bullets, moving around the wall into the park. Using the low-hanging greenery as cover, I move back from the wall and gradually, the hold of the Wildcat enters my sights. The fuckwit behind the door gun hasn't let up, his contorted face mad with the power afforded to him by the gun. I aim carefully and fire. Hitting my mark, the gun whips from his grasp as my bullet hits the steel lever holding the gun. A look of confusion instantly changes the gunner's face and it takes him a moment to recover before he takes hold of the gun again. He immediately starts to fire it again, but the direction of his aim has diverted to another area of the road. I go back over to the wall and sit down with my back against it, staying off the shattered slabs. I have a drink and wait until the onslaught has finished and the helicopter moves off.

Soon enough, the Wildcat powers its engines and I hear it fly out of the area. Whether it has run out of ammo or targets, I don't know—the latter, I suspect. The bottle of fruit water is all but empty so I down the last of it and throw the bottle out into the road, where it disappears nicely into the debris.

Getting up, I walk back out onto the road ready to see the fresh carnage that will be laid out for me. The scene doesn't disappoint, a new haze of dust hangs in the air to blend with the smoke. Beneath the heavy haze, obliterated bodies move, squirming Rabid bodies whose heads evaded a bullet. Dark patches of black blood pool and glisten on the ground as if the numerous wrecked cars scattered around have decided to squirt their engine oil out simultaneously. The blood starts to soak up some of the falling dust particles that are too big to escape gravity.

The destruction and killing has minimal effect on me; I have become so used to it over the last days. I'd always thought that the bloodshed I witnessed on the battlefield in my army days was horrific, and it was. Those images tormented my dreams, but they pale in comparison to the new images my brain has stored up for me. I dread reliving them when this is over, if it ever is.

Chapter 19

Body after mutilated body passes me by as I walk down the remainder of Bayswater Road. I have given up on moving between hold points, as there is little point now. New Rabids are still walking onto the road from side streets, buildings and the park, but they don't show much interest in me. They show even less interest in the bodies of their kin on the ground, moving or not. All they are interested in is the noise of the battle and the fresh prey it promises.

I am still wary of them and try to keep my distance as we file down the road together. By far the bigger threat is the risk of getting mistaken for a Rabid again and getting shot, caught in crossfire or blown up. The dark murky atmosphere isn't helping my cause; the visibility is terrible. The conditions make it unlikely that I will see friendlies to try to identify myself as one too before it's too late. The best I can do to try and identify myself is to attach the torch to my M4 and switch it on. I keep the rifle pointed forward in the hopes the troops will see the light and take a second look at me before they open fire.

Some of the Rabids move along in packs, staying close together. The majority of the packs are relatively small, containing two or three Rabids. Some are bigger, with ten or so creatures moving in unison, like groups of teenagers when school's out.

I steer well away from the packs and not just because they intimidate me. They are a prime target for any troops out here that remain unseen, or for their air support. Whether the packs are familiar with each other and are together for that reason, I don't know. They could all be staff from the same office, a bunch of friends or even a family who were turned together for all I know. More likely, some are drawn together, like objects floating on water are attracted together. Whatever the reason, I stay well clear of them, stopping or changing my direction if I have to, to evade them.

On my left, the Russian Embassy marks the end of Hyde Park and the beginning of Kensington. The impressive tall white building remains locked behind its security gates and walls. The building looks abandoned, however, and the empty flagpole, sticking out from the front of the building, suggests it has been evacuated.

Just ahead, the road widens out as Bayswater Road changes into Notting Hill Gate with its office blocks, shops and supermarkets. The fighting is close now, I can smell it as well as hear it. I look for a vantage point where I might be able to recce the area before going further, without drawing too much Rabid attention.

On the left is a wall with a park bench positioned in front of it. It's the best option I can see that will be easy to mount, relatively discreetly.

I make my way over to it casually, turning off the torch, step onto the bench, step onto its back, put my hands on top of the wall and swiftly pull myself up. As soon as I am up, I take hold of the M4 again, just in case my climb has drawn unwanted attention. Staying sat down on top of the wall, I stay still with my head down, my eyes looking back and right, checking I'm not about to be attacked. The Rabids carry on their march, moving past me with barely a second look. As satisfied as I can be that I'm okay to proceed, my head comes up slowly so that I can see if there is anything ahead.

A flash of light followed by a yellow fireball shows me where I need to be looking. The flash was below my field of vision and the explosion is still some way off. I count to just over three before I hear the boom from the explosion, following the initial flash. That tells me the explosion was over half a mile away. I reach for my monocular and pull it out of a small pocket on my left breast. Twisting the front lens, I adjust the mini telescope to focus in on the area the flash came from. The visibility is clogged by smoke and I'm still too low to see the area, I need to get higher. I take a quick look around me and then bring my foot up to the top of the wall so that I can stand. Balanced on top of the wall, I bring the monocular up to my eye again.

Flashes of light twinkle, penetrating the smoke haze in my magnified vision. The muzzle flashes from the gunshots which also crackle in my ears as I look at the battlefront. Yellow light blazes intermittently as a grenade or RPG explodes into the melee. Short bursts of tracer fire shoot in one direction or another to direct the fire from the heavy gun positions that must be set up or mounted on tanks or other transport. The light show tells me that the fighting is ferocious and constant, but flashes of light are all I can see. I can't see any detail through the haze of smoke and the dimmed light conditions.

In the sky above the battlefront, two Apache Attack helicopters hover, to support the troops below. Both of the aircraft have tremendous firepower at their disposal, but neither is utilizing it to any great extent. My guess is the helicopter's aircrew are finding it difficult to find targets without hitting their own troops. Why don't they turn and fire in this direction and take out the Rabids marching towards the battle?

My answer comes immediately, and I duck in reflex. Two fast jets, one following the other, streak up Notting Hill Gate, over my head and past me up Bayswater Road. The jets are nowhere near full speed as their engines roar by. Instinctively, I know what payload they have just dropped into the air and I catch a glimpse of them as I take evasive action. Notting Hill Gate starts to erupt, beginning near the battlefront. A wave of explosions in a deadly chain reaction moves quickly up the road towards me as hundreds of mini-parachuted cluster bombs hit the ground. The deafening blasts multiply as more bombs hit their triggers on the ground and the fireball increases exponentially.

I have seconds before the wave reaches my position and the cluster bombs end their slowed descent. My jump left off the wall away from the road takes me down onto a small stretch of grass. The kit I'm carrying brings me down hard, and my knees give way to try to put me into a roll, but I come down straight and only manage to fall onto my side. There is no time to nurse my strains from the fall, my arms and legs scramble to get me back to the wall, to take cover. The day blazes bright as the explosions reach my part of the road. I cower behind the short wall, my arms pulling my head down into my body and my legs curling me up into a ball. Flames, shrapnel and debris erupt around the wall and come over the top of it. Pieces of rubble come down and hit my arms and back, I pray that the wall won't succumb and collapse on top of me. Heat sears the atmosphere around my small pocket of sanctuary, and it burns the back of my hands as the ground shakes.

Finally, the heat dissipates as the last of the bombs have spent their fuel. None of the munitions dropped this side of the wall and I'm still alive, burnt, battered and bruised but still breathing. Slowly, my dust-covered hands and arms move down from my head, as pieces of debris fall away from me. More dust and debris trickles down my back, inside my clothes as my head comes up and my legs relax.

I look around and cough, causing more dust to fall out of my hair and into my lungs, I cough again. Rubble is piled up either side of me, the wall has collapsed on both sides. I'm one lucky son of a bitch.

Dust fills my nostrils and mouth as I push myself up from the floor coughing badly and spitting what I can out. I wish I'd saved that last drop of fruit water now. Getting to my feet, I can hardly see anything around me apart from the destroyed wall I cowered behind. Dust and smoke hang like a barrier and the wall now resembles an arch; it has disintegrated around where I was. I stumble over the rubble towards the road, brushing myself down and I then, see what saved me. The bolted-down metal frame of the park bench has only a few pieces of splintered wood still attached to it. Its steel bars are twisted and bent but its ground bolts held as did the wall behind it. If it jumped down either side of the bench, I would have been blasted apart along with the wall.

In front of me, the road of Notting Hill Gate is utterly devastated. Any vehicles that happened to be here are now no more than mangled pieces of metal, the last of their interiors burning to nothing. I put my head down to cough violently, from the acrid smoke and dust that I can't escape. As my coughing eases, my eyes focus on the ground. Beneath my feet are vaporised body parts, barely recognisable, charred as black as the road. My gaze widens, across the road and pieces of burnt, dismembered flesh and bone are smeared over the road like burnt plastic, still smouldering for me to breathe in.

I stumble again to move forward, taking my rifle in my grasp, I have to keep going. A noise from behind makes me turn. A Rabid appears through the haze, untouched and undaunted by the explosions. Reinforcements are on their way to take up the fight. I don't want to get caught up with them, now that the road is cleared. I need the troops ahead to recognise me as a friendly as I approach, if there is any chance of that?

I shoot the Rabid in the head, but more shadows in the haze are already visible and moving this way. I turn my back on them and break into a jog down Notting Hill Gate, towards the sound of gunfire. I reach and unclip the torch from the front of my rifle and raise it above my head, waving it from side to side. I approach on faith that the troops will see the light and recognise I'm a friendly.

That was too close for comfort, Captain Walker thinks to himself as the wave of explosions moves up Notting Hill Gate, destroying everything in its path. The jets came in extremely low and the Apache helicopters had only just cleared the airspace. That would have just about summed up this operation so far, if there had been a mid-air collision or if the jets had dropped their payload a second earlier.

Neither event happened and as the dust settles, Walker sees immediately that it has made a difference to the battle. His troops are pushing forward as the tide of zombies has been cut off. There are still many to clear up but without the constant wave coming up behind, his troops are mopping up nicely, at least for now. He has no doubt more zombies will be coming; after all, that is the plan. The noise of the helicopters and the constant firing, even when there is nothing to fire at is supposed to draw them into the kill zone.

"FALL BACK, FALL BACK!" he shouts to his men. They need to regroup behind the barriers before the next wave comes. Visibility is limited and shadows move everywhere in the swirling, low-lying dust cloud and smoke. He doesn't want to risk leaving his men out there when he can't see what's coming.

One by one, his men fall back through the open gap and back behind the barriers, taking their last shots before they do. Captain Walker slaps all the men he can on their back, telling them, 'well done' and 'good job', as they return. There are too many military uniforms in amongst the piles of bodies on the other side of the barrier. He can't dwell on that now and neither can his men; he keeps talking to them, giving them encouragement, trying to keep their minds off their losses and their spirits up.

"Well done lads, form up, let's get ready for the next lot. That's it, lads, spread out, good job. Does anyone need ammo?" he encourages as he climbs up onto his raised platform behind his men and the barrier is shut.

Behind him and on both sides, the 50-cal machine gun posts will be reloading and getting ready for the next wave. The big machine guns haven't been very effective, as the zombies move too fast over the wide space for them to react. They are deadly when the enemy bunch up though and they first start firing, the awesome firepower also reassuring the men.

"Report, Eagle Eye, over," Walker says into his radio as he looks over his shoulder.

Behind the Captain, perched thirty meters up in the air on top of a swaying boom lift, two troopers act as spotters for the offensive. Nobody had wanted to volunteer for the task when Walker had asked his men, 'who wants to go up?' He suspects most of the men now regret their decision not to volunteer, after fighting off zombies since the early hours. Nevertheless, he wouldn't have wanted to be up there when the jets had flown over low and the explosions had started.

"Nothing to report yet, Sir. The dust cloud is too thick, but it is starting to dissipate slowly, Sir, over."

"Let me know as soon as you can see anything. Over and out," Walker orders.

"Keep your eyes peeled and shout if you see anything. No one fires until ordered," he tells his men at the barrier in front of him, as he walks along their lines.

"Nest 1, give me a short burst." As soon as Walker gives the order into his radio, the machine gun on his right fires its 50-cal for a couple of seconds, the noise designed to draw the zombies to them.

Nothing emerges out of the shadows of the dust cloud. The whole area has gone eerily quiet since the jets flew over dropping their ordinance. Walker doesn't allow himself to think that the worst is over—he knows better.

"Eagle eye to Captain Walker, receiving, over?"

"Receiving, over," Walker replies into his radio, his anticipation building.

"Sir, there is a figure in the cloud coming this way. It is running, but it looks like it is waving a light. Over."

"Waving a light, is it a friendly? Over."

"Uncertain, Sir, over."

"Is it alone? Over."

"Yes, Sir, it would appear so, over."

"All positions, hold fire, let's see what we've got," Walker orders into his radio. "Hold fire, lads, possible friendly approaching. Send it down the line!" he then shouts to his men in front of him.

"Multiple shadows moving behind the possible friendly, Sir, it could be a trap?" Walker hears through his radio from the nest above.

Shit, Walker thinks to himself, deciding how to play it. What are the odds on there being a friendly out there amongst the zombies? He can't take any risks with this position.

"All positions continue to hold fire until I order," Walker reaffirms into his radio. "Corporal Jenkins, report."

"Sir, I have the target in my sight. It could be a friendly; it's waving a torch and holding a rifle. The shadows behind him are gaining on him and closing in on our position though, Sir, over," Walker's best sniper tells him from his sniping position away to the Captain's right.

Walker's brain aches as he thinks what to do. He cannot and will not take any risks with his men or this position. If this position is overrun, it would have ramifications all along the operational lines and could bring the whole operation down. An Apache flies over and past their line,

Walker has no doubt it is about to engage the enemy and it forces him to give his orders to his men.

"Walker to all positions. Fire at will but try not to hit the possible friendly." He barks into his radio as he sees the waving light through the haze and jumps down off his platform to get to the forward barrier.

Nearly there, I think to myself, my legs burning and my arm aching from waving the torch above my head. I trip again over something on the ground and nearly go down. Debris and body parts litter my path forward, but I daren't slow down. Rabids are closing in on me. I can hear them behind. I haven't been shot yet, but if I get swallowed up into the pack, I can expect to be filled with bullets along with the rest of them.

Tracer fire flashes through the air on my left, quickly followed by the loud cracking of a heavy machine gun. The volley wasn't aimed at me and it gives me a glimmer of hope that I've been seen. Bright lights ahead through the haze show me the way and are getting closer. I begin to make out objects coming up, there is a barrier right across the road by the looks of it, with various platforms and positions set up behind it.

As I get closer, the air clears considerably, and I can see what is coming up. It is a barrier across the road that has to be about a couple of meters high, too high to jump over. There is movement all along the top of the barrier. I can feel the rifles aimed at me by the troops positioned there. I trip again, over a leg and now I do have to slow. Dead bodies are piled up all over the road and the piles get deeper as I move forward. I work around them as best I can, trying to find solid ground. The noise of Rabids behind is so close, it's only a matter of seconds before I get swallowed up by them.

I go to shout, to tell the troops behind the barrier I'm a friendly. Gunfire roars into the air all around, before a sound leaves my mouth. Tracer fire and bullets fly above my head as the top of the barrier lights up with muzzle flashes.

The barrier is so close, two or three meters away, but I'm stranded; there is no way to get through it. My head turns both ways, looking for a way in or for something I can climb up. There is nothing.

Bullets hit behind me, forcing me forward, closer to the barrier. Rabids screech at my back as they are shot full of bullets, I'm sandwiched between the barrier and the enemy. Desperately, I look up to the men above for them to help me, nobody looks down. All I see is rifle muzzles pointing and shooting.

A light catches my eye, above and over to my left; is it signalling me? I move without thinking about it, towards the light, climbing over a pile of bodies and down the other side, anything to get to it. I step on a leg, and it rolls as my foot pushes against it and I fall forward, landing on another cold blood-soaked body. Scrambling to my feet again, I jump over the body only to land on another. I keep my footing, just— and look up. Two faces look down at me. 'Friendly', I mouth at them, if they can even see my mouth under the dust, blood and dirt it is caked in.

Arms reach down to me and I reach up and grab hold of them quickly before they change their minds. The arms pull me slowly up, my boots scraping against the barrier, trying to help with their efforts. The loud gunfire attacks both of my ears as I am hauled up and over the barrier.

The two pairs of strong arms keep hold of me as I come down the other side of the barrier and am taken down to the ground. My head is spinning as my feet reach the ground. I don't even feel my hands being secured behind my back with zip ties until I'm released from the men's strong grip and my legs give way.

I go straight down before the two men can get hold of me again. Luckily, my arse takes most of the impact and I roll backwards onto my back.

"Get him up and take him to the rear," I hear somebody order in amongst the noise of battle.

Strong hands grab me again, pulling me up to my feet. I just about manage to use my legs to walk, with the support of the two men as they guide me away from the barrier.

I'm plonked down on a sandbag and eased backwards so that my back is supported. The sound of the battle is lower, and I look around, trying to get my bearings. I seem to be in the middle of a big square. The battle is on my left and in front of me is another barrier with another on my right. Both have troops stationed all the way along them. In the middle of the square is a crane platform, the arm of which rises high above me into the sky.

Personnel are buzzing all around. The two men who brought me here don't move from my side.

"Water," I manage to say through my dust-clogged, dried-up mouth, looking up to them.

One of them moves away and comes back with a bottle of water. He unscrews the top and puts it to my lips. I fill my mouth, swirl the water around and then spit it out onto the ground in front of me. The bottle comes back and I drink the water down.

"Thanks," I say when I'm finished. "Is this necessary?" I ask, motioning to my zip-tied hands.

"Yes, Captain Walker will be over to see you as soon as he can," one of the soldiers informs me. There is no point arguing with him; he has his orders.

Time passes with no sign of the battle quietening down and no sign of their Captain. My arms are going to sleep behind my back, and I need to get moving, so in the end, I have to say something.

"Listen, lads, I'm Captain Richards, carrying out a mission for Colonel Reed behind enemy lines and I need to get back to Heathrow. So, either get your Captain or release me, that is an order."

The two young men look at me raising their eyebrows and in the state I am in, I can't blame them.

"Sorry, Sir, we have our orders," the slightly older-looking one says. "Anyway, Heathrow is compromised, last I heard it was being evacuated."

Blood rushes to my face and my stomach churns at the squaddies' news. Images of Josh, Emily and the others flash through my mind.

"What, Heathrow is compromised, how?" I say desperately.

"I don't know, that's just what I heard."

My body swings forward, giving the momentum I need to get to my feet. I'm up before the two men can react.

"Take me to Captain Walker, immediately, Lance Corporal," I order.

The Lance Corporal looks unsure of himself, but he stands his ground and refuses. I go to walk back toward the battle but both men take hold of my arms to stop me. I don't struggle, I act if I am surrendering to their will and move back voluntarily to my original position. The two men release my arms but move in front of me in case I try it again.

In one swift motion, I raise my arms as high as I can behind my back and then pull them back down as hard and as fast as I can, leaning forward at the same time. My wrists hit my lower back area and the zip ties' plastic locking lever snaps, releasing my hands. My Glock is in my hand before the two men have a chance to raise their weapons. I take a step back with the gun raised.

"Sorry lads, but I need to see your Captain," I say looking at the two confused men, who are wondering what just happened.

"What's going on here, lower that weapon," a man dressed in a Captain's uniform orders from my left.

The two squaddies immediately stand to attention, with embarrassed looks on their faces. I lower the Glock and wait for the man who I assume is Captain Walker to arrive.

"Captain Walker?" I ask.

"Yes, who are you and what on earth were you doing out there?" The tall confident Captain asks.

"I'm Captain Andy Richards, with Special Forces. I am on a mission under Colonel Reed's direct orders."

"I thought you were retired Captain?"

"So did I, Captain. What can you tell me about what has happened at Heathrow?"

"You two are dismissed, return to the front line," Captain Walker tells the two squaddies, who immediately salute and march off.

"Heathrow has been breached, Captain Richards, and is being evacuated as we speak. Command is now off-site. That is all I know at present; I have my hands full here."

"I have to get there now; do you have transport?" I ask him.

"Heathrow is compromised; there is no point going there. Perhaps..."

"I left my children there, Captain." I cut him off.

"Oh, I see." Captain Walker thinks for a moment, before saying, "Follow me."

Captain Walker turns and strides back in the direction he appeared from. He stops at a transit van with aerials protruding from its roof and opens the back doors.

"At ease," he tells the man and woman inside the van. "This is Captain Richards, see if you can help him arrange transport out of here, understood?"

"Yes, Sir," they both say, looking at me as if I am a tramp.

"I will have to leave you in their hands, Captain, I have to get back to my men."

"Thank you, Captain."

"Good luck, Richards."

"You too."

Captain Walker walks off. I didn't even ask him how his operation is going, but I have other things on my mind. The man and woman in the cramped space in the back of the van look at me for orders.

"Can you arrange a helicopter to get me to Heathrow?" I ask them.

"Sir, comms are very sketchy at the moment, and we haven't been able to get hold of flight command for the last twenty minutes," the female Corporal informs me.

"Shit. Can you contact the air support currently up in the air directly?" I ask.

"We have their channels, yes Sir."

"See if you can raise Flight Lieutenant Alders," I tell her.

"Yes, Sir, it could take some time to go through the channels, that is if he is even flying at the moment, Sir."

"I understand that, Corporal. Give it your best shot; it's urgent. I'll be back in a minute; I'm just going to get some water."

I bring back three two-litre bottles of water and stand at the back of the van while the Corporal and her colleague chatter away. I wash my hands off with half of the first bottle, then use the rest of it, pouring it over my head while I lean forward, running my other hand through my hair at the same time. Pieces of debris and God knows what else run out of my hair and onto the ground. I do the same with the second bottle as more debris falls out of my hair. I scrub my face also as best I can, using up the rest of the bottle.

Finally, I shake the excess water from my head like a wet dog, before wringing my hair out with my hands. My hair and face feel much better when I'm finished. There is nothing I can do about the dust scratching my body beneath my clothes, as tempting as it is to strip off and use more bottles.

The third bottle, I take a big drink out of and use it to swill down another two energy bars. I am not hungry in the slightest; I need energy though and force them down while I wait.

"Sir, I have Flight Lieutenant Alders" the Corporal informs me.

"Pass me the headset," I say moving forward to the back of the van.

"Alders is that you, over?" I say into the headset.

"This is Flight Lieutenant Alders, who is this, over?"

"It's Captain Richard, back from the dead, over."

"That's not possible," Alders claims, sounding very doubtful.

"I can assure you it's me, Alders. I survived and managed to get out of the Orion building. I need your help, over."

"How did you survive? You were infected," he asks.

"I'm not sure, but I have and now I need a lift back to Heathrow. Can you help, over?" The headset goes quiet for a moment.

"Heathrow is compromised and off-limits Captain. We are operating out of RAF Northolt. I'm just about to head back to refuel, over."

"Alders, my children are at Heathrow. I need you to drop me off there. You don't even have to land. I'm at the Notting Hill Gate forward position; can you pick me up, over?"

"Yes, Sir. ETA five minutes. Standby at the landing zone, over."

"I'll be ready, Flight Lieutenant, and thank you, over and out."

I whip off the headset and give it back to the Corporal. She reaches for a pack of anti-bacterial wipes as I do.

"Where is the LZ?" I ask her.

"Over there," she says, pointing, with a worried look on her face.

"Thanks for the assistance, Corporal. Do you want the doors closed?" I ask.

"Yes please, Sir."

I slam the van's back doors closed, and turn and jog in the direction I was pointed in. Just beyond where the two squaddies had sat me down is a cleared area with a big white cross painted on the ground. I take a position next to it, put the bottle of water down and start to check my kit, my adrenaline starting to build again.

Chapter 20

Kit checked and ready to go, I stand scanning the sky, impatiently waiting for Alder's Lynx to appear. Two Apaches fly over, both heading in different directions, getting my hopes up while I'm waiting. I have no idea where Alders is flying in from so my head turns this way and that at even the merest hint of a helicopter's distinctive sound.

Military personnel pass me by, looking, wondering what the dishevelled-looking man, armed to the teeth is up to, one or two even asking if I'm lost. Smoke wisps by me in the breeze, caught in the glare of the tall free-standing temporary LED lights dotted around. The sun is straining to break through the clouds above, but the smoke and dust help keep even the most determined sunbeam at bay. The sky has taken on a deep red colour in places, especially lower down near the horizon, as if Rabid blood has managed to stain the sky as well as the ground.

Come on, Alders, where the fuck are you? I think, my impatience growing. How is it possible that Heathrow has been breached? It is a long way from the infected zone and had thousands of troops guarding it. No matter how many times I ask myself the question, I still don't know the answer. It is academic now really, how it happened; the fact is, it has. The more important question is, are my children still there, Christine? I can only hope that they have been evacuated, but that is a big hope. I have seen it all too often in most of the conflicts I have witnessed. Civilians are of little importance to the people who dish out the orders, especially when those same people are threatened. It isn't women and children first; it's women and children last, if at all.

A lynx swoops over my head, from the direction of the battlefront. *This has to be Alders, it's got to be*, I think to myself on tenterhooks. Yes, Alders, you beauty! The Lynx pulls its nose up as it flies past the LZ, bringing its tail up and over to turn. Alders brings the Lynx in quickly, lowering it as he approaches, needing no direction from me. As soon as Alders touches down, I run across the LZ, head down to the co-pilot's door.

"Taxi for Richards!" Alders shouts as I climb into the cockpit.

"That's me, Flight Lieutenant, that's me," I shout back, as I sit down and strap myself in.

No sooner have I shut the door and started to buckle up, than Alders starts his take-off. His ascent is rapid and smooth, I obviously don't need to convey my urgency to him. Before I have even grabbed a headset, he is banking the Lynx around in the direction of Heathrow. He is busy talking into his headset, to what I assume is air traffic control, establishing his flight path. Visibility is too bad to only fly by sight across the city, especially with the number of military aircraft in the airspace over London.

Before we leave the area, I manage to get a brief look down at the destroyed city around the forward position we have just taken off from. Notting Hill Gate is a smouldering pile of rubble ahead of the battlefront. Cars continue to burn in the road and tracer fire streaks up the blackened road as the fight continues. Dark destroyed buildings reach up each side of the road and beyond, some still burn while others just belch out smoke. Battle scars mount as I look out and across the city where other battles have taken place or still rage on, the destruction looks endless.

A couple of taps on my shoulder bring my focus back and away from the horror as it shrinks through my window. Alders motions for me to put my headset on which is still in my hands and not on my head.

"Jesus Christ, you really are back from the dead, Captain. No pun intended. What happened? Everybody was convinced you were infected, they said you were scratched? Josh was gutted!"

"How bad was Josh?" I ask.

"He wasn't brilliant, he was gutted of course. He seemed to be handling it as well as could be expected when I left him if that's any consolation. What happened?" Alders asks again.

"I don't know what to tell you, I thought I was infected too? I woke up a few times, feeling like I was turning into one of them; it was terrible. Then gradually, I started to feel better. I don't know if it was the injections I'd had, if I wasn't infected properly or if I'm immune somehow. I can't explain it?"

"Or you're just one lucky bastard?" Alders says, smiling.

I daren't tell him that something about me has changed, that the Rabids think I'm one of them. He might get the jitters and take me back to where he found me and decide not to take me to Heathrow. I don't know him well and I can't risk it, not now.

"What the hell has happened at Heathrow? That place was a fortress?" I ask him, desperate for some solid information before I dive into the fight again. I seriously doubt he will know anything about my children and the others, however.

"I'm hearing that an ingoing transport got overwhelmed with Rabids, causing it to crash land. Unfortunately, the crash didn't kill them, and it escalated from there. You know how hard these bastards are to kill. I haven't been back since I was diverted to RAF Northolt. I have seen it from a distance, on my flightpath to Northolt; I could see the flames from miles away!" he tells me.

"Shit," I say quietly. "Do you know if everyone has been evacuated?"

"I wish I had better news, but not many have, I'm sorry. Evacuating that many people with Rabids on the ground is proving problematic. I have heard through the grapevine that they are going to take decisive action at Heathrow to stop the infection spreading out of that area."

"What action?" I ask.

Alders looks sheepish, debating whether to tell me any more of what he knows.

"Alders, my children are there!" I press him.

"Okay, this is just a rumour, but last time I was on the ground at Northolt; something big was being prepared. I heard off an old colleague that he thinks it could be a tactical nuclear strike."

I'm speechless, but not totally surprised. A tactical nuclear strike is designed to be used on the battlefield, to surgically aid friendly troops. The warhead is smaller than a strategic warhead, used to destroy a large area such as a city. The warhead is still nuclear though, one has never actually been used tactically on a battlefield, never mind in a city and now they want to use one in London!

"Any idea on a time frame?" I ask, pulling myself together.

"I only know if they are going to do it, it will be soon. I won't be hanging about, let's put it like that."

"I appreciate the lift mate, believe me," I tell him, my mind racing.

"The least I could do. They will divert all air traffic before they do anything," Alders tells me.

"Shit!" I say urgently. "Where is the USB charging port?" I ask, quickly moving to get the two phones out of my front pocket. I should have tried the phones as soon as I boarded.

"There's one," Alders points out.

I plug the one end of Sir Malcolm's charger in the port and quickly plug the other end into my phone. I wait, staring at the screen, willing it to show a sign that the phone is charging. Nothing happens, just as I suspected; my phone is fucked. I pull the lead out and stick it into Sir Malcolm's phone. After a couple of seconds, the screen lights up to tell me the phone is charging. Patiently, I wait for a minute to let the battery draw some juice, then I press the power key. While the phone is starting, I pray that Sir Malcolm hasn't changed his passcode. The phone starts, and I tap in six digits of his birthday backwards and the menu comes up. If only that number had logged into his computer at Orion, I wouldn't be in this mess.

He won't have Josh's number; the only number I think he will have, is Lieutenant Winters'. I quickly scroll, find his name where it should be and press call. Eventually, the call connects, and I get a ring tone in my ear. I press the phone harder to try and cut out the din of the helicopter. *Please answer, Winters*, I think to myself.

"Hello," Winters shouts down the line. "Who is this?"

I'm just about to answer him when gunfire echoes in the background and Winters starts shouting. I can't make out what he is saying.

"Winters?" I shout into the phone.

He doesn't answer. More gunfire erupts into my ear, much closer this time, as if it is Winters doing the shooting. The shooting stops and Winters shouts again, but it's garbled, then I hear him shout Josh, I'm sure of it. Again, gunfire sounds, lots of gunfire and then the phone disconnects.

"Shit!" I say to myself.

Alders is silent next to me. I try to connect again but the call won't connect.

"How far out are we?" I ask Alders in desperation.

"Five minutes, what's happening?"

"Winters is in a fight, lots of gunfire and I'm sure he shouted Josh's name."

"Make that four minutes," Alders says as he adjusts the throttle to increase the engine's output.

The whine from the engines surges as does Alders' look of determination, his eyes fixed ahead. The Lynx flies farther out of the city and the atmosphere outside starts to clear of heavy smoke and the daylight increases. It is by no means crystal clear, but the visibility does improve, however. That enables Alders to point out the tall thick plumes of smoke rising from Heathrow in the distance. Fires at the airport must be extensive, the reprieve for my lungs is going to be short-lived.

"How do you want to play this?" Alders asks.

"Just find somewhere to put me down near Terminal 5, that's where they have got to be," I tell him.

"Finding somewhere safe to drop you off is not going to be easy," he informs me.

"Just get close to the building and low enough so that I can jump down, that's all I ask."

"Rabids will be everywhere, Captain, I'll have to find a clearing."

"No, Flight Lieutenant, get me as close as you can safely, let me worry about the Rabids."

"They will be on you straight away; I can't do that." He tells me earnestly.

"I've just yomped through London surrounded by Rabids; let me worry about them. Get as close as you can. That is an order."

"Yes, Sir," Alders says with a look of bewilderment across his face.

"Trust me, Flight Lieutenant and thanks for the lift," I tell Alders more calmly.

"Don't mention it," Alders replies and offers his hand.

I clasp his hand, give him one last look and then whip off the headset. I glimpse Heathrow approaching through the cockpit window; the airport looks in dire straits. I don't sit and ponder what I am going to do, it's a waste of time. I have no idea what I am going to run into when I jump from the Lynx. All I know is I've got to find my children and the others, and fast.

Pressing the button at the centre of my seat harness, it releases, and I climb out of the co-pilot's seat. I squeeze past Alders and give him a slap on the shoulder as I move into the helicopter's hold and reattach the silenced M4 to my front. My right-hand curls around the rifles grip as my adrenaline starts to spike.

"One minute!" Alders shouts over his shoulder to me.

The hold door is in front of me and my left hand takes hold of its handle, ready to slide it open. Out of the door's window, the ground below rises up to show me Rabids dotted over the concrete below, their excitement growing at the prospect of fresh prey flying in. Alders turns the Lynx fast and all of a sudden, the window is filled with a view of the massive Terminal 5 building, the building where I left Emily,

Catherine and Stacey yesterday. Alders has done well; he has got the helicopter as close as I could have asked for. The helicopter descends rapidly, and then:

"Go, go, go!" Alders shouts.

The hold door's locking mechanism releases and the door slides like a rocket across, slamming into the end stop, surplus adrenaline overloading my power. I jump into the buffeting wind of the rotors and down onto the concrete. Alders has found a gap in the Rabids, but they are closing in quickly. I whip around and slide the door closed. As soon as it slams shut, Alders powers the engines and takes the Lynx straight up.

God only knows what he is thinking as he hovers stationary, above. I feel his eyes staring down looking at me as Rabids speed, closing in on my position.

Letting them come, I don't move, the M4 pointed away from my body at the height of my stomach, ready to fire. Fear grips me as their terrifying faces, baying for blood, hurtle towards me. Their screeches overpower the din of the Lynx above as the Rabids shoot past me in their futile attempt to reach the helicopter, that is now well out of their reach.

Relief washes over me as my ultimate gamble pays off and the Rabids ignore my presence. I can almost hear Alders' gasps of disbelief and shock as he realises my truth.

The gamble won, I don't hang about to celebrate my small victory or to watch Alders leave. I'm off and running towards the smashed glass of the departure gate doors on the ground level of the Terminal 5 building. I will retrace where I know the others were, starting with the departure lounge. I know I won't find them there; the lounge will have been overrun long ago. Next will be, up the escalator and to the First-Class lounge, where I last saw them. They could have barricaded themselves inside there. If they aren't there, I will search the whole building until I do find them or get incinerated by the nuclear blast.

There is no time to take things slow and cautious; my patience won't allow it either. My boots crunch through the shards of broken glass scattered across the ground that threaten to slide my feet from beneath me as I cross the threshold into the building. I adjust to the new atmosphere quickly as I hit the winding staircase that will take me up to the departure lounge. Taking the steps two at a time, I am quickly near the summit and see the door frames that will take me in, their glass panels shattered too.

A Rabid, attracted by my noise echoing up the stairwell, appears at the top of the stairs, beyond the broken doors. The creature looks at me quizzically, until my M4 shoots it between the eyes. I have seen enough of their grotesque faces to last me a lifetime and I can't afford to mess about.

Stepping over the dead Rabid body and onto the departure lounge level, I turn a corner. The lounge is spread out in front of me and it has seen a tremendous fight. Bodies in military uniform and Rabid bodies are strewn across the wide area, their blood pooling on the highly polished floor. Walls are riddled with bullet holes and blackened from explosions. Dust hanging in the air enters my lungs again, along with the smell of cordite.

I move forward more cautiously now, to avoid the Rabid creatures that still shuffle around between the bodies and upturned tables and chairs but also, to avoid getting mistaken for a zombie and shot by any troops that may still remain. The images of dead faces enter my brain, even though I try to avoid looking at them. A young squaddie's tortured face imprints on my mind. His dead eyes look out from under a row of airport seating that is fixed to the floor as if he was trying to hide from the terror beneath the uncomfortable seating.

Pressing deeper into the lounge, I go past the food serving station that my breakfast was served from yesterday. The hotplates still lie on top of the tables, cleaned ready for the next serving that will now never happen. Veering right towards the stationary escalator that will take me up to the First-Class lounge level, I see a body slumped over the table where I ate my breakfast with the others, including Dan. Blood slowly drips from the tabletop and onto the floor below, where it splatters into morbid patterns.

The Rabids look at me as I go, but don't take much notice, my new camouflage still fooling them. Low behind my M4, I approach the frozen escalator where a creature mills around at the bottom entrance as if it is waiting for the escalator to spring back to life. I decide to take the rabid out and focus my aim.

My finger reaches for the rifle's trigger when a dulled sound of shooting vibrates into the departure lounge from above. Could that be Josh shooting, or Alice? Are they in trouble? Panic hits me. Screeches rise from behind me; I am not the only one who has heard the noise. I have missed my easy shot at the Rabid by the escalator. The beast is winding up to climb up the escalator, towards the new sound as it wakens from its stupor. Filling it full of bullet holes as it arrives in between the snaking black, rising rubber handrails of the escalator, it falls forward into the first few metal steps.

The body still twitches but I make my break for the escalator. Rabid noises are rising right behind me as the race to reach the new noise from above starts. I reach the entrance to the escalator first, just, but Rabids are on my back. My feet are unsteady as I trample over the twitching body to get to the steps beyond and I nearly trip over. My left hand catches me and taking hold of the black rubbered handrail, it pulls me along. My legs power as my boots hit solid ground. Releasing the handrail, my left hand goes to my body armour and pulls off a grenade. I pull the pin with my right index finger and drop the grenade. My legs now go into overdrive, straining as I sprint up the awkward escalator, Rabids breathing down my neck.

I open a slight gap as I reach the top of the escalator and I turn, shooting the M4 in automatic. The creatures directly behind me fall back into the others as my bullets rip their heads apart and then the grenade explodes. Rabid bodies erupt into the air as the sides of the escalator concentrate the power of the explosion inwards and upwards. Mangled bodies and limbs spin high into the air as their black blood sprays. Bodies reach their highest trajectory before they drop straight back down back onto the escalator. Others are blown outwards, over the side of the escalator in an arc, their final destination splattering into the floor of the departure lounge below.

The explosion subsides and the smoke clears. My slim hope that the Rabids are dealt with is short-lived. Others are already clambering over the bloody carnage, hell-bent on climbing the stained escalator. I shoot down at the creatures at the front, slowing the ascent, but the fresh bodies are but a small obstacle to the fevered attack.

There is no choice but to grab the last grenade from my body armour and to pull the pin. The grenades lever releases with a metallic click as I throw it down underarm. Aiming for the entry point of the escalator at the bottom where the biggest concentration of Rabids is clamouring to get on, I immediately start firing again. The M4's bullets take down, one by one, the Rabids at the front as they present themselves until the second blast goes off. The explosion throws more bodies into the air and this time the blast explodes the glass sides at the entry onto the escalator. Shattered glass is ejected at impossible speed sideways on each side of the entry and it is joined by pieces of flesh, blood and bone spraying out.

Continuing to fire my rifle again, I despatch the last few remaining Rabids at the front that weren't blown up by the grenade. As the last one falls, I turn and make a run for it. I haven't enough ammo to deal with the throng of creatures that survived behind the explosion and are now climbing over the latest gore to get up the escalator.

Sprinting in the direction of the First-Class lounge. I eject the mag from the bottom of the M4, pull a new one out of my body armour and snap it home into the rifle while I run. Screeches sound off behind me as the Rabids climb, but the First-Class lounge is now in view.

Pushing the solid dark-wood entry door of the lounge I half expect it to be locked or barricaded. I'm wrong; the heavy door swings in deceptively easily. The lounge is deserted, and I don't know whether to laugh or cry. I haven't found them, but at least they won't be in the vicinity of the oncoming hoard of Rabids that are on their way. Hopefully, they are somewhere safe, or safer anyway.

I don't hang about; I exit the lounge and the door swings slowly shut behind me. Rabids are reaching the top of the escalator. I know it, I can hear it. There is only one direction for me to go, right, to keep following the corridor. I set off running again as screeches reverberate along the walls of the corridor to me. The last thing I want is for them to see where I am going and follow me. Luckily, the corridor curves left, so it hides me from the creatures behind as I go, but it sounds like they are gaining on me.

I pass doors on either side of me; my children could be behind any of them, but I don't stop. The odds on them moving such a short distance are small. Quickly, two stainless-steel lift doors come up on my left. I ignore them and stop to push the door to the stairwell open, which is positioned just past the lifts.

Florescent lights show me that the stairwell, at least on this level, is clear. The light also highlights debris on the ground and stairs. Rabids have been here.

Sounds of stomping feet draw closer and I lean against the entry door to stop any inquisitive creatures coming through it. A shadow flickers past the glass panel in the door, then another. More flickers follow, building up to a crescendo. The door vibrates as the horde runs past the stairwell. I apply more pressure against the door as they pass, sounding like a herd of elephants.

My pressure against the door eases as the noise dissipates and they move on, to who knows where? Tightly holding the door handle, I move up to peer out of the glass panel. There is no sign that any creatures have been left behind, all I can see is empty corridor.

Turning my back to the door, I look at the stairs, up or down, which way do I go? Gunshots echo in the stairwell and they come from above. There is no guarantee that it is either Josh or Alice firing, but it's the only clue I've got. I move for the flight of steps that go up. I turn once, as I climb to the two flights on my way up to the next floor's door, which I approach cautiously. There is only empty corridor again as I peer out of the glass panel in the door. I then crack the door open slightly and listen.

The sound of Rabids is immediately audible through the crack; they are definitely on this floor too. Gradually, I pull the door open wider to be met with the blast of more gunfire, automatic gunfire, coming from my right. The coast is clear, and I step out of the stairwell and into the corridor, turning right as I do.

Moving swiftly along, behind my raised M4, I stalk down the corridor following the sound of Rabids and sporadic gunfire. I don't have to go far to find the fighting. Another corridor splits off from the main one, on my left, and I stop short of it. Screeches mixed with gunfire are now loud as the sound is carried down the smaller corridor that is branching off left. I approach the corner of the two corridors and look around it.

Trampled dead bodies are a short distance up from me, ten or twenty of them. Some of them still twitch but there no active Rabids in sight. This corridor is also curving left, so I can't see what is happening farther up. I turn the corner and head up the corridor, adrenaline fizzing in my limbs as I prepare for the inevitable battle.

Stalking to the right of the corridor to get a better view of the way ahead, I reach the trampled twitching bodies. Stepping around and over them, gradually Rabids come into my view as more of the corridor and then an open space presents itself. Rabids are thronged at the far end of what looks like a foyer with rooms off it, thirty or forty of them, more even. Above the heads of the Rabids, I spot a sign attached to the wall that reads, COMMAND ROOM.

My hope rises; if I am going to find Lieutenant Winters anywhere, surely it is at the command room. I'm banking on him knowing where my children are if he isn't with them, and if Colonel Reed has anything to say about it my rifle will be breaking his jaw.

Another volley of gunfire explodes as I assess my tactics. The blast comes from the left of the command room, where another door is situated. The door is partially open and that is where the Rabids are concentrated. Somebody must be in there, fighting to keep the mass of Rabids at bay, Winters?

I hear the scream above the screech of Rabids and through the gunfire. *EMILY, EMILY IS IN THAT ROOM!*

My body is overtaken by panic and desperation to get to her and to kill every one of the fucking Rabids that stand between us. I twist off the silencer from the front of the M4, discarding it, unclip it from my front, raise the rifle and pull the trigger without a second thought. If the throng of beasts is attacking me, then at least they aren't attacking Emily. The M4 blazes into life, spraying bullets into the back of the Rabids. Heads explode and bodies fall as my first volley catches them by surprise. The new blast of noise gets their attention immediately and Rabids turn in my direction. My first magazine empties and I swiftly switch it out, opening fire again. More Rabids fall, but my element of surprise is gone. Beasts scatter from the back of the pack in too many directions for me to shoot at. They come for me, screeching their battle cry to alert others to my threat.

No longer invisible to the Rabids, my camouflage has evaporated. Just as happened in the Orion building, I am drawing them to me and that is the reason the M4's silencer is lost on the floor. Changing my tactics, I fire shorter bursts at specific targets as I fall back to the more confined space of the corridor behind me. Rabids follow my retreat, some falling from my fire as they are forced to group together, the narrower corridor closing in on them.

My mag goes. I was expecting it and again I reload the M4, so rapidly it surprises me. Ferocious creatures fly at me, but I make my stand near to the junction with the main corridor. Rabids go down, the M4 whipping through the air in multiple directions, picking out targets and firing. My aim is astonishing, it's holding the tide back. Bullets hit heads, shattering skulls and exploding brains.

As the next mag goes, I know exactly where to reach for the next one with my left hand as my right ejects the spent one. The delay, as quick as the switch is, gives my enemy vital seconds to breach the gap to me and I'm now playing catchup. The Rabids are too close now though, I can't keep up. The angle has changed, and the rifle has to move too far, through the air to each side of the corridor to be effective.

I spray the whole magazine into the legs of the oncoming Rabids. Many have their legs taken from under them. Others behind fall over the ones that go down but not enough of them. There is no time to change the mag again as a Rabid launches at me. Its eyes are filled with hatred and determination, not to feed but to kill the betrayer.

I am no zombie, I think to myself as I bring the butt of the M4 swinging around and smash it into the back of the Rabid's head. The beast's skull cracks from the force of the blow and it crashes to the ground at my feet, headfirst. I release the empty M4 to drop to the floor.

Most of the Rabids are dead or down but more still come and are on me. One slams into me as I reach for the

Sig in my shoulder holster. Hit backwards, my hand comes away empty as my arms flail backwards to try and break my fall. Managing to save myself from the brunt of the fall, I recover enough to bring my arms back up to defend myself from the vicious Rabid snarling inches away from my face. My arms push, trying to force the determined creature away. The fucker has gripped hold of my shoulders though, and is pulling itself down; no matter how hard I push, it is too strong, it is winning.

Gunfire erupts from back in the foyer. *I hope I have given Josh enough of a chance to kill the rest of the Rabids and protect Emily*, I think to myself as my arms weaken and the Rabid nears its victory.

Wretched Rabid blood splatters across my face as the sound of cracking bone fills my ears. The attacking Rabid is sent rolling sideways off me as its head is whacked sideways. My head is spinning as I try to recover myself from the attack, unsure what has happened. Blood is in my eyes and my hand comes to my face so that my fingers can wipe it out.

My senses start to return, and my eyes focus. A figure is standing over me, holding their rifle like a baseball bat. They are talking to me and finally, I hear what the female American voice is saying. "Are you okay, buddy?"

"I wipe my eyes again, "Alice, is that you?"

"Captain Richards, it can't be, you're alive?" she replies as another figure comes and stands over me. "Yes, it's me, Alice," she tells me as she drops her rifle and bends down to me.

Her hand comes across my face and she starts to wipe it, mopping up the Rabid blood.

"How did, erm—I didn't recognise you with that blood over your face. I can't believe it; can you sit up?"

I push myself up with Alice's help and sit up. Alice stays next to me and there are two other sets of legs in my view. My head rises to see Winters and Dixon standing over me with looks of disbelief etched across their faces.

"Josh and," Alice cuts me off.

"They are safe, back there in a conference room with Stacey," she tells me.

"We need to get out of here, now!" I tell them all. "Ask your questions later."

"I have an evac, we need to get down to the loading bay on the ground floor," Winters says, immediately getting on point.

I go to stand up and again Alice helps me. Back on my feet, I look around the floor.

"Looking for this?" Dixon says as he bends down to pick up my rifle.

"Thanks," I say as he passes it to me. "Alice, Winters, go and get the others while we secure the route to the lifts. We haven't got time for Josh and Emily to see me now. More Rabids are one floor down and they could be here any second, especially after all that noise." I don't mention the possible impending nuclear bomb that could arrive at any moment.

Alice and Winters move without question, going back up the corridor. I reload and then Dixon and I move out to secure the lifts. The route is clear and halfway to the lifts, I speak to Dixon.

"Opinion on Winters' evac?" I ask.

"It's the only one we have," he answers bluntly.

"Fair enough, any details?"

"We need to get the lower ground floor, which is separated from the main building, so it should be clear. I'll fill you in with the rest of the details when we are off this floor, okay?"

"Okay, I'll go down first as soon as we hear them coming to save any drama," I tell him.

"Yes, they are going to be elated, when they see you, especially one little girl I know. I'm quite pleased to see you myself," Dixon informs me with a grin across his rugged face.

"Thanks, mate. They aren't the only ones who are going to be excited, I can't wait to see them. It has been a very long road," I tell him, exhausted.

"I can imagine and I'm looking forward to hearing all about it, with a cold beer in my hand. Here take these, I think you'll need them before you see your children." Dixon delves deep into a pouch in his body armour. His hand reappears holding a small packet of wet wipes, a soldier's best friend.

"Ideal, thanks," I say as I take them from him.

"Here they come, see you down there," Dixon says.

"Okay, watch that stairwell, that's where they will come from," I tell him as I go.

"You got it," he replies.

The lift door pings open just as the rest of the group turn the corner, back down the corridor. As tempting as it is to steal a look at them, I don't take the risk. The last thing we need right now is noise and confusion. I step into the lift and look for the button for the lower ground floor. Funnily enough, it has the letters LG printed on it and that's the one I press.

Thankfully, the lift's buttons have a mirrored panel above them, and I take a look at myself in it. I'm not surprised Alice didn't recognise me straight away, what with my new wounds down the side of my cheek and the blood on my face, which is still considerable even after Alice has wiped it. I rip open the packet of wet wipes and quickly go about trying to clean myself up. The small packet of wipes manages to last long enough to clean off the blood from my face and around my neck. I can still feel blood in my hair, and it is still splattered across my body armour. There isn't much I can do about that now; I doubt Emily will notice when she sees me and hopefully Catherine won't notice how haggard I look.

I am poised behind my reloaded M4 as the lift door pings open onto a confined, narrower corridor than the ones on the floors above. All is quiet as I move to the lift door and aim the M4 up and down the corridor. There is no sign of any Rabids and no Rabid noises. I exit the lift, covering the corridor while I wait for the other lift to arrive.

Butterflies dance around in my stomach as I anticipate the lift opening and my children seeing me. I find myself trembling nervously. There was a point when I thought I would never see them again; in fact, there were several points and I tell myself it is only to be expected.

Eventually, the second lift pings and I step back from it. To give everyone room to get off, but also out of trepidation, my trembling increases rapidly.

Dixon and Collins disembark the lift first. Collins looks so surprised to see me, for a second I think he might actually shoot me with his raised rifle. He gathers himself quickly, gives me a nod and moves past me to cover the corridor beyond, like the consummate professional he is.

In quick succession, Emily and Stacey appear, closely followed by Catherine and Josh. Emily has her head down and doesn't even notice me to start with, and Stacey's concentration is taken up with Emily. Catherine and Josh behind them come to a sudden stop as soon as they see me, with looks of disbelief and bewilderment on their faces. Stunned, neither of them says a word; they stand there like statues, eyes wide, their brains trying to process who is standing in front of them.

"Dad?" Josh finally manages to utter.

Emily's eyes come up to my face, her small face appears frightened and afraid. She cannot understand that it is me; she looks like she has seen a ghost and she even takes a step back towards Josh.

I move down to her level, onto my haunches. "It's okay Emily, it's me, it's Dad."

Her eyes start to well up, as she begins to understand that it is her Dad in front of her and not an apparition.

"Dad?" She takes a small step forward. "Dad?"

"Yes Emily, I'm here. I am not dead, I survived." My eyes well up too and tears start to roll down my cheeks as I hold my arms out to her.

"Dad!" Emily shouts and runs into my arms.

I pull her to me, tears streaming down my face and savour having my little girl in my arms again. Emily sobs as I lift her up, her legs moving around my body as she grips hold of me tightly. I look over to Josh whose eyes are red and wet. He looks unsure, guilty, I hold my arm out to him. Josh comes over and I put my arm around him, pulling him in.

"I'm sorry dad." He says, quietly to me.

"Don't say that. You did what you had to do. You did what I wanted. You couldn't have known," I tell my son.

"But."

"No Josh," I cut him off. "There is no way, I'm proud of you for the decision you had to make."

Josh pulls away and looks at me as if to double-check he isn't dreaming.

"Forget it, son, it had to be done," I tell him earnestly, gripping his shoulder.

He gives a small nod of acknowledgement as Catherine comes over. She puts one arm around Josh and one around me.

"You are full of surprises," Catherine jokes, which breaks the tension slightly.

"I like to keep you on your toes," I retort and kiss her on her forehead.

"Sorry to break up the party, but we need to move," Dixon says.

He is right and he doesn't know the half of it.

"Come on Stacey," I say as we all follow Winters down the corridor. I feel a pang of guilt that I haven't time for her now, but I will when we reach safety.

Dixon catches up to Winters and I see them talking as we go. Something tells me the evac isn't going to be straightforward. I need to get in on that conversation and that isn't going to be easy, what with Emily clinging onto me.

"Emily, I'm going to have to give you to Josh. I have to talk to Sergeant Dixon." Emily makes a long grunting protest. "Josh, take your sister please."

"Let them handle it, Dad, you've done enough," Josh replies.

"Now, Josh," I order him sternly. He has no idea and I haven't the time to explain.

Josh relents and goes to take Emily off me as we go. Emily won't release her grip and I have to prize her off me. She protests again but I have no choice but to ignore her.

Free of Emily, I break into a jog to catch up with the two men ahead. Skirting around Alice and Collins, I reach the backs of Winters and Dixon. They turn to look at me but don't break their stride or stop their conversation, thinking they have the situation under control, without my input.

Unfortunately, on this occasion, they don't know all the facts, so I have to barge my way into the situation. I put my left arm out and push my way between the two men, taking them by surprise.

"Steady on, Captain, we have things under control. You can't keep out of it, can you?" Dixon half-jokes.

"I'm sorry, Sergeant but things are happening you aren't aware of."

"Like what?" Winter asks as the two men walk on either side of me.

"It looks like they are planning to stem the outbreak at Heathrow with a tactical nuclear device. It could be inbound as we speak," I inform the two men, who both go quiet. "What is the evac plan?"

"I have cars in the loading bay, ready to go. Unfortunately, there are approximately twenty Rabids also trapped in the loading bay, which we will have to clear. One of them is Colonel Reed," Winters says, and I look at him shocked. "I'll tell you later," he says.

"I will clear the loading bay," I tell the two men.

"No fucking way, you wouldn't stand a chance against that many," Dixon insists.

Telling these two wily operators just to trust me isn't going to cut it. There is no way they are going to let me go into that loading bay alone unless I tell them, so I tell them straight.

"Since I got scratched, the Rabids think I am one of them, I don't know why but they do. I can get into the loading bay and set them up," I tell them.

"What do you mean?" Dixon asks.

"I'm invisible to them, like camouflaged."

"It didn't look like that when one was about to bite your face off before Alice intervened," Dixon points out.

"That was because I was attacking them and making a lot of noise. Believe me, they walk right past me unless I threaten them. I've just walked out of the city surrounded by them for god's sake."

"Are you infected, then?" Winters asks.

"Look, I don't understand it and didn't believe it myself until it happened, but it's as if they think I'm one of them."

"What do you suggest then, Captain?" Winters asks.

"I go in and kill them, that's it."

"No way, your little girl would never speak to me again if I let that happen and you didn't survive."

"It's the best plan we can't afford to delay," I tell them.

"Okay, a compromise, you go in, set them up and as soon as the shooting starts, we come in," Dixon suggests.

"Agreed," I say. "Just don't shoot me in the crossfire!"

"Funny fucker." Dixon smiles.

"That's the entry door on the right," Winters points out.

"Okay, get ready, I'll speak to Josh and Catherine to stay back with the girls," I tell them.

Dixon and Winter move to brief Alice and Collins, while I go back towards the others.

Emily is still in Josh's arms when I get back to them, her head is up though, and she is looking at me. Heaven knows what is going on in her mind, but there is no time to spend with her now.

"Can you two move back with the girls?" I ask Josh and Catherine. "There is going to be shooting, so be ready for it, okay?"

Josh and Catherine nod and start to move back. Emily looks at me and I think she is about to say something, but her head turns away and she buries it into Josh's shoulder. I try to give them a reassuring smile before I turn back towards the loading bay door.

"Is everybody ready?" I ask. They all nod and I look at Winters. "Open it up," I tell him.

Winters punches a code into the keypad on the wall, next to the door. My hand takes hold of the handle as the keypad beeps, showing a green light. Winters nods and my hand pushes the handle down.

Slowly, the door pushes open. Winters moves back, his rifle coming up to aim at the opening gap. Nothing springs out at me as I open the door ready to slip through into the loading bay. I scan the bay and sure enough, Rabids are inside, milling about as they do when they are waiting for something to happen. One close to the door, in a green General's military uniform, looks at me through the gap. The former General bares its teeth at me before turning its head away. That is all the invitation I need, and I slip through the open gap and into the loading bay.

There are indeed about twenty Rabids shuffling about inside the large loading bay. On my left is a roller shutter that has two black cars and Colonel Reed's Defender lined up behind it, our transport out of here. On my right is an open space that has wheeled storage cages and a few pallet trucks scattered around. Then in front on the opposite side are a couple of offices with a forklift parked up beside them.

The Rabids are spread out across the loading bay. I wish I had the silencer reattached to the front of the M4, I could take them out a few at a time if it were. I need to get them together into one bunch so that we can deal with them easily, in one place. How to do it without getting attacked again—I'm not sure I have the strength for another fight?

The solution presents itself on the wall on my right; a bonded storage cage is attached to the wall there. I presume it is used to store valuables in when they arrive, and it will be perfect. I slowly go over to it, not wanting to re-energise the Rabids with any sudden movements until I am ready. As I move, I look at each of the Rabids, looking for Colonel Reed. I definitely owe him one, but I'm just not sure I wanted it to be like this. He appears, shuffling out from the back of his Defender as if he is waiting by it to be driven somewhere. He is unmistakable, with his tall stature and short-cut grey hair, I could spot him from a mile off.

Reaching the bonded cage that has boxes of various sizes stored inside, I see it is padlocked shut. I release my hand from the M4 and go to reach for my Sig, but I stop before I take hold of it. If I shoot the lock off, the others will bowl in too soon. Instead, I unclip the M4, take aim and swipe it down, handle first, smashing it into the body of the padlock.

The loud crack is followed by the body of the lock hitting the floor with a thud. A screech sounds out behind me. I don't look around, but unhook the remainder of the lock from the doors clasp and quickly pull the door open and move inside.

Pulling the door closed, I don't delay and start banging my fist against the steel mesh; at the same time, I shout "Come and get it!"

In no time, the Rabids are heading towards the new noise and coming back to life. I hope that the others don't mistake the banging for shooting as I carry on hitting my fist on the mesh. Glistening yellow teeth and angered black eyes are quickly piling up on the other side of the mesh, their throats belching out high-pitched noise and foul smells.

Waiting for them all to crowd around, I move back a few paces from the mesh, still shouting. Colonel Reed is one of the last ones to join the fracas, his head bobbing around above the others.

Finally satisfied, I take aim. I have Reed's head in my sights, his face looks angry and tormented. *Oh, how the mighty have fallen,* I think to myself as I pull the trigger.

The Rabids are quickly despatched; it's like shooting fish in a barrel, especially when Dixon, Winters, Alice and Collins join in on the action. It takes a minute to shift some bodies away from the door of the cage so that I can get out, but I am soon leaving the loading bay to go and get the others.

Emily is standing next to Josh as I emerge, and she runs down to me as soon as she sees me, and I sweep her up in my arms gratefully.

Quickly, we all get into the cars, without delay. Winters is behind the wheel of the Defender, Dixon next to him with Alice and Collins in the back. Josh is behind the wheel of one of the other cars that is nearest to me, with Stacey next to him. Emily and Catherine are in the back of Josh's car with the back door open, waiting for me to press the roller shutter's button and run over.

Winters and Josh start their engines, and both give me a thumbs up. I press the roller shutter green button and run for the open door behind Josh.

As soon as the roller shutter is half a meter up, Rabids are coming in under it. The shutter rises quickly and before the Rabids have a chance to attack, Winters is gunning the Defender out of the loading bay, leading the way. Josh hits the accelerator and we fly forward, tyres squealing. Two Rabids hit the bonnet as we exit but both spill off quickly.

Outside, many more Rabids are scattered around the concrete expanse. Winters and Josh speed between them, swerving when they need to, to avoid hitting any. Even the fastest creature is no match for the speeding cars and Winters is soon leading us out of a gate and onto the roads beyond the terminal building.

Before we know it, we are exiting the airport grounds completely and heading for the M25 motorway that will take us out of London completely.

"Where are we going?" I ask.

"Devon," Catherine says, taking my hand.

"I love Devon," I say as Emily climbs over Catherine and me, to sit on the other side of me and she takes my other hand in hers.

Exhaustion starts to take hold of me; I'm completely drained and my eyes won't be open for much longer. As my eyes flicker, a bright white flash ignites the whole sky. I don't even have the energy to look behind to see the mushroom cloud rising over Heathrow.

"What was that?" I hear them all ask as I drop off to sleep.

Epilogue

Out of the darkness, a creature's hand curls its fingers around my arm. I can barely see the beast in the low orange light, but its low Rabid snarls are unmistakable. The strong hand grips my arm tighter as it pulls me into its clutches. I don't resist; my limbs are paralysed with fear as it brings its teeth closer to my wide eyes.

I tremble as its drooling mouth gapes open, ready to sink its teeth into me. At the last moment, the creature's head goes back ready to strike and I see Dan's face staring back at me.

"NO DAN, NO!" I scream.

I am suddenly awake as the bright light streaming into the room blinds me. A dark figure beside me, looks over me, her soothing voice trying to calm me.

"It's okay Andy, it is only a dream." Catherine's voice settles me, and I remember where I am.

My wits return quickly and my eyes focus on the beautiful vision above, looking down at me.

"I'm sorry, did I wake you again? I ask Catherine.

"No, I was awake and please stop apologising, there is no need to. It is completely understandable," she insists. "It's nearly ten, we had better get up."

"Five more minutes, or maybe ten?" I ask, as my hand smooths down Catherine's naked side.

"Stop it, Captain. I need the loo," she scolds.

Catherine rises out of bed and goes over to the door to get her robe and my eyes feast on her curves as she goes and then reaches up for her robe.

"Don't be long," I plead as she ties the robe and opens the bedroom door.

"There is no time for that now, Mr Richards, Emily is already up." She smiles as she leaves.

My arms go behind my head to prop it up and I look out of the window, where lush green grass meets the blue sea in the distance. Five days have passed since we arrived on Catherine's friend's farm in Devon. Her friends have been very accommodating and are happy to have us. I think it makes them feel more secure in their house, which is a short walk away.

Catherine, Josh, Emily, Stacey, Alice and I are sharing this holiday cottage at the moment. The cottage is plenty big enough for us, although it was a squeeze when Winters, Dixon and Collins were here too.

Winters was going to leave first, the day after we arrived. He had been called back to duty by the new military command and was going to leave immediately. Dixon tried to convince him to make his excuses and stay another night when he and Collins would accompany him back, and eventually, he agreed. It did all three of them good to have another night of R & R before getting back into the fight. We had a great night, a massive barbeque and plenty of beers were enjoyed by all. I told my story of events after I was infected, and they told their stories. There were some sore heads in the morning and Winters did not look like he should be driving.

The fight continues, the infection still hasn't been eradicated from London and there are reports of cases outside the city. I am not sure where it will end if it ever does. Some plans have started to form in my head to make sure we all stay safe but none of them is fully formed yet.

I have an appointment at Plymouth's Derriford Hospital in a couple of days with some military doctors who are experts in viral infections. Winters arranged it before he left, to see if we can get to the bottom of what happened to me. I still haven't decided if I will keep that appointment, however.

Emily seems to have recovered as well as can be expected from her ordeal, as Josh has. They both have nightmares and I can only hope that they calm over time, as I do with mine. If not, we will look into maybe getting them some help. Stacey is grieving for the loss of her parents; we are all here for her and she seems to take strength from that. Alice, on the other hand, seems to be unaffected, she may be putting on a brave face, though, and I plan to keep an eye on her.

The bedroom door opens as Catherine returns. She sits on the side of the bed, looking at me.

"Are you okay?" she asks.

"I will be when you get in here with me," I tell her.

She stands smiling, then undoes her robe teasingly before dropping it from her shoulders. I pull the covers back and she slides in, on top of me.

The End.......

CAPITAL
FALLING

For more information on Lance Winkless
and future writing see his website.

www.LanceWinkless.com

By Lance Winkless

CAPITAL FALLING
CAPITAL FALLING 2 – DENIAL
CAPITAL FALLING 3 – RESURGENCE

THE Z SEASON –

KILL TONE
VOODOO SUN

Visit Amazon Author Pages

Amazon US - Amazon.com/author/lancewinkless

Amazon UK - Amazon.co.uk/-/e/B07QJV2LR3

Why Not Follow

Facebook www.facebook.com/LanceWinklessAuthor

Twitter   @LanceWinkless

Instagram @LanceWinkless

Pinterest www.pinterest.com/lancewinkless

THE Z SEASON - *A series of standalone books that don't hold back and all with a zombie twist...*

KILL TONE

The music has a pulse… The hungry revellers do-not.

Jack Foster's life has fallen to pieces, and now it's time to pick them up. Sex, drugs and alcohol have long blinded him to the one person that matters to him; his daughter. Now, however, he has a chance at radical redemption.

Jack is nothing but bold, he will take the gamble… and the risk. While one profitable weekend of business at the upcoming music festival could set him up to be a proper father once again, more than financial ruin awaits if it doesn't go to plan.

A sickness is spreading, and crazy crowds spell catastrophic danger.

A festival of feverish, exhilarating tension with a rock 'n roll crescendo that unleashes hell itself, this is not for the faint hearted.

__KILL TONE__ proves the perfect blend of decadence and undead carnage, whilst never losing sight of its predominant humanity.

VOODOO SUN

Paradise Lost ...... The Undead Found

Max had the perfect wife and the perfect life, but his happiness proved a house of cards, and on one fateful night, the whole structure came crashing down. Facing unbearable heartbreak, Max resolves to clear his head beneath the Caribbean sun. Perhaps some respite will give him the chance to find a new path forward.

Despite his initial doubts, Max finds that island life is just what he'd needed. As new friends and eye-opening encounters bring him back from the brink, peace and purpose appear within reach. The beach existence begins to soothe his troubled soul at last.

But it isn't time to celebrate just yet, as paradise has a dark side—one that Max could never have imagined in his darkest dreams. Undead beings surface, and nirvana soon runs red with blood, transformed into a hellscape.

Voodoo may have caused this nightmare, and nothing short of a miracle will help Max get out alive.

A tale of undead carnage and mayhem, VOODOO SUN embarks for bliss but lands in true perdition.

Praise for THE Z SEASON

★★★★★ *GREAT BOOK*
Just read the Kill Tone what an amazing book. the story had me
captivated from start to finish. great author love his books.

★★★★★ *JUST A BRILLIANT AUTHOR*
Another great book by the author lance brilliant from start to finish
kept me on the edge like the others so will have to wait for next
one now hopefully

★★★★★ *ANOTHER GREAT READ*
Action packed from the beginning. So realistic that you could
actually imagine this happening! Just wish it didn't end so soon. I
would like to see how the virus spreads so roll on the next one.

PAPERBACK – KINDLE & KINDLE UNLIMITED

Printed in Great Britain
by Amazon